Renfield's Journal

To Marilyn,
Death is nothing;
I fear nothing!
D.

George DeVein

Renfield's Journal
Copyright © 2018 by George DeVein

ISBN 978-1-7246-3789-5
Printed in USA

Preface

The manuscript within these pages has been handed down to me from my father, as it was handed down to him from his father. With it comes the responsibility of presenting it to the world. The connection between my grandfather and the manuscript is somewhat of a mystery. Clearly he believed this to be a work of some importance. In his short foreword he explains how he came to have the manuscript, but does not explain why he wished 100 years to pass before publishing it. The executors of my grandfather's estate placed the manuscript in my hands until such time as it may be shown to the public. Now, since no living relatives of the original author could be found, I have been entrusted to carry out the provisions of my grandfather's will.

This journal was written by a late nineteenth-century curate who, after the strain of serving 30 years as a missionary in Rhodesia, succumbed to mental collapse. He was later confined to a psychiatric hospital near London where he completed most of this odd, yet fascinating account of his journey into the further reaches of consciousness.

My grandfather believed that this journal, and subsequently the letters and patient records that he spent his life collecting, belonged to the book *Dracula*. His reasoning was simple: Rev. Renfield, the author of these pages, was an integral part of the lives of those whose journals and correspondence was included under that title and he is mentioned frequently in them. The actual justifications of the original publisher for neglecting this journal are forever lost to us. However, it is not unreasonable to conclude that they either were not aware of the existence of the Renfield diaries or doubted the value of the contribution of one who was considered mentally ill. My grandfather believed that Renfield's account did indeed contain something of value. Moreover, he believed that this exclusion was a slight to the man and the manuscript. My grandfather wished, by publishing these journals, to right the great injustice dealt to Rev. Renfield by excluding his accounts from *Dracula*.

This manuscript was left as close to the original text as was humanly possible. I have done some small editing where needed; however, the narrative has been left in its original journal form including the archaic spelling. Several of the passages in charcoal were smudged and illegible. Some passages were water-damaged. Other entries were not dated and I supplied the dates using the previous and subsequent entry dates as a guide. Also, in the case of missing dates, journal entry dates from *Dracula* were an invaluable source.

October, 1997   George de Vein

Foreword

It was by accident that I came across the manuscript I now put before you. I was familiar with the journals recently published as *Dracula* and found them thoroughly entertaining, but I never thought them to be actual accounts of real events. I believed the Dracula journals to be fiction, probably scribbled by some university student neglecting his studies. And yet, these stories, though it seems silly to admit it, became a part of me. At first vampyre lore was simply a topic at dinner and then became the subject of humour, until finally, when the excitement of the story had died down amongst my circle of friends, it rested in my private fantasies.

So intrigued by this tale was I that, on an excursion to the North Country, I paid a visit to Whitby where so much of the story takes place. It was in Whitby, so the journals tell, that Mina and Lucy were staying and where the Russian ship, The Demeter, ran aground. Whitby is a small, out of the way, fishing village in North Yorkshire, a pleasant place to be in the fine weather of the summer months, drawing vacationers from all parts of England.

Whitby's points of interest, in respect to the journals, are the ruins of Whitby Abby and the graveyard of St Mary's Church that overlooks the North Sea. In that graveyard, I sat on the stone bench described as the "suicide seat" and took the air. Lucy, the sweetest invention of a man's mind, sat here. If you sit on this seat you may be distracted, as I was, by the beautiful ocean views. But when you turn back and head down the steps, the town is so picturesque that you wish to explore that as well.

Before returning to my room I stopped to visit another church. This one was a little chapel near the old market square, just a short jaunt from the east side of Baxtergate Bridge. I thought perhaps that something of interest would be there. The door was locked, but no sooner had I decided to depart, than a jet carver from a nearby shop appeared and inquired of my interest. I have always found these villagers unstoppable in their musing about their local history and indefatigable in the praise thereof. He produced a key, and nodding to the door, suggested I might have a look about.

Centuries ago, the chapel had been built so that the old and infirm would not have to climb the 199 steps to attend services at St Mary. The chapel, being in great disrepair, had been closed some four years earlier, after the Gale of '93. The damp, musty air gave a close feeling, hardly like a church at all. The cracked windows were so thick with coal dust and dirt, the light passing through seemed grey.

Seeing I was enjoying the rather eerie atmosphere, my host offered to tell me the *real* reason for the chapel's downfall. "There is a tale told of the new curate who had disappeared on this very site. He was an odd, little man who, though seemingly weak and ineffectual, could deliver a sermon that changed people's lives. Animals immediately took to him and strangers confided their innermost secrets to him. It was said that he could see a person's soul. Then, one day after evening services, he had refused a ride home saying he wanted to take in the night air. The next morning the chapel was found open, the candles burned down to the nub. The curate had disappeared."

Such a remarkable story. I suggested that perhaps the curate had just fallen into the Esk. "His ghost still walks here," my guide assured me. "On the nights of the full moon he watches the bridge from the chapel roof so the devil cannot cross the river." He added that the chapel was soon to be gutted and turned into a shop. Then he left me to ponder his tale alone.

I decided to view the altar more closely. The pews had been damaged by water as well as the floor which now sloped toward the river. The pulpit was spared this indignity being located on the raised floor where the altar stood. On either side of the altar were two semicircular plaques painted over in heavenly blue. No doubt during the reformation the figures in these paintings were deemed to be icons. On a whim I decided to rescue them and have them restored. The first was firmly attached to the wall, but the second lifted off easily. Behind that panel I found the diary of one R. M. Renfield.

It was then I knew that there was more to the tale of Count Dracula. The madman of Dr Seward's asylum was a real person and had lived in, of all places, Whitby.

Thus began my search for the truth concerning Count Dracula and R. M. Renfield. From this first journal and the ones I subsequently found amongst Dr Seward's papers, come startling new insights into the history of Dracula. These I have placed in safekeeping with instructions to publish them after a period of 100 years to protect the good names of those involved.

I wish to thank the executors of the Seward estate for the use of Dr John Seward's records and their unwavering support. And I must express my deepest thanks to Arminius Vambery for his painstaking translation of the several passages in the later section of the manuscript from Old Rumanian.

Here, I place before the reader the journals of the Reverend R. M. Renfield. I have also included other writings, i.e. letters and case histories, to give you, the reader, a gauge of time and place. Though I cannot insist that you take these writings as true, I do wish you find truth in them

.

London, England, 1912   S. de Vein

BOOK I

Repression

Reversal

Regression

Projection

Rationalisation

Displacement

Transference

Chapter 1

PRIDE

RENFIELD'S JOURNAL

15 March. — Happiness has made me careless. I wanted to share my gift with others and this has led me into grievous error. It seems to-day's visit to my superior, Bishop Fairfax, was premature; I did not have the proof I needed. To my shock and consternation, I was chastised for my blasphemous thinking. Blasphemous! The bishop went on to state, unconditionally, that if I had such a gift it would be "evil incarnate"—a fancy way for him to say the Devil. Imagine my dismay to hear a grown man, a learned man, a clergyman talk of devils. And I was the instrument of the Devil—possessed! I was sent away with a scolding (am I a child?) and told never to mention this to anyone. I remain, though, steadfast. I will find a way to prove my ability so that even this unenlightened cleric will be unable to deny the scientific fact.

I fear that the bishop has hammered down his opinion of me—an opinion forged two years ago during my installation here at Whitby—and cannot look past it. He has never hesitated to make his opinion known and that opinion invariably holds sway. Bishop Fairfax considers himself Queen Victoria's representative here in Yorkshire, and as such, adjudicator of morality and defender of the faith. He even boasts that it was he, himself, who pointed out Sutcliffe for the scoundrel he was, thus instigating the artist's excommunication.

The bishop always saw me a free thinker. At our first meeting, I had to defend my "Darwinist views," as he called them, to the board while he sneered at me from high behind his desk. I got the distinct impression the board wanted to put me out to pasture. I was too young for that. I was only fifty-seven.

After much deliberation, the board did reluctantly grant me a position. I was installed here as curate of the St Ann Chapel of Ease, yet only on the condition that I shield my congregation from my "modern" views and refrain from any and all comparisons between Eastern religions and our most holy and righteous Anglican Church. To this, the bishop added, if I persisted in thinking like a dissenter, then I should "go ahead and join them." I am now convinced that this post was granted only in deference to my almost thirty years in missionary service.

These past two years have not been without difficulties, yet I feel I have had some success in building a strong sense of community and commitment in my small congregation. If not for my unfinished business in Africa, that constantly occupies my thoughts, I would be quite content. That is, of course, until God granted me this gift.

It was the events of last week that caused me to believe I had proof of my psychic abilities and to make the grave error of reporting my findings to Bishop Fairfax.

Thursday last, I was enjoying my usual pleasant evening stroll with Ham while on our way to services in the village. Certainly I could rely on someone in the congregation with a carriage to collect me, but I preferred to walk, for lately I am possessed of a renewed vigour. I have always much enjoyed walking along the cliffs where the waves dash against the rocks below, releasing the pleasant taste of salt in the air. And on this evening, as we looked down on the village, the daffodils, like ladies in their Sunday bonnets, lined my path, a yellow colour guard in my honour.

The sun still lingered in the west. It had rained that day so I made a point of getting to chapel early to mop up. St Ann is precariously close to the Esk which rises and falls with the tide. A bit of wet weather at high tide is all that is needed to flood the nave.

With the lengthening of days and our early departure we were not surprised there were people about. And as we were about to descend the 199 steps to the chapel, we heard young Nicholas Mathews singing to himself as he approached along the narrow cliff path. *The Minister's Cat*, he recited as he clapped in rhythm. He marched as he sang and just as he got to "is a curious cat" the clouds, still agitated from the earlier shower, moved in front of the setting sun. And there in the twilight, I saw the pale beacon of death upon him. This was a sad day, for I realised that my proof and his death would be the same event.

Three days later, the once happy child chanced to slip on the rocky ledge by St Mary as he played in the graveyard that overlooks the sea. It was this event I brought to the bishop, wanting his advice on how I could use my gift to benefit more people. I thought surely he would consider the positive change in me and its benefit

3

to the parish as additional proof of my gift. I was terribly, terribly wrong.

My only solution is to write down my observations and seal them with a dated, post office mark. I watch my parishioners as closely as I can for signs. If I chance to meet someone in the road, I invite them to sit in the shade and talk. This, however, has brought about a general feeling of unease where once was an almost idyllic calm. I must try to conceal the fact that I am watching them. Yet, I pray for vigilance, lest I miss the sign from the heavens. God give me strength.

I have placed a clean sheet of stationery on my desk and beside this my special pen and a new pot of ink. Finally, I have addressed an envelope to Bishop Fairfax. All this I have done in preparation lest time be lost between my next vision and my vindication.

Now I have only to wait and pray.

March 25. — After almost a fortnight without visions I now feel relaxed and myself again. No mention of my visit to the bishop has come back to me and I am now confident that no repercussions (other than a probable lack of future promotion) will come to me. This is no worry to me for I love my people and my parish. I am content with my small cottage and living. My reward is in knowing I make some small contribution to the Lord's works.

Before I approach the bishop again, I will create a record of all the times since my installation here at Whitby that I may have had a vision.

It was shortly after my coming here that I realised visions from the pulpit. During one Thursday evening service, I chanced to look down into the face of Capt John Colbert, his hat in his hands, as we sang Abide with Me. Though the rest of the congregation delicately swayed to the mellifluous hymn, Capt Colbert stood transfixed, a beacon shining down on his face. This light had no origin and was harsh and unwavering. Was I the only one to notice? What a fool I was to take this visitation of God's grace as a mere physical phenomenon: perhaps the setting sun's rays refracted through the stained glass or the candlelight reflected off the gilt cross behind me. But these are impossibilities! No light of such intensity enters my small, dark chapel.

The next week I was called upon by poor Mrs Colbert. Capt Colbert, a fisherman, had returned to port early the day before, having injured himself. Without knowing it, he must have caught his trouser leg with one of the fishhooks that line his net. Then with the force of casting the net, the hook made two small punctures in the skin just below the knee. At least that is what he claimed. This seemed nothing at first, but when it continued to bleed he became worried and returned home. Mrs Colbert fetched the doctor thinking it only a small matter. He was pale but still in good spirits. However, during the night there came a fever said to be as virulent as those caused by malaria.

In the morning when I arrived, Capt Colbert's condition was grave. Dr Thompson, exhausted after the long night's vigil with Capt Colbert, turned the helm over to me and returned home to sleep. The knowing look he gave me on his way out, indicating Capt Colbert prostrate in bed, led me to know that a doctor was no longer of use there, and I was to take over.

I sat with Capt Colbert at first uneasy, for I did not know my parishioners as well as I should. If I only knew what price that knowledge would exact from me, I would have been glad that I was ministering to a practical stranger. Capt Colbert accepted my comfort not so much for me, myself, but for the collar I wore which symbolised to him, and the others of his mean education, a representative of God.

That afternoon he died. May he rest in peace. The day before, he had been well and working, a credit to the community. Now he was dead from a scratch that would hardly catch another man's notice. Then I remembered the beacon of the Thursday before, but how could I have known what it was? Had God warned me of this event? Had I been chosen to know what no man should know? And what am I to do with this knowledge? Could I have prevented this tragedy?

I saw this beacon again, but it is only now that I know what it means. Mr Slope and Mr Wicks died last year of the influenza. Since they were both elderly men, anyone would say these were natural enough deaths. And yet, what is strange is that I saw a glow from without which followed them in the shade. The glow, as I said before, was like a beacon and was not visible in broad daylight. I thought perhaps that others might be able to see it, if only they knew what to look for. Yet, no one volunteered any corroborating sightings. I was then a shy and retiring man, and I had not the courage to point out these "beacons" lest I become the object of ridicule. If only I possessed my new strength then, I would have done so much.

My visions are not only of death, but of life. I foresaw Miss Harth's pregnancy. The young girl of sweet nature bent to pick a wild flower in the kirkyard. As she rose, a pink glowed in her cheeks giving her colour that contrasted sharply with the grey of that cloudy day. It was as though she were the glass of a lamp with a candle burning within. The light came from inside her! I do not know how I knew she would soon have a child, I just knew. I also knew to be unconcerned that she had no husband. Yet, I kept this a secret. Soon she came to me requesting to be married to a young man from the next village. I was unacquainted with him, but I acquiesced gladly. She now has a baby girl and a seven-months' baby at that.

This scenario would be difficult to prove as miraculous because certainly young girls of good character marry and it is not surprising to conceive a child during a honeymoon. Still the fact remains that she displayed this glow before she had ever met her young man. Yet I feel that no one would believe this as a vision in itself. It is only that it came between my first vision of Capt Colbert and the vision that I have just had, that it must be relevant.

I now know the nature of my gift: it is the ability to see the spark of life—that which distinguishes the singing bird from the one that lies prostrate in the cage. Perhaps it is even the soul, the part of God we all share, that I see. I was taught that only mankind has souls, but I see this glow of life in animals, birds and even insects.

I have had much success as a preacher as of late. This is due to my ability to see life's glow. Ham always agreed with me on this point. My congregation loves me for my new-found confidence. I have no fear of the "Devil" or any other such nonsense. I know who is to live and who to die, and I plan accordingly. I see life all around me and it has given me a confidence that I can share with my congregation. Not since I first realised my vocation, more than thirty years ago, have I ever been so happy.

Though my interest in nature brought many, including my mother, to believe me to become a naturalist, my tutors at Oxford steered me toward theology for my graduate studies. Upon graduation, I was pleased when called to missionary service.

Missionary work suited me for I am fascinated by exotic cultures and landscapes. I immediately accepted and asked for a post in China. The East always intrigued me and now I would go there to pursue the Lord's work. Zealously, I sought out books on Chinese custom and language. The reading room at the British Museum provided me with a wealth of information including maps as well as books. I soon was armed with a modest yet useful knowledge of the customs, language and layout of the land. But, it was not to be.

Imagine my disappointment with the London Missionary Society's change in plans. They said it was God's will. I now suspect that it was not God's will, but rather man's will that sent me to Africa so ill prepared. I went where I was needed.

I arrived with little more than my wits. Dr Moffat took me north from Cape Town and then westward into the interior where Dr Livingston was to take me from the border to his mission by the Zambezi. Dr Livingston, however, sent word that I must set up my own mission farther east, so as to keep communication open with our neighbours in the Cape Colony. It was arranged that a small group of young Shona men would escort me to the new mission site. I spoke no Bantu and they spoke no English; yet, within a short time I was to earn the title of n'anga or diviner!

The young children followed me everywhere with their insatiable curiosity. Word of the new visitor spread quickly. Much was made over my hair which was still red then. The older children were shy, but the younger ones approached unabashedly and touched my hair, finding delight in the texture as well as the colour.

They watched amazed when I wrote down their words (trying to learn their language). I drew a sparse sketch of each thing described and as near an approximation of the spelling of the new word. They were astonished that I could remember everything they taught me by looking at these simple markings on the pages on my note-book. Later, when I read back a story I have been told weeks earlier their enchantment faded. Their faces showed shock and fear, and, one by one, the children fled.

Soon the headman called for the spirit mediums. It seemed that they were told that a white n'anga had come. At first I had no idea that they were speaking of me. Later I learned that they believed I was possessed of a strong spirit that earned me the title of "White N'anga." I paid no mind. Surely they were mistaken; they had never seen writing before and could not believe an ordinary person could possess such an ability. Where, of course, I thought, anyone could learn how to write.

The n'anga are clairvoyants who are possessed of ancestral spirits. Their talents are to heal the sick and to see the future. Back then I dismissed this as nonsense.

Now I see that they were right, I am an n'anga, I can see the future.

Years later, when I had settled far to the west in Matabeleland, I was taken to a sacred place, a place only a few can ever go. The Ndebele n'anga took me to the top of a cliff where the Zambezi plunges hundreds of feet. They called it *mosi oa tunya*, the "smoke that thunders." I stood on the precipice watching the pounding falls below. A rainbow arched above me, and the damp wind and mist tousled my hair. I was wearing my frockcoat, all the fashion back in England, but too hot for the southern climate. I liked to wear it because the ample shoulders made me appear larger and more robust. Casually leaning on my walking stick, I contemplated the misty horizon. Oh yes, I stood alone in the vast wilderness, yet it filled me with satisfaction that God had smiled upon me and made me a man. As long as it was in my sight, I was ruler over all I surveyed. There was nothing to do but watch and be.

I believed myself the simple wayfarer, yet deep within lurked the White N'anga. The native n'anga could see it all along.

March 26.— God is testing me! Never was a man burdened with such tragedy and responsibility. I cannot help but think that God is punishing me for my vain and selfish ways. I dare not pray for forgiveness when I know I have many sins and I have not made amends for them. I know not what I must do, but I fear that I will have to make a great sacrifice to win redemption.

The task put before me has moved me to tears. I write in my journal more to delay, if only for a few short minutes, the writing of my vision on the blank sheet before me. Please God, have mercy on me. Take back your gift. I ask only that my vision be false. Take all that I have. Take my life! Only please preserve the innocent lives of my congregation. I am unworthy of your largesse.

Letter, R.M. Renfield to
The Right Reverend Bishop Fairfax

"County of Whitby
"1 April.
"Right Reverend and my dear Sir,

"I humbly submit to you my account of the events of Sunday last. As you know, I have been given by God the ability to foresee the future in that it pertains to the life and death of a person. I bear alarming news. I have delayed in sending this letter hoping that my vision would prove false. I cannot, however, delay any further for my visions only tell me what will happen and not when. Since this account must reach you, sealed and dated, before the vision comes to pass, I pray God it reaches you in time.

"You see me the fool and I am that and worse, yet I am not a fool in the way you think. I sat contentedly by the peaceful seashore when I should have worked with those in need. I preached to the converted when I should have brought new sheep to the fold. I fear my people are to be punished for the sins I have committed. I, and I alone, am the guilty one.

"In this brief account, I must tell you that never before has any vision come to me with such clarity. Not only the fact but the method has been revealed. If this were not so, I would not have the courage to disclose what I write here.

"While delivering my sermon Sunday last, the faces of the congregation were shone upon by beacons that had no origin in earthly things. Their faces grew ashen until they resembled skulls, their eyes and noses dusky black holes. As if this were not terrifying enough, flames sprang up around them and they screamed in pain. Never before had sound accompanied my visions. And this sound, this horrifying sound, lingers in my ears still.

"Drawing on my previous experience, I can only conclude that this is a sign that somehow my people will perish soon in a great fire. I pray continuously that this is a false vision. I only write to you lest my prayers are not answered. Though I fear that if my vision proves false you will think me an imbecile, I pray that it is counterfeit.

"Yours most sincerely,
"R.M. Renfield."

RENFIELD'S JOURNAL

2 April.— I awoke to a persistent knocking at the door. Could it be the bishop? I ventured to the doorway of my room to listen and perhaps find out who it was. A faint voice called my name. It might have been a female voice though I could not be sure. As the knocking became more urgent my heart began to beat faster. Fear prevented me from taking action and I returned to bed remaining under the bedclothes long after the knocking had ceased.

7 April.— Bishop Fairfax and his "entourage" have just left. I still feel uneasy as their odd behaviour was unsettling. Not only did they arrive without warning, but just before tea. The bishop was accompanied by a Dr Seward and two large men who were not even introduced to me. I offered them tea, the best tea, of course (it was all I could offer, for I had no other left) and my last tin of biscuits. These the two mute hulks greedily ate while the others kept me occupied with their endless prattle.

Dr Seward had a pleasant manner that was most disarming. He inquired after my health and the health of my family. He took great interest in the death of my mother and asked many questions.

"When did your mother die?"

"Oh, that was when I was seventeen. I hardly think of it now," I answered.

"Dr Seward is a very prominent physician. He tutored under the famous Dutch physician, Dr Van Helsing, and it is only by coincidence that he should be here in Whitby today at all. Back in London he has his own hospital and is doing groundbreaking work," said the bishop as though these accomplishments were his own.

"How interesting," I replied. I had never heard of him before, but Dr Van Helsing is the author of several papers on carnivorous bats that I have enjoyed. To bring out our mutual interest, I asked the doctor about his research.

"I emphasise the scientific explanations for illness," said the doctor. "Once people believed that certain illnesses were caused by evil spirits and that these spirits had to be driven out of the body. Now science teaches us that illnesses have physical origins and thus must be treated with medical, rather than spiritual means. The unsound of mind were once thought to be possessed, thus exorcism was used. In this century, research is finding medical treatments for a variety of illnesses. For instance, blood transfusions have been used to cure manias by removing the impure blood and replacing it with that of a dog or sheep."

"Isn't that amazing," I replied. His manner had been cool until he hit upon the subject of transfusions. When he talked of these new treatments a warmth coloured his cheeks. It is clear that the young doctor bears a childlike attachment to his new toys. I talked with the doctor for some time about this new science for I found it fascinating.

Ham came in to interrupt (possibly because he was also interested in the subject—Ham often made reference to blood) and asked for a bit of meat. I told him politely that he should wait, for I had company. This upset the bishop for some inexplicable reason. The bishop then, to my astonishment, got down on his hands and knees and examined Ham as if he were a prize rosebush whose purchase he was contemplating.

"Does he speak to you often?" he asked from his undignified position.

"He does have a gregarious nature," I replied.

"Yes, but does he speak to you?" he insisted in an irritated tone.

"We have many pleasant conversations," I said, which quite amused the doctor.

"Surely he is speaking metaphorically," said the doctor.

I found this most odd, for Ham had just spoken clear as day in front of him. Ham speaks in a haughty manner and acts superior, but that is no reason to be rude and speak about him in the third person as if he were not there. The doctor ignored Ham's inquiry about the effects of chloral hydrate, whatever that is.

"Why have you never married?" the bishop asked perhaps to speed things along.

The doctor swayed slightly as if he had become suddenly light-headed at this, though the question was directed toward me. The doctor did not wait for a response, but quickly interjected, "Are you quite happy with your position here?"

From this latter question I am convinced he was trying to subtly bring up the subject of my letter. I avoided the subject for no proof has come of my vision, true or false. I assured them that I was quite happy. This did not satisfy either of them and they looked at each other for agreement. This made me most uncomfortable and my face began to feel moist.

I needed to blow my nose, but I could not let them see my pocket handkerchief in its deplorable condition. (I had had a fit of melancholy in the afternoon and did not have time to take out a fresh one as my guests had arrived unexpectedly.) I tried to excuse myself for a moment, but my guests would not have it. When I rose to my feet, they became restless and rose as well, even the two raiding my biscuit tin.

After an awkward moment the bishop made hasty excuses to leave which I did everything I could to accommodate. I even helped him on with his coat, which I later realised was the only thing I have ever done for the bishop that he did not find wanting in some way.

8 April.— I slept well but awoke with the uneasy feeling of last evening, only deeper. I am sure that the bishop is up to something.

The bishop, so pleased with himself for personally initiating the excommunication of Sutcliffe, stands—no looms—with an attitude and bearing that makes one wonder "who is next." One cannot escape the feeling one is being scrutinized. The picture that caused all the fuss (as it was described to me) depicts the backs of several young boys in their altogether. They stand knee deep in the ocean playing around a beached fishing boat. The row of bottoms is seen at a distance. I am sure I have seen the Ndebele equivalent of this many times. What innocent infraction will bring down his wrath upon me?

He has never been impressed with me. At our first meeting, the spring of the great gale, he explained that there must have been a misunderstanding. "The position of vicar is not available and is not expected to be vacated for some time."

The documentation of my creditable record at Magdalen and my missionary work were received with a yawn. I suggested that surely there must be a position available somewhere in England.

"London alone harbours millions of souls," I said.

This he seized upon saying I had not the background for a position in London. He expostulated about modern education, industry, and social refinement. Thus, without saying it, the bishop made it clear I was only fit to minister to a lower caste of humanity. I thought for sure he would recommend another missionary post. It is clear to me now that only my delicate physical condition, caused by mean living in the bush, kept me from being sent to back to Zambezia.

It can be no mistake that it was the bishop who saw to it that I was given only the position of curate. Thus, I am not allowed to preach in the main church of St Mary, but only in the St Ann Chapel of Ease. The congregation is tiny though it does swell a bit during the tourist season. Instead of the vicarage, I was provided with a humble cottage, which stands on a rocky cliff three miles from the chapel. The chapel roof was in such disrepair the rain came in unimpeded in some spots. Also not surprising was the fact that no money to repair the roof could be found in the budget, so that I had to replace the tiles myself. Yet the most damaging encounter with the bishop occurred because I was on that roof the day he arrived on his initial inspection.

This disastrous second meeting no doubt sealed his deleterious opinion of me. He arrived without forewarning as I was applying tar between the tiles. I had no work clothes so I did the work in my spare suit. My collar had unhitched and it took ever so long to set it straight before I could inch my way over to the edge of the roof to speak to him. He asked me to come down, but I could not. I should have explained that I was quite tired, for I had been at it for several hours. Coming down ladders was then so frightening to me that I had worked as long as I could to avoid it. Yet, somehow his gaze made the prospect of mounting the ladder, at that moment, even more loathsome. I became drenched with sweat. (This is a perfect example of how I have changed for the better. I am no longer prone to such fears.) I must have looked the fool standing up there in the hot sun

17

dressed in black coat and trousers. The bishop left as abruptly as he had arrived, giving up all hope of me. Later, after he had departed, I realised I had made a square black thumbprint on the front of my collar.

The bishop still sees the old me and he is manoeuvring to get rid of me. I am sure of that. Why else would be have shown up yesterday like an inspector general?

I must get things in order. Mrs Stimpson left to take care of her family four weeks ago so the state of the household is dismal. This alone could get me sent back to Africa, perhaps even to a French-speaking province.

Luckily, the snoops arrived after dark so they could not see the condition of the garden. I will try to straighten things up outside by lamp light to-night.

13 April.— Last night I had the fright of my life! I planned to spend the evening tending the garden, for it could reflect negatively on me in its present condition. I ventured out just after sundown with a lamp hoping to pull weeds and trim the roses. The lamp offered little light, but I found that the moonlight was almost sufficient in itself to work by. I began by pulling weeds from between the bushes on either side of the front door. With the lamp beside me, I crouched down on my knees and was making some headway when I saw something under the bushes.

I pulled a large, leafy weed and behind it two red eyes were staring at me. These eyes were as flame and held me transfixed. I could not but stare back at them. When the eyes slowly started to move toward me I broke their hold, found my legs, and ran inside. No sooner did I catch my breath, when there came a scratching at the door startling me for the second time in as many minutes. At first my blood ran cold as though I were encased in ice. Then the ice suddenly began to melt—a ring of heat passing slowly downward leaving everything above it flushed. The scratching continued. When at last I recognised this scratching as Ham indicating he wanted to come in, I had to laugh. I must admit I opened the door only a crack and peered through it before I risked letting him enter.

"Did you see anything odd out there, Ham?" I asked.

"Odd?" he asked back as though nothing should be amiss in the minister's garden, and I had to give him that.

"I just thought I might have seen something."

"Something?" he queried, giving me cause to realise I would get nothing out of him that night.

At first, when I sat down to write, my intention was to omit this episode with all the other innocuous incidents of the day. Now, however, I feel it is best to include it for it might be a new variation of my gifted sight.

16 April.— Even Ham has turned against me! He says the bishop and his cronies will come back for another inspection. When I asked him how he knew this, he replied that any rational being would notice that I have not attended my own services for the last three weeks.

"The bishop isn't smart enough or interested enough to understand that you can't leave the cottage anymore. If he doesn't believe in your previous visions, then how can he reckon your need to avoid future ones?"

As usual Ham found the logical thread of events, and though he expressed himself honestly and without malice, I tossed a book at him which made him yawl and scamper from the room. He looked so comical, his claws scraping at the floor furiously, but making no headway until seconds later.

Later.— When Ham returned he seemed no worse for wear and was downright smug. I could tell he knew something by the way he circled the room pausing to stare at me, only to turn and move to a new spot when I addressed him. I tried to coax him with a bit of cheese but to no avail.

"I only want live meat," he insisted.

I had none to give. I have been reduced to eating porridge for the last two weeks now, and even that is almost gone, though I eat but only once a day.

"When Mrs Stimpson returns we shall eat well again," I assured him, but as soon as I said this I knew it was a mistake to mention the housekeeper. Ham does not like Mrs Stimpson. She would throw the dishwater at him when he caught birds. She did not mind him catching mice, but scolded him for catching birds. This, Ham insisted, was an idle prejudice. "I am meant to catch birds—it's the natural order of things!" he would always contend, but Mrs Stimpson refused to talk to him. This is understandable for Ham had once attacked her without warning or provocation. He ought to be ashamed for attacking her the way he did, biting her leg so furiously that he drew blood and left two permanent marks with his canines.

"Mrs Stimpson won't be back," he said in a casual manner. "The bishop will be back though—that's a fair fact!" he taunted again before I could ask about Mrs

Stimpson, and promptly left the room through the open window.

20 April.— Ham returned this morning, having been gone for four days. He demanded my attention, not to ask for food, but to give me the devil. (His firm body and casual air prove he must be hunting for himself.) He began to taunt me with his views on the bishop's opinion of me, saying I was "really in for it now." What if Ham is right? I asked him to explain, but he would only talk in riddles.

"Do you know what Sunday was? Not Sunday last – say about three weeks ago." I gathered from his demeanour that it must be something trivial.

"A birthday I've forgotten?"

"No." He lingered on the "o" to let me know I was close.

"An anniversary perhaps?"

"Right! You're so clever to get it so quickly. I thought you'd never remember."

An anniversary in April—what could he be thinking of? I cannot even remember what has happened this last week. How did I spend my time? I have noticed that every little thing seems to take ages to do. Life has slowed down for me so that getting dressed and having a cup of tea for breakfast takes all morning—though I do rise late to catch up on lost sleep. Reviewing the mail and reading the paper takes me until dinner. Then I eat and spend the afternoon with my scientific journals. After years of neglect, I have finally organised them and have started to read them anew. They are my only pleasure.

Tea is just that, a cup of tea. In the evening I work on my sermons. I have started six in the last week but finished none; they take on a morbid tone that reminds me of my terrible vision.

At night I do not sleep, but go over and over the events since the vision. Or I picture myself in the future explaining lucidly and clearly the danger that hangs over my people. Invariably, my listeners doubt and mock me. They throw things at me, and then I realise that I am actually ducking and flinching, when the hurled objects are merely in my thoughts.

21 April, 3 a.m.— I remember! Am I going mad or is worry and lack of sleep dulling my capacity? While lying in bed trying to rest, I remembered so vividly that I could hear the soloist practicing the opening to Part III of Handel's *Messiah* which was to be performed at Easter services three weeks ago.

"I know that my redeemer liveth, and that he shall stand at the latter day upon the Earth; and though worms destroy this body, yet in my flesh shall I see God."

Please God forgive me.

Chapter 2

ENVY

RENFIELD'S JOURNAL

(*Date supplied by the editor.*)

28 April. The Asylum.— Here I begin a new journal to record the details of my false commitment. At first they were reluctant to grant my request for writing materials. Then, after some terse interactions with George, I found it was not the content of my writing that concerns them, but the fact that I wanted a fountain pen. Recognising this, I successfully suggested that I might have paper and any humble means of marker so that I might continue my sermons. I was provided with this bit of charcoal, which though messy, is adequate.

Thanks to Ham's warning, I have concealed my Whitby journal in a safe place. I will use it as evidence that I am, indeed, quite sane when my vision comes to pass. God help me. The warders here give me no credit for rational thought; Dr Seward and the others believe me quite mad. I must prove to them their error. This journal I will hide behind the headboard of my bed for it is best my "keepers" do not see it until I am vindicated.

Later.—I am loath to pen, or should I say charcoal, the details of my confinement for they would unfold a tale of humiliation and degradation. The Bishop Fairfax was clearly the instigator of the whole plot. Dr Seward, the bishop and two henchmen (including George, who is the chief warder in my ward), showed up unannounced on my doorstep just as Ham had predicted. Ham seemed amused by my predicament and watched the whole incident from atop the bookcase. He even egged them on at one point.

The bishop did most of the questioning. "Why have you not delivered services? Why have you not left your cottage for three weeks? Where is your housekeeper?" I tried to answer as best I could, but I had to avoid talking about the visions which they would only use as proof that I was mad. They questioned the fact that Mrs Stimpson had family matters to attend to and asked: "Isn't it odd that she left when she did?" I insisted that I never doubted Mrs Stimpson's veracity. To this Bishop Fairfax and the doctor gave each other a knowing look that made me feel that I had been left out of the game.

When the subject came back to my not attending church services, I stammered trying to think of a good excuse. I explained that I was ill which as soon as I said it, seemed in some queer way, true. Come to think of it, my stomach felt somewhat queasy at the time, and I had not slept well in weeks. A lie it was nonetheless, because I was omitting the fact that I was afraid of having another vision. Since I am not practised in deception my excuse sounded hollow, so my inquisitors dismissed it out of hand.

They loomed over me and I began to perspire even though it was chilly in the cottage. I had not lit the fire for I had no more firewood and I thought my "company" might be cold. It is strange that I thought of this at that moment. Here I was sweating so profusely that my collar was losing its shape and yet worrying that I was being a remiss host. I turned to Ham for help, but he just yawned a wide yawn that caused his ears to slowly meet at a point behind his head.

The bishop asked if I would accompany the doctor, but he did not say to where. When I declined the two thugs came up behind me so closely that their shoulders, one at my right and one at my left, actually touched mine. Naturally, this behaviour unnerved me. I made excuses that I was busy and that they must leave, but the pair never moved. I looked over my shoulder and saw the villain was smiling at me. Perverse curiosity forced me to look over my other shoulder to see yet another toothy grin. Surely, they were not going to hurt me? It was at this point that Ham voiced up. "Don't be so stupid! Can't you see they're taking you to Bedlam?"

Dr Seward approached me and said, "Perhaps you should come along with me."

"I thought," the Bishop broke in, "that is, the board and I thought, that it is best you should have a rest." Board indeed; the bishop dictates how they should feel, let alone think.

The doctor continued, "I have a place just outside London where you can stay. I am sure that once the pressure of running things here is gone, you will be quite your old self again."

The bishop gave a sniff that suggested that my old self was not up to snuff either. If he only could see the new me, the confident me, then he would not act so superior. He has not forgotten the humiliating time he caught me on the chapel roof. If it were not for this infernal waiting I could have shown him the new me.

I do not remember much after that except half waking in a sort of dungeon by the force of a fire hose. My clothes were taken from me and when I awoke they were on a stool beside my sickbed. They were cleaned, but my collar, belt, and shoelaces were missing.

My room is clean and I have my own bed, stool, and little table. The dimensions are small, yet the ceiling rises perhaps as much as 12 feet or more. The window, though small, affords a view of an old ruin as I sit at the table. If the door did not have an observation-trap (a little barred window for the warders to peep through that can be opened only from the outside), one might think that this was an ordinary room. In fact, it is much like the room I had during my seminary retreat. My guess is that the board must have paid for this, for I saw yesterday that most of the inmates live in the general ward in such squalor that the stench makes one gag. I do not know why the board has suddenly become generous toward me, but I am grateful to be sheltered from suffering the humiliation of being chained to the wall of an open ward.

PATIENT LOG

(Entries kept by warder, George Simmons.)

Patient: R. M. Renfield, PAID

23 April. 2:35 p.m. New patient. Violent. Wash, purge. Slept good. Very naughty talking says he wants to go back to Witbe[*sic*]— no such place. Padded cell for now.

24 April. 9:30 a.m.—Patient much quieter to-day—keeps asking for ham and won't eat nothing else.

8:30 p.m.— More awake but still talks jiberus[*sic*].

26 April. 9:30 a.m.—Patient better to-day—gave me no trouble—moved him to Ward D. Room #7, ground floor, west wing.

27 April. 9:00 a.m.—Patient no trouble to-day. Talked to me—wants bible, paper and pen.

28 April. 10:00 a.m.—Patient busy to-day—reading and riting[*sic*]. Dr Hen. says all right to give him paper but no pen.

29 April. 9:00 a.m.—Patient nervous—don't know why. Not eating.

10:00 p.m.—Patient very upset—cried loud for over an hour. Gave him a dose.

30 April. 9:30 a.m.—Patient quiet.

1 May. 10:15 a.m.—Patient in good spirits—asked to see Dr Seward. Ate to-day, wants shoelaces.

2:00 p.m.—Didn't eat lunch, won't talk. Riting[*sic*] mad.

REPORT OF DR PATRICK HENNESSEY

23 April.— Record of new admittance. Subject Raeford Morton Renfield of Hollow's Den, The Cliff, Whitby. Admitted by Rgt. Rev. Bishop Fairfax. Age: 59. Hair: white. Eyes: blue. Height: 5' 5".

The patient was admitted after succumbing to delusions. He is pale, thin, and nervous, with an unusually strong sense of disorientation. When reviving from chloroform, the patient became violent and insisted on being released. Laudanum was administered, and the patient was temporarily placed in solitary confinement.

The patient is suffering from feelings of persecution, the object being one Bishop Fairfax. The patient has requested immediate release to attend to important matters of an unspecified nature. Patient is extremely agitated: pacing, muttering, and displaying disorientation with regard to his surroundings.

With great distress, I must disclose the patient apparently does not distinguish between doctors, warders, and servants, for he speaks to everyone in the same familiar tone and has made the same request to all: immediate release. Recommendation: seclusion, constant watch.

29 April.— Patient, Renfield, reported as being agitated. Administered: two drops of chloral hydrate in water.

2 May.— Patient, Renfield, is settling in nicely. He is quiet, respectful, and very clean in his habits. He spends most of his day looking out the window, reading, and writing. The last I have encouraged by supplying him with paper and an artist's charcoal stylus. Writing is a soothing occupation and can be therapeutic, especially for the agitated patient. It is to this I attribute his relative calm (compared to the agitation in which he arrived) though he is still, however, nervous with strangers.

His appetite is good; he chews each mouthful of his food with relish, though a little longer than is usual, and, after each mouthful, cleans the tips of his fingers by rubbing them together. This habit of cleaning his fingers is the result of a fixation, for the mannerism continues though it is no longer mealtime. Mr Simmons reports that he is often dyspeptic and has trouble keeping down his food. Yet, this indigestion is most likely merely due to a nervous stomach.

Recommendation: careful watching; change in diet.

RENFIELD'S JOURNAL

(Date supplied by the editor. G.D.)

29 April.— I seem to have been drugged. I forgot about the fire and my visions. I did not even care that I had been kidnapped and thrown into a lunatic asylum, which I am now certain that this is (though it is not Bedlam as Ham suggested). When I read my journal entries of yesterday, the detached narration was that of an observer and not the subject. I remember more clearly now that I sat on the floor of a windowless room for hours, even days, alone, frightened, and humiliated. My appetite has deserted me and I am plagued with pains in my side.

I do not know how long it has been since I prayed. Merciful God, forgive me. I must tell my people of the danger I foresaw. I do not know how, but I will not sleep until I have devised a way to warn them. God guide me.

I must return home immediately. I will discreetly observe my doctor for he shows signs of receptivity.

1 May.— Dr Seward, the man who came to see me in Whitby, has just left me. I must confess that the man is an imbecile! I explained to him that I had important and urgent business to attend to, and his reply was: "Have you purged today?"

Through the course of our conversation he continually returned my questions with *non sequiturs*. It became clear that I was to answer all of his questions, yet he need answer none of my own. I asked him, trying to disguise the urgency in my voice, "Why can I not leave here now?" He did not answer, but went on to insist I eat more of my dinner. Resolute, I asked again. Astonishingly, he acted as though I had indeed answered him and affirmed I would eat. I do not understand this. He seems pleasant and open, yet he can divert a direct question without giving any hint to the incidence. I could feel myself flinching, my eyes growing ever smaller, with each instance of miscom-munication. With difficulty I asked again, "When may I leave here?"

"Sleeping better now, Renfield, are you," he suggested. How does he know how I have been sleeping, and to what has he attributed my change in sleeping habits? Most likely my body finally resigned to much needed rest. And this addressing me by my surname—I am not his school chum.

I became lightheaded as the pain that has been plaguing me increased. Though it was growing difficult for me to speak, I pressed on. "You realise I must leave at once, for my people need me. When can I expect the return of my shoelaces that I may be about my business?" I asked with all the command I could muster. I left out asking for the door to be unlocked, but of course, that is understood.

"I'm glad to see you're sleeping better. I'll speak to you again in a few days."

I smiled and said good-bye. Perhaps I should wait before I tell him of the vision for he seems unlikely to be receptive at the moment. I have an idea—I will write a letter and thus be relieved of needing the doctor's trust.

3 May.— The asylum is truly a "mad" house for here everything is reversed: here, everyone ministers to me. George's tasks are simple: wake the patients, measure and empty the chamber pots, and get us to bed at night. He is a credit to his class. George is a textbook example of the ignorant ruffians who breed with abandon in the city's overcrowded tenements. How he loves to lord it over me. Does he not know clergymen are gentlemen? Oh, he acts kindly enough when Matron is watching, but would he bother to tell you that it's time for such and such treatment? No. And before I know it, I have been grasped by the collar and moved bodily to the tub room or put to bed.

Our only protection from George is Matron. He would not cross her. I have never seen the matron, but one knows that she is present when the ward goes silent—even the inveterate curser in the room next to mine. Her main duties are supervising admittance, manning the front desk, and attending the women's poor ward upstairs. She recites this daily to George—as if he could forget. When she comes to attend the women in our ward each morning, George finds himself busy elsewhere.

Dr Seward was on rounds. Evidently he is the proprietor of this establishment (I should have reckoned this from that cretin Fairfax's comment the day of my incarceration). He is obviously young, presumably successful, and probably does not have a care in the world.

Dr Hennessey, or Mother Hen as he is called behind his back, visits the ward frequently. He looks in on me but is not as loquacious as Dr Seward. I see what makes him tick! Dr Hennessey is older, yet Dr Seward is the master. We are all but pawns in their endless struggle for power.

I know I cannot confide in them—my visions are a contradiction to their philosophy. And obviously the bishop has not spoken of them either. Perhaps the bishop believes that if he told of my visions it would reflect negatively on the church. The church is dead set against miracles.

Later.— I cannot find the words to express my fears to my people. God give me strength. Each attempt at a warning is a dismal failure. How can I write a warning that does not sound like the raving of a lunatic? If only I had shared the knowledge of my visions with someone in Whitby, then I could contact that one with the message. I have torn out seven pages of my journal in disgust, for even I, who am confident in my powers, cannot see fit to let anyone read these attempts lest they think them comical and thus neglect their import.

5 May.— I am greatly relieved; I have instructed George to post the letter of warning, but I did not tell him of its

content or urgency. As he took the letter into his clumsy hands, a twinge of fear shook through me. He ran his fingers over the address, as if those fingers might discern the content through the envelope. The wait begins. Tomorrow morning the letter will have arrived in Whitby and on Sunday the letter can be read to my congregation. Then I will have peace.

As I watch the sun set I think of the village in the spring and my long walks back to the vicarage after evening services. Just a tiny place, really. A family of herring gulls had nested in the chapel spire. No doubt the smoky chimneys of the fishing shacks discourage them from nesting there. Just a peek of the cathedral's spires is visible through the leaded window above the front door. St Mary looms down on the chapel in much the same way as its three-tier pulpit towers over the lectern where I read the scripture. Oh, how I longed to deliver a sermon from that lofty place. So high up, one must be very important to occupy such a place.

Letter, R. M. Renfield to the people of Whitby
(Found amongst Dr Seward's files)

"5 May.

"Dear people of Whitby,
    "As you know, I have been called away suddenly. I am sorry I can no longer be with you to see to your

spiritual guidance. Do not be alarmed; only take care to stay away from fire, especially if you are in large groups.

"Your faithful servant,
"Rev. R. M. Renfield."

PATIENT LOG
(Entries kept by warder, George Simmons.)

Patient: R. M. Renfield

3 May. 9:30 a.m.—Patient agitated—tearing his paper, pacing until late in the night.

4 May. 10:00 a.m.—Patient still nervous, don't eat much, got stomach pains.

5 May. 9:00 a.m.—Patient calmer, didn't give me no trouble for the first time. Asked to have letter posted—gave to Dr Seward for approval.

6 May. 9:00 a.m.—Patient slept through night first time this week. Not eating nothing but will take some milk.

7 May. 9:30 a.m.—Got litararry[*sic*] itch already—better watch this one as is the ritters[*sic*] are the looniest—should take paper away or he'll get worst.

8 May. 9:00 a.m.—Complains of pains in stomach, hardly eats nothing.

REPORT OF DR PATRICK HENNESSEY

9 May.— Patient, Renfield, has become interested in his surroundings. He spends much of his time, when not writing, watching the goings-on from the observation window in his door, and, though this surely cannot afford him much of a view, he seems quite interested.

I have denied the patient's request for a candle which he insists he needs to continue his writing at night. It is good to encourage a patient by supplying certain luxuries, but I am reluctant to allow candles in the patient's rooms or dormitories, for their misuse is too tempting for the unattended lunatic.

Due to nervousness, the patient is now offered milk rather than coffee or tea, and seems much the better for it. Mr Simmons informs me that the patient is now sleeping better, but his appetite continues poor. I believe this is, no doubt, a reaction to his sudden change in scenery, and I recommend waiting rather than intervention, for a period of adjustment, as with all new patients, must be allowed.

RENFIELD'S JOURNAL

6 May.— The strain of incarceration is too much for me I fear. A pain in my side that started over a week ago is now demanding my constant attention. I take this as a welcome sign of imminent death; some roaming disease has chanced upon me in my weakened condition and taken hold. I will write to distract my mind from the pain.

The window of my little chamber faces west onto the ruin of an old estate. Most of the structures are obscured by a high wall, but the chapel steeple and original keep (this of course built on some pagan sacred spot by early missionaries) stand high above it. The single windows up high in each give the impression of two one-eyed giants, a tall, thin Cyclops and a shorter, squatter gorgon, each shamelessly, relentlessly staring at me. The chapel tower is likely over 300 hundred years old, but the keep, of course, would predate that by centuries. This is the view that accompanies me as I write. This evening the sky is orange and the grey stones of the ruin are black. As the sun sets, the eyes slowly close. Soon I will have no light to write by—I must ask George for a candle.

I have yet to be allowed to leave my room, but I have determined there are three other rooms on this corridor. The comings and goings of the warders and patients give hints to their occupants; and I have made detailed pictures of them in my mind, using the tiny fragments of information gathered each time they pass my door.

The stairway is all the way down to the right. At the other end of the corridor is the tub room. Next door, to my right, is a silent woman called Mary. The warders speak to her in an apologetic, coaxing tone. I never hear a response. Apparently neither do they, for they must constantly repeat each command or request.

In the next room to the right is Angie. Angie is my champion, giving George and the others "what for" whenever they pass. I know that she does not taunt them for my sake, but since I, as a clergyman, certainly cannot ill-use my fellows, and since she doles out as much abuse as it would take two costermongers in their cups to heap, she makes up for my silence. I cannot help but feel that, in her common way, a small personal justice is made.

Angie is certainly unlike anyone whose company I kept before coming here. Her brash manner and crude language are most out of place in this ward, even if it is a lunatic asylum. Ribald comments are turned with a quick wit that the warders cannot ignore—though I am sure they try. Just this morning I heard her say to George: "It must be hard—dressing and undressing young girls." (She was most likely referring to Mary.)

"Now Angie, you mustn't talk to me that way," he said.

"But George, what did I say?" she replied in the most perfectly innocent of voices. When George reached my room and looked in through the trap, I could see his face was still red.

In the last room before the tub room, to my immediate left, is Tom. Tom is restricted to his room (as am I). Though not common, he possesses a most violent temper and laughs a wicked laugh after he performs a lurid act or utters a coarse remark. During the night I hear him mutter about his wife. It would seem that he loves her a great deal. George, the heartless beggar, turns a deaf ear to Tom's pleadings to visit his wife.

Shall I become as he? Oh God, is mania in store for me? I fear the loss of my dignity and humanity. I do not believe that I will lose these due to illness of the mind, but that they will be stripped from me by cruel abuse and callous neglect.

Letter, Mrs Johnston to Rev Renfield
(*Found amongst Dr Seward's files*)

"Whitby, 1 May.

"Dear Rev. Renfield,

"I do hope this letter finds you in good health. I have entrusted this letter to the care of Bishop Fairfax. He says that though you are not to be disturbed in your pursuit of deeper spiritual awareness, he will give it to you all right.

"I trust you are enjoying your much deserved holiday retreat. Though the bishop was vague as to the suddenness of your departure from us, he did assure us that you are being well looked after.

"The members of the Women's Charitable Society have pitched in and restored your cottage for you. Mrs Stimpson should never have left a man alone for so long. On your return you will find Hollow's Den respectable again. We took special care with your prized Chinese pottery. I do hope you do not mind that we burned the newspapers and old science journals you had piled in the sitting room. There were so many of them they heated the cottage for quite the entire day of cleaning.

"Ham was glad to see us. He stayed with us the entire day watching our every movement like a palace guard. He is so dear. He must be very attached to you for he would not let any of us take him with us, but insisted on remaining like a sentinel on the porch of Hollow's Den. I am sorry to say Ham seems to have damaged the yellow wallpaper in your room. We shut the door so he will not be able to enter. We have created a schedule so that each day one of us will leave food at the door for him.

"Please write soon that I should know not to worry.

"Yours, Mrs Johnston."

8 May.— My stay here is far from pleasant. Though I find that I am now sleeping well, I have little interest in food. I have developed an aversion to even the most common fair. Tea and coffee have a most stimulating effect on my bowels, so George is now bringing me milk with my meals. Milk, however, acts as a soporific and leaves me sleepy for hours. These effects I have never experienced before. Also, vegetables and grains give me intestinal gas. At first I believed it was a malignant disease that caused the sharp pains in my side. Later I grew suspicious of the nature of this disease, for it had no particular preference for one side of my abdomen or the other. Now I am aware that this pain only comes after eating, and is considerably less intense since I abandoned both tea and coffee. Alas, my life-threatening disease is but a puff of the wind.

I content myself with just the meat portion of my meal, and though this is usually small, it is all my poor stomach will hold. Dr Seward, of course, is greatly distressed and feels it necessary to remind me to eat. Could he possibly believe that I have merely forgotten to eat?

Why do they keep us alive? It cannot be Christian charity for they mock these beliefs. Their purpose is simply to keep us alive and thus their purpose is to strip us of our purpose. I am alive, but my existence is as nothing. The warder's rough treatment of me will not break my spirit, however. I will carry on with the grace of God.

11 May.— I have studied the ward's daily routine, and I know that I will be able to write undisturbed in the afternoon hours between lunch and tea (or I should say milk). Matron attends the women's ward at this time and George slips away during her absence.

For the last three days I have been unable to eat for my stomach will hold nothing. But more important, is that during this time I have discovered that I smell, hear, and see better than I thought was humanly possible. Yesterday afternoon, while lying quietly, I thought I heard an insect run across the room. Its tiny footsteps rang clear on the tiled floor, a minute drumming like a reed on stone. When I investigated, I found I was correct, it was indeed an insect. I watched it closely for some time as it sped along, sometimes dashing for yards with what looked like great purpose, only to stop suddenly and change direction. When the little fellow stopped, so did the drumming, then the drumming resumed when it moved on.

At first I was alarmed when it disappeared under the bed. Some latent fear caused me to sit up on my knees and listen closely. It had stopped. What was it up to? Curiosity is the devil of me; I had to look. The light was poor under there, but by pulling my blanket up on the bed some light reached underneath. My little friend was nowhere to be seen. If they would let me have a candle I could have used that, but instead I had to squint in the darkness with the failing eyesight of old age. Needless to say, I saw nothing. I gave up, stretched out on my bed, closed my eyes and rubbed them to relieve the strain.

It was then I saw it silhouetted in the twilight, carefully running its forelegs down each antenna much like a cat washing its face—or no, more like a woman combing her long hair with long strokes from the temple to the ends, a lock of hair sweeping forward with each stroke. In my mind's eye the ant was magnified as if under a microscope and in perfect focus that my lenses no longer afford.

She was combing her antennae before her barbell eyes one at a time. When she got to the end, the antenna sprang up and arched above her head like a youthful bud bowed by a zephyr. She then licked her wrist-combs with her horizontal pinch-jaws. (I do not know the lovely Latin nomenclature for these things so I have made up my own descriptive names.)

I have felt this presence before. I noticed the living glow of insects and spiders back in Whitby, but I took hearing them for granted. No, it was not hearing then, it was sensing. One day I went to the cupboard and I felt the pull on my face to look to the right and see a new web and its triumphant occupant framed in her matrix of concentric, octagonal rings. The next day the pull was gone, and so too was spider. What made me look? Yes, made me look—to resist would have resulted in an uncomfortable feeling of restlessness, which could only lead to distraction and *ennui*.

When I opened my eyes the room came into sharp focus. It is a miracle! I now can see perfectly without my spectacles. God restored my sight and, even more, he has given me hearing and sense of smell better than I thought possible. These new abilities, clearly another gift from God, I will put to good use.

12 May.— When I was a child, my maiden aunt took me on nature walks. Her speciality was flowers, but she imparted what little knowledge of animals and insects she had to me as well. It seems ants, like bees, live in tightly-knit ordered societies. Each class of ant has his (or I should say her, as Auntie did) own job. Ants are to me now even more wondrous than I found them as a child.

The first ant from yesterday must have been a scout for now a steady stream of ants comes marching in, single file and heads directly for my plate. If the plate is moved they become frantic and run in circles. By the time the sun set yesterday, most of them had returned home. Apparently they are daylight creatures, though one would expect them to be blind being that they are tunnel builders and spend most of their time under ground.

My excellent vision allows me to see the ants quite clearly. I was able to capture one of this tribe and keep her with me. Discreetly, I poured the milk from my cup out the window. This will be her home for the night. Exhausted, no doubt from running in circles under the cup, she is now still. She is of a common black variety about one half inch long. I consulted the Bible for a suitable name and found a good match. I will call her Leah for she is dull-eyed and languid.

14 May.— A most curious variation of my new abilities has occurred. I must explain this carefully, though I do not expect anyone will ever read this, and if they do, they surely will not believe its content, for it is too miraculous. Nonetheless, here are the details of my new discovery.

I can easily tell that George is coming by his ambling, yet heavy, footsteps. Angie, her voice as unsubtle as the mixture of cheap cologne and sweat that radiates from her, I can never mistake. But what is fascinating is that I can sense Mary, who is mute and sedentary. She is sad from the loss of her child—I know this, but how? When she is near I can hear—no, feel—her thoughts of rage pressing on my skull. She never looks up, but I sense that she is as aware of me as I am of her. George and the other warders ignore her and I can understand this for she never acknowledges another's presence. Her thoughts do not reach them and it is only since my fast that I have become aware of her thoughts.

Her melancholy is a company to mine and I feel less alone. I have tried to speak to her as George walks her past my room. She answers only in thought, not in thoughts formed into words, but in pure thought unhindered by the imperfection of language; raw emotion reveals its cause and effect seamless without punctuation. Her thoughts cry out for life, not for the mortal flesh of life, but for the immortal soul of her fatherless child who was denied the sacrament of baptism. These cries repeat so that the repetition becomes a rhythm and this rhythm in turn entwines with the songs of others and of birds and trees so that they are a whole, a song of the earth.

George has no such thoughts; his wants are simple and he is oddly happy in his work. He does have one small problem, however. He, like the other attendants, does not get enough exercise. This causes a restlessness that is only released by brusque performance of his duties. (I must keep my tongue at bay lest I be the object of this brusque-ness.) Poor fellow, little, if anything, is happening inside his head.

Dr Seward, however, has many feverish thoughts, displaying a wonderful variation between thinker and animal. His careful essays in logic are interrupted by sinful lust of the most vile and carnal kind. He desires a woman called Lucy. She is a comely maiden of some rank. The doctor has made a study of when is the best time to pop the question. So far he has declined to ask for his young woman's hand, because she has not eaten and thus might become faint from hunger at an inopportune moment. On another occasion, he reasoned it too early in the day and thus she would have too much time to make her decision. And of course, hours later, he deemed it too late and he did not want her too tired to appreciate the gravity of the matter. All this, he does not realise, is just an excuse to put off the inevitable rejection. He has aimed too high and his professions of love cannot overrule the disparity in their levels of wealth and station.

15 May.— At first Leah was more interested in escape than her tea. She quite enjoys running up and down my fingers. When she heads too far down my arm, I circle my wrist with the thumb and forefinger of my other hand; and when she mounts this barrier, I release my wrist so the cycle begins again. Leah is tireless in this game and has amused me for hours.

As she stands and stares at me from the wall, she reminds me of a Portuguese nun. Her antennae tilt in reflection, not unlike the wide cornette they wear over their wimple. Yes, they are much like the holy sisters, uniformly dressed in black, industrious, sacrificing themselves to endless, humble toil, and shunning male society and reproductive duties. Dedicated to calm virtue, their stares are free from judgment, yet they make me feel uneasy.

Later.— Loneliness fills my small sparse room. Aggregated from atomies to form a Colossus, it sits hunched and boxed against me, sucking all the air so there is scarce enough for me to take a breath. I long to be free—to stand in the open air and feel the breeze on my face as in Whitby when I stood on the roof of the chapel. I was frightened, but I felt a freedom from the pressures of the world.

The red roofs of the fishing cottages huddled up to the cliff all the way down to the sea. Looking down on the Esk, I watched the busy townspeople below as they crossed the swivel bridge. They seemed so small, their voices so far off. Cormorants lined the jetties, their outstretched wings held in ungraceful arches to dry. The herring gulls circled and called at eye level. I was high up but not so high as St Mary and the Abbey.

The ruined cathedral known as the Whitby Abbey looms down on the town—a reminder that politics and religion do not mix. By order of King Henry VIII, the abbey was closed. The lead was removed from the church roof leaving it exposed to the weather. Over the centuries, the once great cathedral was allowed to fall into ruin so now only the bare bones stand. Even the mansion built near that site burned under suspicious circumstances over forty years ago, producing a cloud of scandal. But the little chapel-of-ease survives by the grace of God. There once was another chapel on the further side of the river, but, ravaged by the weather, another was built further inland to replace it. (It was suggested me, when I first arrived in Whitby, that the chapels were built to guard the town, lest evil cross the bridge.)

The cottage chimneys, constantly billowing out black soot, discouraged nesting. Thus, the chapel became the most desirable roost on the east side of the river. And every week I was forced up on the roof to clear them out. I was tempted to leave them be, but the noise of their ceaseless calling made services impossible.

From the roof, I could see St Mary standing high on the cliff above me. It is not with motherly care that she looks down upon my chapel. St Mary, renovated many times over the centuries, presents a fine example of "too many cooks." The chapel-of-ease, set at the bottom of the hill, exists for the old and infirm who cannot climb the 199 steps to the main church. My small congregation and I lived in St Mary's shadow.

Dr Hennessey has given me this journal so that I may search my past for the origins of my fears. He believes I can relieve my fear of high places by finding the earliest time I experienced this fear. High places once made me dizzy, but now I have no fear of them.

I remember clearly the first time I had such a fear. The day I attempted to discover what creature had taken up lodging in the roof of the mission chapel back in Zambezia I shall not forget. The chapel, which doubled as a school, was only a thatched roof held up with twelve sturdy poles. Four wooden poles stood on either side and two more front and back. Several youths had lifted me up onto the roof and stayed to watch me go about my business.

The thatch gave off a musty odour. I knew something was there for I heard the rustle as it burrowed deep beneath me. Tamping a stick into the thatch yielded a flurry of activity. A squirrel poked its head out defiantly. I reached for it with my stick. No sooner did I chase it away, but it poked its head out another hole to stare at me, but this time, just out of reach. Out popped three more. Each made a high-pitched, chittering sound and bobbed its head repeatedly. The squirrels, rooted from one spot, quickly burrowed into another. The situation had got out of hand for I found the thatch riddled with tunnels.

To their delight, the boys found themselves an amusing distraction. They rolled in the dust laughing at me and my predicament. Their mothers, clapping their hands to get attention, scolded them and insisted that they should be inside for their midday nap. As I see it now, I was more a curiosity than a religious man to the people of my village.

Then, Matata, a round-faced boy of about ten, ran up to the chapel and called up to me urgently. He bobbed up and down excitedly, bursting with news. He breathed heavily trying to catch his breath. "Dr Livingston," he cried, "the good doctor—he be mauled by a lion!"

I peered down at him, my heart in my throat, thinking now I would never meet the man. I raised my head toward heaven to pray and looked up at the sky. It was so blue. Up there above the village the firmament was solid and intense. The sun shone high above the distant trees unimpeded. No cloud disrupted the pure expanse above me.

"He be hurt only, he strong, he live," the boy explained. (No doubt the look on my face betrayed I feared the man dead.)

I felt the urgent need to stand on solid ground, but when I asked for help the boys no longer seemed to understand me. With mock concern they looked at each other for help trying to comprehend the situation. I was forced to try to slip down a support pole without aid. While mounting the pole I lost my grip and slid bit by bit over the edge. I felt myself falling slowly as if buoyed up by angels, and just as I began to enjoy the lightness of the fall, I hit the ground, landing squarely on my back. I remember hearing the thud but not feeling any pain. Blackness closed in on me as I faded from consciousness.

When I awoke some minutes later (I do not know how long I was unconscious) an unfamiliar face peered down at me. It was a white man's face, the first I'd seen in years. The boys lifted me onto my feet to greet him. His sparkling eyes searched mine as he delivered these words in a slow, measured intonation, "Dr Livingstone, I presume?"

It was he, a newspaperman named Henry Morton Stanley, who had informed Matata of the lion attack of what? Months? years ago? He had travelled to Africa from New York to interview Livingstone for his newspaper. I do not know if I was more shocked by the fall or the realization that people in England and even America were better informed of Livingston's affairs than I.

Stanley did not linger in our mission long, the urgency of his mission pressing upon him. The boys led him out of camp on the east path, though I had always been told that Livingston's camp was to the *west*.

Thank Goodness I was not seriously injured. Dr Livingston had been mauled by a lion carrying out his duty. The irony that I had travelled all this way to be pestered by squirrels was not lost on me.

This event affected me in such a way as to make me avoid heights from then on. Yet, there was a positive outcome to this incident. After that day, the boys and their friends attended school regularly, though it was probably in hope that they could witness another entertaining escapade of the "white *n'anga*."

PATIENT LOG
(*Entries kept by warder, George Simmons.*)

Patient: R. M. Renfield, PAID

12 May. 10:15 a.m.— Patient Renfield staring like seeing things.

13 May. 10:00 a.m.— Patient didn't sleep last night. Didn't drink milk—just played with cup.

14 May. 9:30 a.m.— Plays with fingers and cup. Watches with madness in his eyes.

15 May. 11:00 a.m. — Riting[*sic*] again—should be getting larger dose.

16 May. 10:00 a.m.—Patient talks to hands—getting worst—must be kept away from other patients.

REPORT OF DR PATRICK HENNESSEY

16 May.— Patient, Renfield, has been exhibiting a new fixation. This week, he was observed talking to his own hands for extended periods of time. It seems he stares at one hand and then switches to the other, repeating the

49

pattern over and over. As of yet, the cause of this behaviour is unknown.

Fearing he might become over stimulated by this, I went inside his room to talk to him. As I entered, I found the patient busily writing on his papers. When I asked what he was writing, the patient shrank from me, grew alarmed, and held the pages to his chest. Though he responded pleasantly, he appeared nervous and evaded questioning. This pattern of behaviour, that of cradling his papers, has arisen most unexpectedly. He holds his papers for comfort when approached, for he is still unsure of me.

The patient is, however, much improved and I think more freedom is in order, starting with an hour in the dayroom during the afternoon recreation period.

RENFIELD'S JOURNAL

(*This passage has been extensively edited for the benefit of the reader, the original being essentially only one sentence with little punctuation. G.D.*)

17 May.— I awoke in the night my flesh burning. My head pounds as if a bell, the sledge, sounding the screams of the banshee for the clang, striking my left temple. I fear the worst. No one has spoken of a fire, but I know that it has happened. My shoulders feel heavy with the burden of knowing, yet I should not know. How can I be so sure? Oh God, make it not so. I needed only a little more time. If I had only insisted that the doctor tell them,

they would have listened to him. But I was afraid, afraid he would think me mad. I am not mad.

I called out to George, but when he finally came, he would not listen and told me repeatedly to calm down. He assured me that the letter had been posted, but I did not trust him until he gave me his solemn oath. But his thoughts betrayed him— "I give 'em de ol' G."

What is the use—it is too late. He brought me a drink of water which made me feel a little better, but I cannot eat. Oh dark despair, the consciousness of my people cries out to me for help, but how can I help them now? Oh, cruel Providence! Why should it be that I, the only one who could help them, should be restricted in body and tongue? The bishop could have told them—he knew. He knew!

God! Why has this happened? You could have prevented this. The most perverse part is that you gave me the knowledge only to have me suffer. You knew of my devotion to my people. You knew I was without support from the church, intellectually alone in this world. You gave me the gift of vision, but no way to use or impart the knowledge it brings. You showed me the lot of the innocent, only so that the anticipation of their demise would drive me mad. Do you delight in my suffering?

Life is no longer of use to me and I am resolved to die. Let us find out the truth of heaven and hell. Is it all a lie? Will my passing be just that—a passing? The wretchedness in these four walls and the pain in this skull is Goliath. If there is a hell it must be a hideous place to frighten me now.

Chapter 3

SLOTH

RENFIELD'S JOURNAL

(*Continued*)

19 May.— My head is quiet now and is clear and aware. The worst has passed. I am calm now, almost serene. The stillness is sublime and the birds' calls from outside have cheered me. Leah, after three days under the cup alone with only a tea-sopped crust of bread, seemed a bit dazed at first, but is fine and playful again.

I spent the last three days in what is euphemistically called the "quiet" room. It seems they do not know (or care) about the purpose of my "destructive" behaviour, thus, the confinement was simply to punish me. I am glad of this, for I do not want the warders to know of my shameful reasoning. That reasoning, produced in a cloud of fear and doubt, led to most foul action.

Leaving my journal entry of 17 of May as a suicide note, all that was needed was a method. I had never thought of taking my own life before and so was ill prepared to carry out the deed. After much analysis, I realised hanging was the only option open to me. Though I had no idea how to tie the knot, I began to tear my sheet into strips. These I planned to roll and braid using the technique we used to make mats in Zambezia. Tearing a strip of sheet first required biting the edge until it was weak enough. Then a couple of quick pulls on both sides of the tear yielded a nice seven foot strip.

I heard something at the door. It was George, his face squeezed into the trap. The noise of the tearing must have carried in the hallway. I stopped, but said nothing.

"Right," he said, closing the trap.

I hesitated only a moment and then began to hide the strips under my pillow. He and a burly, unshaven lout returned moments later. George had a serious expression, but his companion smiled wickedly and approached me without the slightest apprehension. Foolishly, I fought his grasp but soon he had me helpless, wrenching my right arm behind me, forcing my fist toward my neck. Using only my eyes, I appealed to George for help. He did not look unsympathetic, but it was then I noticed he was concealing something behind his back.

We stood like this for some moments. He was waiting for the pain to sap my energy. I was new at this; they were old hands and I realised they would most likely win. The lout sensed my thoughts (or had my muscles relaxed slightly, signalling my thoughts?) for he lowered my arm, though without loosening his grip.

George brought the strait-waistcoat from behind him. As he did so, I saw myself as if through his eyes: thin, pale, and frightened. Never had I guessed I would be brought to such indignity. He studied my reaction. I knew it would go more easily for me if I submitted, but I could not. As the tears rolled gently down my cheeks, my captor's thoughts touched me.

Until that moment, desperate thoughts had flooded my mind and that resolve had directed my mind utterly. In this pause, George's thoughts took hold of me and filled my consciousness. Perhaps it was the excitement (that I now shamefully admit that I caused) that directed his thoughts—made them "louder" if you will. Or perhaps, and I do think I am on to something with this, since he was trying to press his will on me, he said in his mind what he acted with his body.

"Ow come on, come on, don't give me no trouble. It'll all be over in a minute and I can git back to my nap. This is what I git for a-lookin' arter 'im. 'E's calmin' down. 'E's calmin' down." These thoughts I heard in my head. Clearly, from the tone, these were George's thoughts, but where were the thoughts of "Burly?"

For a moment Burly stared me straight in the eyes and I pictured myself huddled in a small room, trussed up in the strait-waistcoat.

"Bet that 'urt," thought George as the other pushed my arm up further toward my neck again, breaking the truce.

They could not hear my thoughts, or if they could, they displayed an unsportsmanlike conduct toward my inner cries of "uncle".

I beg understanding of my next course of action. The warder thought, "'E's chuckin' it in. If 'e relaxes, I can git 'is togs off."

At the time I was shocked, but now I can concur with the wisdom of saving one's good suit from the dangers of the quiet room. I did as he "ordered," and though at first surprised at the suddenness of my capitulation, he laid the waistcoat on my bed and began to undress me. I tried to help with my free hand. He reacted as if I were a child, incapable of unbuttoning myself; he gave me a parental look, shaking his head and waving his finger. It was not these actions, but the tightening of the grip on my arm by the other, that forced me to abandon this small attempt at self-rule.

Stripped down to my underclothes, I was asked to stretch my arms out before me. I knew that if I did so, I would be totally helpless and if I did not, I would be punished.

"Come on you _____ stupid ol' man, I 'yaven't got all day," thought George before he said, "It's all right, we won't 'urt ye."

The big ruffian was now holding me by my left arm, having had to switch to allow my shirt to be removed. Without thinking of the consequences, I elbowed my captor in the ribs using an old rugby move I learned at school. I surprised both of us when I was able to break his grasp. I ducked past George, who was not quick enough, and took a sharp right down the corridor. The way was blocked by a gate. Locked! I doubled back, and finding no exit, hid in the tub room. Hiding crouched on the cold, damp floor, I soon knew why they had let me run here; there was no escape. I was naked and cold, and now they were angry. My mind raced but time dragged its feet. There was no sense in delaying the inevitable. I stood, walked to the door where they were waiting, and stretched out my arms.

Alone in the quiet room, I had no distraction from my thoughts. Heartless self-doubt and merciless self-pity whirled about me. Reasoning held no sway over them, for a devil's advocate spoke on their behalf with debating skill far beyond my ability. Finally, exhausted, I slept.

I awoke, groggy and hungry, with a buzzing in my head. When I closed my eyes I saw crimson waves splash and sputter like molten metal. Nausea set me coughing up bile from my empty stomach. My nose ran and tears steamed from my eyes. I longed for the simple dignity of a handkerchief, though it would be of little use with my arms bound around me.

Soon I realised the "buzzing" I heard was not from inside of me, but coming from the wall. The inmate in the cell next to mine was trying to communicate something that I could not make out. It was some kind of a code. The inmate must be trying to send a message to someone—surely not to me, for how would he know who I am?

I could not sense his mind. Perhaps this was due to the thick padded walls. Closing my eyes and directing my mind to the origin of the sound, I simply saw red. The red focused into scenes of blood coursing through veins, then spattering on clothing and finally, spilling onto the ground. What morbid, inner instinct caused me to linger on these scenes? I concentrated on the humming to block out the scenes. Forced to keep my eyes open, I lay my head on the cool floor and watched the padded walls spin slowly around me.

I do know my companion was a man from his tenor voice. Was he just moaning, as is not uncommon in this den of suffering? No. There was a pattern and I set my mind on figuring it out.

"O hm-mm-mm, tha haa-aa-haa ve-sli-i." Though he repeated it over and over, this was as close as I could figure the first line. It went on for several lines before it repeated and at that point, the end, it became quite fervent and rose in pitch (where before it was monotone) until his voice broke. This "code" was familiar and I can't think why!

This afforded me some distraction until the rhythm of the code reminded me of the drumming, the drumming in my head, as I lay alone in my straw thatched hut by the shallow Shangani. Driving drums called for action as I lay, fully clothed, listless, perhaps for weeks, with the fever. It seemed the dry season would never end. The rains had not come even though the msasa leaves had flashed their signal in pink and gold. There was talk of *shangwa*—famine. None of my young students came to see me, only the medicine man who chanted prayers and waved his boar hair whisks outside my hut each day. He was praying for rain. I prayed for rain too, rain or death.

When the weather finally broke, the fever broke as well, simultaneously, miraculously. Each year when the rains came, they transformed the stark plains into gardens. Countless dots of reds, yellows, and brilliant whites blended in the soft breeze—a constant, yet ever changing French impression of the landscape. Watching the rain from the doorway, I got the impression that the rain had transformed me as well.

I ran outside to praise and thank God for my worthless life. Standing in the drenching rain, the combined force of the thousands of individual drops tried to spill me. My clothes clung to me. Heavy with rain, theirs were the burden of chains. I stood in the clearing between the creek and the river allowing the cold rain to cool the fever in my brain. More likely it was my restless spirit that needed to be cooled.

I tried to remove my clothing, but each piece fought me and seemed to cling harder, the harder I pulled. The force of removing my coat brought me to my knees, which sank three inches into the newly made mud. Sitting on the ground it was easy enough to remove my shoes and stockings, but my trousers would not go past my thighs and I fell sideways into the sucking wet earth.

When finally I was bare, I stood to let the rain cleanse me. It cleaned off more than the dirt that covered my body—it cleansed away the muck from my eyes revealing a clear vision of my duty in life no longer clouded by the trivialities of a distant social order. From that moment I was truly free, reborn.

I was in Africa, alone. Oh, there were many who came to the mission, but I could not talk to them of the important things. They could not understand my preaching and I could not understand theirs. I knew the clingers that populated the compound were watching but I did not care. Clearly, I baffled them more than they baffled me. They were naked but I was not. I was clothed in shame. I was to lead them but to what? English sensibility? I was to teach them, but teach them what? All they needed to know they learned from the bush. I, the Latin scholar, was humbled by the purest of ignorance.

As I sit here in my small room unable to sleep the voices—perhaps just remembered voices—of the people of Whitby, beg and scold and taunt me. Their faces appear to me, one by one, each more accusing than the last.

The Widow Johnston's face appeared. The widow, whenever I chanced to look her way, was always looking at me. Her large brown eyes betrayed the smile which her lips seemed to be trying to hide. Now, in my delirium, she looks at me in much the same way and for the first time she finds the courage to speak. Her shy face looks down upon me much as it did when she sang in the choir on Sunday mornings.

"We are together now," she said before her visage faded back revealing the others.

I recognised them all as they spoke in turn and then cried all together. Their souls, they said, are in my keeping.

Later.— After a long, uninterrupted stay in the quiet room the sound of the key in the lock, rough and impatient, the other keys on the large ring jangling loudly, was to me as a mother's forgiveness. George rules here and the ring of keys is his magic sceptre. He opened the door and I averted my eyes from the unaccustomed light, thus granting him the bow of deference that his looming stature over my crouched body demanded.

George and Burly observed me from the door for a moment and then approached. I had always hated being subject to George's bedside manner, but when Burly lifted me into his arms to take me back to my room, it felt strangely comforting. Owing to this weakened state, I found myself confiding my fear that there had been a fire.

"Ere was no fire," he said trying to soothe me.

"In Whitby? Was there a fire in Whitby?"

"No, I'm sure 'ere wasn't."

"Perhaps the news has not travelled to London. It is just a small place; no one in London would care. Can you find out for me? Perhaps get a newspaper? *The Whitby Gazette* would tell."

"You are ready to go back to ye room, aren't ye? You don't want another night 'ere, do ye?" George asked in a hauntingly pleasant voice, his face close to mine. During this discourse George's thoughts wandered to his other duties. It seems having to fetch me from the basement had interrupted a routine, and thus a catnap and a snack pilfered from the larder were now in jeopardy.

"No, I am quite all right. Thank-you."

George, changing his mind, turned from the stairs, and, taking my other arm, redirected me to the washroom. Grateful, I gave them no trouble. We passed the door of my noisy neighbour and on the door was tacked a card with the initials G. P. I. An image of a frail man, huddled in a cell much like the one I had just left, seized hold of my mind. His face turned slowly toward me, gaping with sad, hollow eyes that were strangely animate compared to the pale stillness of his emaciated face. George veered away from the door dragging me with him.

George bade me use a clean pot, then carefully poured the liquid into a graduated cylinder and weighed the remainder on a scale. He added the figures to a chart which he handed to Burly instructing him to bring it to Dr Seward.

During the short trip to the washroom I was relieved from the images of blood, but as we were about to pass the door of the quiet room again, the images returned. George became angry and pulled me toward the cell. Frightened and distressed, I resisted, but I was still bound in the strait-waistcoat and George managed to throw me into the dark again.

As before, the humming and voices filled my head, and the backdrop of blood filled my eyes.

Later, in what I guess were the early hours before dawn, one voice became stronger than the others. I did not recognise this voice for I had never heard the voice of God before.

"Renfield, why are you afraid? Are you not deserving of my gifts?" God called me by name and I was uplifted!

I kneeled in supplication, saying: "Yes, Lord I fear your wrath."

"It is I who sent you to this place to do vital work. Everything that has happened is to prepare you to do my bidding. Do not resist, for I will come to you soon and you will be greatly rewarded."

After this I slept. And the next day when George came for me I was meek as a lamb.

This test has strengthened my faith. God has not yet revealed to me his great purpose, but he has touched my mind and healed it. He has revealed to me the error of my thinking. I am not responsible for the lives of my people. I am responsible for their souls and they are here, within me, for safe keeping. We will live together until the Lord is ready for us. Then we shall all have eternal life.

20 May.— Now I am confident that God wants me to live and will give me a purpose. I am sorry for my doubt and beg forgiveness. I will busy myself with my pet Leah and be cheerful. I heap pleasantries on both the doctors and life is much easier for me with their approval.

Dr Seward is distracted. He has been paying little attention to his patients. He has occasionally looked in on me and by sensing his thoughts I have learned something very important. In his mind he repeats a betrothal and a train schedule. By now he is on his way to Whitby where his Lucy is staying. It was she, the luminous, nubile Lucy, he was visiting the day the bishop coerced him to investigate me.

I am also fostering a pleasant relationship with George. Now he is willing to grant my simple requests. I have received more paper and charcoal and have begun negotiations for a lead pencil. Also, I have a little pocket-book, much like the one Dr Hennessey uses to jot down notes about the patients. This he gave me to record my scientific observations of the asylum's fauna. Most gratifying was the presentation of a handkerchief, which I wear in its proper place in the breast pocket as the true badge of a gentleman.

PATIENT LOG
(Entries kept by warder, George Simmons.)

Patient: R. M. Renfield

17 May. 10:15 a.m.— Patient quiet. Still moody he spends his time lying on his cot or at his desk writing.

3:47 p.m.— Heard noises. Patient Renfield found destroying his room and hiding things while I was keeping careful watch. Not talking. Put in padded cell.

18 May. 4:13 p.m.— Patient raving. Vomiting. Not tidy. Wants newspaper left in padded cell.

19 May. 4:30 p.m.— Patient quiet. Behaving — returned to room.

20 May. 10:15 a.m.— Patient is good and happy. Wants more charcoal as he is run out and paper.

21 May. 10:00 a.m.— Patient thanked me for paper and charcoal but now wants lead pencil.

22 May. 11:00 a.m.— Patient writing again and now drawing. Making loud noises like yelling at nothing — banging on table and walls.

REPORT OF DR PATRICK HENNESSEY

23 May.— Patient Renfield has undergone a change in disposition generating concern among the staff who must attend him and his fellow patients. Though melancholy for a long period, he seems, now, to have become agitated, and was found, owing to George's unwavering vigilance, tearing his sheets and hiding the pieces, no doubt for some later use, under his pillow. Warders were compelled to use restraints, though I strongly object to their use, especially for paying patients. There was necessity for these, however, in that Renfield, though usually well behaved, struck a warder.

The patient was then removed to solitary for observation. The warder on duty reports that Renfield was wakeful during most of his stay. George Simmons reports that on the second day in solitary, the patient was still agitated and resisted him. Later that night he is reported as saying: "I fear God." The third day brought happy news of a much improved patient. Though there is no way of telling, at this point, if this episode is short-lived and temporary, or if this is a signalling of times to come, I recommend that Renfield be restricted to quarters until further notice.

RENFIELD'S POCKET-BOOK

(*Found in Dr Seward's files.*)

De Animaculis Animadversio

22 May.— Flies are constantly flying in through the window so I have made a study of them. How free they are. Flies appear to be omnivorous, feeding on animal and plant life, and seem to enjoy everything on my plate. They feed while standing on their food. (Such ecstasy: imagine enough mashed potatoes that a man could lie down in them and eat them at the same time!) It is sad I never took the time to observe flies before. Observing them is difficult for they do not stay still for very long and fly too fast to be studied on the wing. Perhaps they were observing me. They circled my head endlessly and occasionally darted at me. I could not resist ducking at their approach. Such tenacity!

I grew impatient with their antics and decided to catch one and observe it more closely. A large one stood on my dinner plate. Watching carefully for a while, I observed a pattern. The fly stood on the food (apparently feeding); then rubbing them together, it licked its front feet and lastly it flew off only to circle and return to the plate beginning the cycle again. Between feeding and flight, I reasoned, was the best time to strike. I caught the fly easily with one quick snatch. It was not, however, my careful study that allowed this. It seems that I am more agile now than I ever was in my entire life. Languishing confined in a cell could not possibly trigger this; it is yet another gift.

23 May.— Flies may stand motionless for minutes, but when approached they take flight with remarkable speed. To test their response I devised a simple experiment. First, I threatened them with only sound. Loud, sudden "whoops" and "ahs." No discernible reaction to sound. Then I tested their tactile sense by banging the object on which they stood, but at several feet away. Again, the response was minimal. Lastly, because I have observed this effect before and thus made the hypothesis that flies are sight oriented, I made gestures near the flies. They reacted to movement, and also it appeared, to the shadow of those movements on them. I am not sure, however, that the wind caused by this movement was not the cause of their reaction. (Odd, it seems they were irritated by my actions. I've observed yellow wasps become more tenacious after being waved away from a picnic luncheon. Can an insect have such complex emotions like fear, anger, and frustration? Surely they must feel pain.)

A more careful study is necessary to test whether it is sight or wind that the flies respond to.

26 May.— I am collecting flies in a box so that I may observe them better. So far I have caught seven.

Greenbottle flies remind one of little, fat, mechanical dolls with shiny, greenish-black armour that fades into burnt gold where the plates of its back meet. Their bodies are about one half inch long with only one pair of wings.

These wings are transparent and delicate with an opalescent sheen. The wing's strength is derived from a strong lattice of veins not unlike those found on a leaf. Their legs are disproportionately thin, with sharp angled elbows, which would seem to be bent by the weight of the relatively large body. Their legs are strong, however, for flies can run with as great agility as they can fly. Their eyes are magnificent; dull orange-red, they contrast the fly's shiny body in texture and colour. The pattern of the eyes, like tooled leather, is a tiling of hexagons fitted neatly together to cover the curved surface of the eye. It would appear that there is no room for a brain in a head that is so dominated by such relatively huge eyes. They circle the crown of the head leaving no doubt that flies can see a predator's approach from behind. The mouth is surrounded by tiny "fingers" that remind one of scraggly whiskers.

28 May.— I observed the six "feet" of the fly as it easily walked down the wall. Their secret is revealed to me! Each foot has sticky pads and an array of tiny hooks. It is these pads it uses to scale the smooth wall. This demonstrates the strength of their legs. These tiny pads are enough to securely hold the fly to the wall yet the legs are strong enough to pull away when taking a step forward. Since the fly moves two legs at a time to walk, only four groups of pads are holding the weight of the fly from the pull of gravity as it moves about. Though the fly cannot weigh much, the relative strength in a man would be tremendous.

RENFIELD'S JOURNAL

24 May.— Thank Heavens. I now have the freedom of movement I need to catch more spiders. Was this freedom discovered by mere chance? No! He has pointed the way. "Ask and ye shall receive."

To-day God has shown me how to gain access to the entire institution. I can now roam the institution at will. A vent opens under the counter in the tub room. This vent is small, yet much larger than the one in my room, and, removing the grate, I find that I can just fit into it though with some difficulty. The vent follows the corridor and leads to the stairwell landing beyond the gate.

Angie, whose room is at the end of the corridor, keeps watch for me. The matron, it seems, has a habit of eavesdropping from the stairs. And Mary, who can call me by her thoughts, helps me as well. After a quick dart to the tub room, and a slow crawl along the vent, the stairs lead down to the main floor. The stairwell grate (now held up with only one screw, having had to break the others) I loosely fasten in place after me.

I follow the stairs down to the ground floor. Here the main building joins the west wing at right angles. A corridor leads off to the left to the main foyer where the matron has her desk by the front door. I watch from the stairs, and when the moment is right, slip around to the door under the stairs leading down to the basement. Here, I soon discovered, all the buildings of the hospital connect by tunnels.

Later.— Last night in my loneliness I got up to play with Leah, thinking to enjoy the tickle of her tiny steps on my hands. To my astonishment, I could see the faintest of lights under the rim of the cup that held her. In the dark her glow of life was strong. She did indeed glow! To make sure this was no reflection on her shiny shell I stood with my back to the window to block the dusky moonlight and holding her between my thumb and forefinger in front of me, observed her carefully.

Then I felt the presence of another. I turned to look behind me and found another ant faintly shining on the windowsill. She must have been from the same nest as Leah for she was the same species. I must have trapped her here when I shut the window for the night. I decided to call my new friend Rachel for she is more beautiful than her sister, Leah.

I found a spider. And since spiders eat flies, I want to test the rate at which spiders prey on them. With my food as bait, the number of flies increases steadily. The left column of this notebook will be reserved for tallies.

Ham ate flies. Indeed, Ham enjoyed flies even more than he appeared to enjoy birds. Flies, even as agile as they are, were no match for Ham. Ham liked birds. He talked to them. The language he used was distinct from his former vocalisations and his later thought projecting; it was more like a chattering, earnest and attentive, his lower jaw moving rapidly up and down. Flies were not granted this respect; he dashed and pounced at the first buzz and soon after was licking his chops. The lace curtains of the sitting room, completely ruined by his climbing claws, are a testimony to his tenacity in catching flies. Ham was a strange bird.

(*Dr Seward misquotes this date in his phonographic journal concerning Renfield. His entry dated April 25th was most likely recorded on the May 25th. This error may be due to stresses outside his hospital duties. G.D.*)

25 May.— To-day Dr Seward was on rounds, though not at his usual time. Tom cried out "Dr Sewer, Dr Sewer," at his approach, warning us and teasing the doctor at the same time. (Tom, no doubt, derived this name from the doctor's preoccupation with our bodily fluids. One would think he were German.) Dr Seward appeared tired and dejected, and he is the one supposed to be looking after us. He has done it! He has gone and asked for the young lady's hand and I did not have to read his mind to get this information or guess at the sad result. *Omnis amans amens!*

Our good doctor spoke to me at length to-day. He stayed almost an hour and for the first time he seemed interested in what I had to say.

"How are you?" he asked.

I was automatically about to say, "Very well, thank-you," but then I hesitated. What did he mean by that? His face was difficult to read but his thoughts betrayed a great deal of emotion. He was very concerned with my answer. Was he asking after my physical health or does he simply mean, "How was your day?" Coming from a mad-doctor this could have meant, "Are you quite yourself (sane) to-day?" or was he simply using the question as a greeting?

"Good afternoon, doctor," I replied. This seemed to suffice, for his mind opened up and he thought, "He's in good spirits to-day."

"Do you enjoy the food here?" Ah-ha! He is up to that old trick again, so I thought.

"I'm eating quite well, thank-you." He accepted this! My trick of moving the food around on my plate has worked.

"Are you sleeping well?"

"Yes," I replied and then realising that this did not satisfy, added, "I find it most restful here."

"Then you do not miss Whitby?" he probed, but his thoughts were on his own experiences in Whitby.

"My work continues."

"Work?"

"I do God's work."

"Is that what you did in Whitby?"

"No..., I mean yes, different work, but God's work all the same."

"You did God's work in Whitby." He began to think I was not free enough with my "thoughts" and wondered at my reticence. What astonishes me about this discourse is that he should know all the answers to his own questions.

Could I not read his mind, I would have thought he was trying to bore me. I found his simple questions provoking and had he not been actually interested, would have been angered by them.

"I've been a missionary since before you were born."

"Missionary. Why did you first decide to become a missionary?"

Beginning my discourse with my childhood questions about life's purpose and explaining my appointment to Africa, I soon knew this was not what he was after. Apparently my entire career counts for naught in the cause of my "illness." He continued his enquiry hoping to answer two questions. Firstly, he wanted to know of my relationships with women and secondly, of my childhood relationships with my family. This I gleaned from his thoughts; he does not impart his intentions to me.

I took great exception to his questions about the women of my mission. He was unaware of it, but his questions were lewd! As he probed me he described these women (whom he had never seen) to himself, dwelling on his assumptions concerning their scant clothing. Then he recited the virtues of his beloved Lucy in his mind. He began, "Her round hips, her tiny waist ..." (The rest I must Bowdlerise.) After dwelling on her physical characteristics a while, he then waxed on the lady's sweet, childlike nature, her cheerful disposition, and her quick wit. I was much moved. We talked at length on the subject of women, and with each question I was saddened more, until I became visibly bewildered by his pain.

"For his sake," he thought to himself, "I will try to change the subject to his childhood."

"Are you from Whitby?" he said aloud.

"No, I was assigned there when I returned from the mission."

"Assigned," he repeated and said nothing more. It is only now that I realised he was expecting me to continue. "And what is it you say you do?" he asked, finally resigned to talk of my work. His openness and honest interest led me to confide in him.

"I collect souls."

His face was stoic as usual, but his thoughts reacted sharply to this and confirmed my statement. "Yes, he collects souls." Then, to my disappointment, he thought, "Of course, he's a missionary—he collects souls."

Sensing him now sitting in his office just above my room, I am overcome with loss. It is his loss I feel. He is still. Most likely, he is sitting at a writing desk feigning to be working. Oh, doctor, look where your impure thoughts have led! Considering that the man has no spiritual guide, I must help him through this crisis myself. God does not test us beyond our ability, but we must help ourselves by looking for God's grace. God's grace is freely given, and now if I must shoulder this cross as well as my own, I will fill his lamp, so to speak, so he will be ready for the Bridegroom.

Chapter 4

AVARICE

RENFIELD'S JOURNAL

(*Continued*)

26 May.— I must confess I ate my friend Leah. She was small but good. There is a certain satisfaction found in securing one's own nourishment. Ham would have approved. I ate Leah live on instinctual impulse. Though she was hardly a bite, she was quite satisfying; it was more of a fusing of one life to another than merely predator ingesting prey.

This behaviour must be explained, for at first I did not understand it myself. The first day in the quiet room no food was brought to me and I became very hungry. Ravenous, I ate everything on my plate when I was finally served on waking the next morning. At first, the reason why the food did not satisfy me seemed clear: I just needed more. Then my body rejected the food altogether. I spent the day on my knees hanging over my cold, enamelled chamber pot. A bulge in the padded wall above my bowl gave mind to the protruding belly of a Buda. I pictured myself a monk in a Tibetan temple genuflecting before some steely-eyed, golden idol. Though ill, I could not help seeing the humour in this as I offered up my food. The pot does resemble a temple bell, but I could not get a good sound out of it—too tinny—not the broadly dull, soothing tones of the genuine article.

What is the good in regaining one's appetite when one cannot keep anything down? Now even meat repulses me. I do not know what is happening to me. Though I am not seriously ill, my indigestion has reached a crisis. Where there once was just a trace, is now a total revulsion to the sight of food. If all the food on my plate causes this stomach rumbling, then what am I to do? I suffer from a hunger that I cannot satisfy.

Hunger evolves slowly. First there is a distant call from within, a faint, unsure sensation, easily ignored. Later, this is replaced by nervousness. I feel the need to rush somewhere—to do something—but what? Still able to function, I busy myself with writing or some such employment until the faint call reappears and gradually becomes a dull, thick pain in my abdomen, a phantom fullness that grows larger as my energy is drained. My head aches destroying my concentration. Listlessness sets in, making even lifting my arms difficult. This is the oddest sensation for I know I can lift my arms if I must. They ache on the outer sides between my elbows and shoulders. I ask myself to lift them to prove I still can. All the while another, more sympathetic side of me, claims that that effort would only sap what little energy I still possess, and yet reassures me that it is still possible to raise them. I can no longer sit up straight but must remain reclined. Though I need food I have not the vigour to ask for it. I wait, not with the patience of self-restraint, but rather with the lethargy of a will past caring.

There are stronger urges than are recognised in polite society. Without food we all would surely die. I am not the first to indulge in insects as nourishment and I will surely not be the last. The strange reasoning of a guilty conscience provided excuses that sounded perfectly logical if not pressed by the rules of rhetoric. They are not dirty, I insisted to my absent dissenters, they are continually cleaning themselves. The attendants may stop feeding me at any time. I am responsible for myself and should not allow myself to become a burden on others. It was then I noticed the glow of Leah go round and round under the rim of my cup. Lifting the cup slowly, I pinched Leah between my thumb and forefinger. Hesitating, I watched her struggle to get free. Could she know the fate about to befall her?

The flies, of course, were next. Flies, I find to my unexpected pleasure, are quite filling. (Ants, even when engorged, the plates of their abdomens extended to their maximum, are too small to bother with.) I catch flies with my eyes closed. Visualising their movement using only sound, I track them in my mind. Up close their bodies are surprisingly hairy. Venturing to feel the fly's down, I snatched one and carefully placed it in my mouth, alive. I could not feel the hair, but the wings, fluttering frantically, tickled my tongue. Blowing out my cheeks gave it room to fly about inside. Finally, it adhered to the moisture on my tongue so I swallowed it whole.

Ruth, the spider I caught, has spun a web in which she hangs upside-down from long spindly legs. She only eats one fly a day; sucking out its body fluids slowly and then dropping the dry, hollow carcass from her web. (I will consume the excess, for flies do not survive the week in the box even when they are well fed. Their lives are quite short.) Dead flies dropped into her web were of no interest to her. Clearly, it is the struggle of the trapped prey pulling on the web that signals the spider: dinner is served. Thus, I will only give her live flies. The warders will not let me keep food in my room at night and thus I cannot raise my own "flock." No matter, there are plenty "on the wing" that I can pick.

Later.— I have expanded my thesis to include the people of our community. They afford a very interesting study. Taking one subject at a time and using careful observation, I study them. Dr Seward will be the main course. The doctor is out, however, so George will be the subject for to-day.

George is not difficult to understand for his mind dwells on only his immediate needs. Though it was, at first, difficult to read his thoughts, I could easily understand his intentions. When on his rounds, George starts at the end of the corridor. He first goes to Angie and then to Mary before checking on my condition. To-day his thoughts were focused on Mary as he entered my room. Her shoulder appeared as if seen through a spyglass. The view travelled down her arm and so too did George's rough hand. The sleeve of her dress dropped to her elbow.

I glared at George and at once came to the girl's defence. "How dare you touch a patient in that manner?" I insisted, but George just stared at me blankly. "Get out," I demanded, "Get out, you scoundrel." George backed out of the room quickly. He was afraid. Hands reached for his neck—strong hands, choking him. I recognised them—they were my hands! He thought I would attack him. In my entire life I cannot recall anyone ever being afraid of me.

As I stood looking down at my hands, I heard the bolt of my door rammed into place, jarring me back into consciousness. Reaching out my mind to Mary's, I found no trace of his assault. She was calm, and when her thoughts felt mine, she said she had missed me and was sorry I had to endure a padded cell. George's thoughts, it seems, were just daydreams. He had pictured my hands in his mind just as he had pictured himself touching Mary. It is clear now that George more often thinks in pictures than in words.

There must be a way to figure the difference between someone's actual thoughts and simple musing over one's alternatives. Or is there? In the future more careful attention must be paid before action. It is quite embarrassing. If George knew that his shameful reverie was being "observed," he would be embarrassed, too.

PATIENT LOG
(Entries kept by warder, George Simmons.)

Patient: R. M. Renfield

24 May. 5:30 p.m.— Patient nervous—keeps folding handkerchief over and over—not eating good. Still won't give me his cup.

25 May. 5:00 p.m.— Patient sick and lies in bed all day. Still not eating. To-morrow he will be allowed to eat in the common dinning room. Gave small cardboard box.

26 May. 4:30 p.m.— The patient is very
             nervous—violent. Shouted at me in his
             room—no reason. Restricted to room. Not
             eating.

27 May. 5:30 p.m.— Patient Renfield not eaten
             to-day. Sat for hours staring at the wall.

28 May. 5:00 p.m.— Renfield quiet but still
             nervous. Sits looking at his plate which
             had to be removed as it was drawing flies.

REPORT OF DR PATRICK HENNESSEY

*(This notebook "pocket-book" has been preserved and all
intelligible passages inserted by date. GD)*

30 May.—Patient, Renfield, has now clearly entered the
manic stage of his illness. He shows a great deal of
energy, is quite restless, and is no longer melancholy; in
fact he is elated for long periods. To sublimate this
nervous energy a pocket-book has been provided, thus, he
may divert his attention with writing and drawing.

RENFIELD'S JOURNAL

27 May.— Dr Seward has returned and I have learned a
great deal from listening to him recite into his
phonograph with my acute hearing. His Lucy is a young
woman with chestnut hair. She is a virgin, but only
because their shameful fornication exists only in his
thoughts.

It seems the doctor spent the night with two old
friends, Quincey and Art, drinking to excess. The doctor

is thinking slowly to-day and repeats the same few phrases over and over. "Why did I drink so much?" is the phrase most often recited. Quincey, it seems, is a "social climber," unlike himself, who "knows his place."

After his mind began to clear he asked himself why Lucy has chosen Art over himself and Quincey. Oh, it seems Art is a Lord. Dr S. taunts him calling out, u "yes, Lord G. Congratulations, dear fellow. Well done, Lord G." (It seems the girl had many suitors.)

Later.— I noticed an ant on the wall. It has been there for five hours and has not moved. Could it be watching me? Is it accusing me of eating its sister? Though it seemed silly, I checked my sheets for ants lest they bite me in my sleep.

1 June.— I have found that even a small quantity of flies fills me with strength. There can be no doubt for I have eaten nothing else. This tally I keep in my pocket-book for it is of great interest to me to know how many flies a man of my size needs to survive. Making excuses to keep my plate with me longer, I pick the flies one by one, relishing each morsel as if it were an *hors d'oeuvre*.

Storing flies is easy enough once you get the knack. I fitted my fly box with a flexible cardboard flap that covers a hole through which the flies are inserted. The flap is held in place with a bit of wax. Once a fly is inserted through the hole, the flap swings back and the slight mastic qualities of the wax hold it in place.

Removing a fly from the box is a different matter. Holding open the flap with my thumb, I shake the box rigorously over a bowl of soup. This shaking stuns the flies and one or more will fall out into the liquid and float there. When a fly's wings are wet, they cannot fly. Picking the fly out of the soup is easily achieved.

5 June.— Dr Seward spoke to me for the first time as a fellow man of learning. He expressed passionately the reasons why I may not keep such a quantity of flies in my room. I objected to his statement that they were dirty, but had to admit their buzz was annoying the other patients. It is not only that he spoke to me man to man, but that he deigned to converse with me at all that I wonder at. Just two weeks ago he was probing me with his circumlocution—treating me as if an underling—and to-day he uses rhetoric to convince me that his argument is sound. And sound it was. I took only a moment to calculate how many flies I must eat each day to reduce their number to the "daily catch"—certainly, I did not want to merely dump them out the window. He agreed, without gloating, to my suggestion of three days. His thoughts indicated that he did not know how I would rid myself of them.

I am getting to know him better than he is getting to know me. He is pining, poor fellow. He truly believes he loves the girl, but if he could hear his thoughts from where I stand, he would right his thinking immediately.

PATIENT LOG
(*Entries kept by warder, George Simmons.*)

Patient: R. M. Renfield

2 June. 9:00 a.m.— Lots of flies in patient's room making lots of noise. Patient behaving himself accepting[*sic*] he wont eat.

3 June. 9:30 a.m.— Patient been seen eating flies. Told Dr Hen. Patient wont give his plate back after meals. Says he needs it.

4 June. 10:30 p.m.— Noise getting worst — others complaining.

5 June. 9:30 p.m.— Dr S. says I must take away patient's plate after meals. Patient eating flies.

6 June. 9:30 p.m.— Still too many flies but less than before.

REPORT OF DR PATRICK HENNESSEY

6 June.— Patient Renfield. The patient, possessed of a sanguine disposition, strives to accommodate the peculiarities of his fellow patients and please his doctors; to wit, he is, at times, obsequious and fawning. His habits are clean, as mentioned earlier, in all but one aspect: the patient is enamoured of consuming insects. His careful studies of the asylum fauna have deteriorated into a mere tallying of their number and variety in his note-book. This, in and of itself, is not a concern, yet, one must wonder how he may keep such a large number of flies in a box without mutilating them in some way, such as, removing their wings. The patient, protective and secretive of his nature studies, declines comment on the subject.

7 June.— Prayers are always answered and this time the answer was yes. Early this morning I awoke with a sticky thread on my face. This cobweb stretched from high on the wall to the bed's headboard, down across my pillow and up to the headboard again. Broken, the fairy-fine thread reached out toward the window, gently waving as if signalling to its lost owner to come and retrieve it and restore it to its former connectedness. It did not take long to find the climber who had so carelessly left this trail.

Samson, for that is the name I have chosen for him, walked slowly across my desk and stood on my notebook gaping at me with all eight eyes as if to say: "Here I am." He cleaned his long moustaches with two tiny extra legs that extend from either side of his face. Yes, and what a remarkable face! It is flat with its two larger eyes placed forward like a man's. (Ants and flies, like other insects, have their eyes on the sides of their heads.) Large, strong, and remarkably hairy, Samson has a commanding presence. (I must, of course, guess the gender of my little friends. Ruth is likely female for she spins a web and, as with many species of orb weavers, only the female builds a nest. With Samson it is anybody's guess what sex he is.) Samson is a large jumper spider and is much more voracious than Ruth. He is attentive as I write and is still watching me.

A fly placed in Samson's box may run free for hours. The next morning, however, the fly has been drained and its outer body discarded. Strange how perfectly intact the fly appears. The interior of the body is totally hollowed out, yet the outer body receives hardly a scratch. I can easily tell which flies are still alive. I blow on them and the dead ones, so light and hollow, roll away with just the force of my breath.

Samson is my new friend, for not only will he eat flies that otherwise would be wasted, but he has shown me the benefit of waking early. It is pleasantly quiet in the early dawn and I must take advantage of this time to write. The sun's rays from the window are diffused, giving a soft, warm brightness to the room. It is still cool then and pulling back the covers is refreshing.

I have made a box out of bits of cardboard to be Samson's new home. It is of simple construction and of course is aerated with tiny holes in the sides and lid. Samson's box has a floor of damp earth in which he enjoys digging. Also, the box is supplied with a water dish made from the cap of a calomel bottle. He must like it for he spends his day in his box sometimes even when I leave the lid open. At night, however, he is on the prowl and does not return until sunup.

RENFIELD'S POCKET-BOOK

10 June.— There are, I have observed, two distinct patterns for spiders: building webs (orb weavers, I believe they are called) and running about in search of prey. My names for these are sleepers and runners. The sleepers wait patiently for prey to happen into their webs and the runners are in constant motion, hunting. I should not say constant motion for occasionally they do stop and remain motionless for long periods. I cannot fathom why. It is very disconcerting when they decide to stop on the

ceiling just above me as I lie in bed observing them. Perhaps they simply need rest.

Runners do not mind standing upside down, or running upside down for that matter. I have heard them called jumping or "wolf" spiders. Though it may only be the giant spiders of South America that are called wolf spiders. I do like the term wolf spider for their colour, size, and tenacity in catching prey make it a good analogy and thus, a good name for the big hairy fellows like Samson.

The faces of these spiders are much like human faces in that the eyes face forward and the forehead arches above the eyes like our own brow. Their seemingly harmless walrus moustaches are actually rather large, hair-covered fangs. These fangs are hollow, having within them a tube that emits venom. Sometimes, when I open the box to feed them, the venom drips from the sharp tips of these fangs as if they are salivating.

I now have eight impressive specimens which I keep in my box.

RENFIELD'S JOURNAL

13 June.— As my abilities increase I am able to learn
more and more about the others here. It seems I cannot
read everyone's thoughts—some people's thoughts read a
blank. Though I concentrate on them, their thoughts are
obscured by my own thoughts or stronger thoughts from
others. Simple minds are easiest and highly developed,
directed minds, like the doctor's, are also quite

accessible. Most people, however, think in a jumble of vagaries, which I cannot make out until they choose to think of a specific idea.

Tom, the violent patient, often thinks of his wife. When he is not secluded in the quiet room, his thoughts show tranquil scenes of his home life. He pictures his wife sitting in a garden spilling peas from their pods into a large bowl or picking flowers. He sees her at a distance and I cannot make out her features, though I am sure she is a comely woman. It is odd that he does not picture himself with her.

I have begun to remember Whitby as if I were an observer and not a participant. I see the scenes in my memory with me in them, but it is a self I do not know. In physical appearance I am exactly as I am now, but my actions and words in these memories cannot be correct. In one recurring memory, I see myself standing in the pulpit delivering a sermon and I am quaking. This causes my voice to shake as well and I am scarcely loud enough to be heard in the back of my tiny chapel. Is this a true picture of the past or is my mind recreating the scene differently?

As for Tom, he does not picture himself in his thoughts. This caused me to think that these scenes of the woman in the garden were part of my past—a misplaced memory. I did not connect these scenes with Tom until I was near him in the tub room yesterday.

George ordered him, "Keep your fas' nin on!" although the man was far from showing any resistance. The dirty brute of a man cowered as I was brought in. The warders have beaten him and placed him in solitary confinement so often, he has become cowed in their presence. He speaks constantly, asking to see his wife or uttering nonsense until a warder or the matron draws near. Then he retreats into himself and becomes silent.

The garden scene, which was until then always faint, crowded my mind as I entered the room. The garden was filled with large, flat stones and the woman sat on a broad, stone bench with a flower basket in her arms. She was tossing away daisies, one at a time, from her basket, which curiously remained full though she cast away many flowers. An intense feeling of desire surrounded her, but she was unaware of it. This feeling caused my face to sweat under a hot and heavy weight as if the air had become denser. Had this weight not lifted as Tom retreated from me, I might have fainted.

At first I was not aware it was his desire I was feeling. I delayed as long as I could in the washroom and lingered by the door watching flies circle the full basins that lined one wall. When the two warders coaxed him out, he no longer pictured the garden. His wide blue eyes, filled with fear, spoke silently to me. They said, "Help me! help me return to my wife, Father." (I'll excuse the "father" for he clearly does not know better.) This was most telling for these thoughts began abruptly when the garden picture ended. I told him with my thoughts that I would do whatever I could, but my thoughts did not register in his mind. He cannot sense my thoughts as can Mary. In fact, as he stared out from under the hair that shadowed his eyes, he realised that I am the one who keeps the flies. He became upset and began to tug at the warders who held him on either side. They hurried him out and he cursed me as he passed. Since then he has added: "Flies! buzz buzz. Make them go away," to his litany. Poor soul.

1 July.— Dr Seward visited me to-day, so while he was here I took advantage, for I want to get to know him better. I need more information about Lucy so that I may help him. I tried to turn the conversation to his private life, but he is much too clever and changed the subject to me and my own private dealings almost immediately. (I am still not sure how he does that.) This had the further undesirable effect of turning his thoughts to me as well. Thus, I learned nothing new of Lucy, to-day.

Dr Seward would have us believe that he lives without care, only the dark circles beneath his eyes betray him. He is not sleeping or if he does sleep, it is not restful sleep. Is he still pining for Lucy? I could help the man if he would only let me.

His thoughts were focused on my room—he was searching for "clues." He eyed the box on my desk. Without a word I picked it up and handed it to him. Pleased, he opened it and looked inside. I felt the sudden shock pour, as if liquid, down from the top of his head, over his shoulders, and through his arms to his fingertips. This resulted in a minute, but violent, shake to the box. All my lovely little predators fell to the bottom of the box and rolled themselves into tight balls. At the moment of the shock the doctor thought: "They're so big!" and he pictured a huge spider—as big as a cat! —in front of his face. That was the first picture the doctor has sent, and the only one, for he immediately began thinking in words again. In fact, his thoughts accused me of purposely making him uncomfortable. My goal was just the opposite, so closing it gently, I took the box and placed it by the window. Just then a large fly flew in. I caught it, and seeing it was only a blow-fly (which I have already described in my pocket-book) popped it into my mouth without thinking.

"What are you doing?" asked the doctor who was again shocked.

I could not speak for I had not swallowed yet.

"Renfield, you mustn't do that."

"Doctor, there is no harm in it. In Africa people eat insects every day. Flies are tasty. And they are quite nourishing because they are all meat and no waste. A more wholesome food one might never find."

"You are given plenty enough food to eat."

"But flies are alive and their life gives me strength—they give me life!"

He, of course, did not understand. He is a dull pupil, sometimes so thick he does not see what is in front of him. He "corrects" his observations to fit with what he already "knows." I tried to be patient and let him sit and observe me. I sat at my table and recorded the fly I had just caught. This small action piqued his interest and he eyed my pocket-book longingly thinking: "If I could get a look at that book I might find something important." To his astonishment, I handed him the pocket-book. He looked quizzically at the tallies for only a moment. Then, feeling uncomfortable about keeping it too long, he handed the book back to me.

On his way out, Dr Seward turned and said I must rid myself of my spiders. I was taken aback for I believed that he was supportive of my research. Speechless, I held my spider-box to my chest trying to decide what argument I could make. Before I could speak, the doctor decided that I must merely reduce their number as I did with the flies. He gave me only three days to do so. I thought it best to comply without a fight for I did not want to wound his vanity.

2 July.— The trees outside of my window are full of birds and that has sparked an idea. The weather has been fair and the window is left open all day. My plan is to conscript aid in reducing my flies and spiders, and get a new subject for my nature observations. The plan is simple: leave flies on the windowsill and imitate bird calls. I had to crush the flies, of course, lest they fly away. It is much easier to count them as "splats" than while flying about, anyway.

5 July.— Success! A sparrow lighted on the windowsill this morning. Busily, it hopped about gulping every spider placed on the sill. (Dead flies were of little interest to the sparrow; it preferred the live spiders. Such a waste.) Cautious of me, it flew back to the trees when I approached. I placed more spiders on the sill, removed to the far corner on my room and quietly sat on the foot of my bed. It returned. It hopped about excitedly twisting its head with wary curiosity all the while jabbering away like a child with too much to say.

But what was it saying? Perhaps it says: "Stay away, I'm afraid of strangers." It did seem nervous. Or maybe it says: "Thank-you for the scrumptious spiders," and it was in jubilation that it jumped about. It may be that, to a bird, spiders are tasty. I find them bitter and tough—even the meatiest of them. They are more texture than taste. And, where flies panic when placed inside the mouth, spiders play dead. They roll themselves into balls and remain very still. With each spider I wait patiently expecting them to "wiggle and jiggle and tickle inside me" as the song goes, but to no avail. I nudge them with my tongue to get them to move, yet, far from tickling, they bite back!

Thank-you, oh Lord, for this sign of your presence.

6 July.— The sparrow is manic. Though it should feel more comfortable with me by now, it still jumps about nervously at the slightest movement or sound. It is awkward to enter a new situation. I will make an effort to make the sparrow comfortable in his new position as chief spider controller. I will show him the hospitality that I was shown by a king.

It was to be my crowning moment in Zambezia. I was called to the royal *kraal* at Bulawayo to speak with King Lobengula, himself. At first I was uneasy for I misunderstood what was wanted of me; you see, Bulawayo means "place of the killing." I soon learned, however, I was called only because of my singular talent—the virtue of being able to read English. The king had arranged that as many white missionaries as possible were to study a new treaty.

A camp, swelling with Europeans, had grown around the royal *kraal*. Just a few years before there were almost no outsiders in Matabeleland and now there were dozens. The king tolerated missionaries like myself, who, on the most part, were unsuccessful in converting his people to Christianity. Now, however, gold prospectors, adventurers, elephant hunters, ivory buyers, traders, and seekers of cheap labour were quickly finding success converting them to a life in pursuit of material wealth. The enterprising whites, following our missionaries' paths, set poor examples of western morals and culture. Each needed permission from the king to travel in the land, for the Ndebele are fierce warriors descended from the Zulu. On this occasion, however, it was the traders who had to wait and we missionaries were invited in.

King Lobengula had serious doubts about the treaty after our most beloved Queen Victoria wrote to him expressing her feeling that there was something irregular about it. Indeed, upon reading it, it was quite odd. What struck me most peculiar was that this was not a treaty with England, or with any country for that matter, it was with a mining company from the Cape Colony. Also, it was not drafted for a king or other ruler, but for a businessman, one Cecil Rhodes. The treaty (concession) called for all mining rights from the Limpopo to the Zambezi and, what caused us the most concern, the company was to have full power to "win and procure the same."

The king had signed this treaty with the mining company several months earlier. A group of white men, headed by a Mr Rudd, was sent to overlook the signing. Scouting parties were sent out ahead to watch Rudd's party and bring back information.

The parties brought back stories of magic and fear. Mr Rudd's *induna* was a powerful wizard, they said, for they saw, with their own eyes, the man step into a vat of boiling water. What man could do that unless he were a wizard? He then proceeded to rub himself all over with a strange vegetable that foamed and bubbled until a fearful froth had covered his entire body. And though the froth and boiling water quite covered his entire body, he was calm, so calm in fact that he hummed and sang cheerfully to himself. He emerged from the vat unscathed, scattering the brave onlookers into the bush. But this was not the end to their magic.

Another white man of the party, putting a touch of powder on a tiny brush with a long handle, rubbed it in his mouth. A red froth grew in his mouth which he spat into the river, bewitching it.

The *induna* had warned the king against signing the treaty for they had proof that Mr Rudd was travelling with powerful wizards. Yet the king was promised a gunboat on the Zambezi, and besides, he did not believe the rabbit-faced man (as he called Mr Rudd) was accompanied by wizards.

Now the king was having serious doubts.

The *induna*, I recall, had serious doubts about the concession as well. They said the mining company meant to take their kingdom, they said they feared war would come soon, they said this was all the missionaries' fault for did not the son of Reverend Moffat tell the king that the concession was just to let a few prospectors in and were there not already hundreds more waiting for mining rights as well. The king said that his fortune tellers had known this all along. He seemed resigned to their divination. We advised the king to cancel the concession and send emissaries to England.

The Pall Mall Gazette, 7 July

(*Found amongst Dr Seward's files. Though no name is used, the patient mentioned here is most likely R.M. Renfield. G.D.*)

THE MIND READER

Interview with the chief alienist of the Purfleet Lunatic Asylum

A new curiosity can be found in an asylum just outside London. Dr John Seward, the curator and chief alienist, is attempting to fathom the unbalanced mind and discover the inner workings of the insane. Dr Seward challenges the belief that madmen lack the power of reason. "Madness is not a lack of reason but a corruption thereof. The lack of reason is the lot of the dumb animal. The doctor must seek the germ of this corruption, the *idée fixe*, to gain insight into the workings of the unbalanced mind."

In his courageous struggle, it is ignorance that wields the strongest blow against him. Old myths about insanity persist even in this, our modern age. Some warders insist that patients are more likely to give them problems during the full moon (hence the term lunatic). The doctors, however, say that this is nonsense. Many melancholy claim that in winter, when the days are shorter, they feel their sadness more acutely, and, in the spring their spirits are lifted. Again, the doctors cry "poppycock." Dr Seward will look inside the patient for the cause of madness rather than outside. That is, he will probe the patient's mind rather than search for an external physical cause.

To his contemporaries, Dr Seward's methods are seen as a throwback to earlier forms of treatment. Dr Henry Maudsley, author of *Natural Causes and Supernatural Seemings*, states there is a physical cause for insanity and that that cause is determined by heredity. "Survival of the fittest does not always mean survival of the best," he says, "... it means only the survival of that which is best suited to the circumstances, good or bad, in which it is placed." Dr Maudsley explains a rogue may survive among rogues or a savage succeed in a savage medium or a parasite flourish where a parasite alone can live. Maudsley finds that the tenements of London are a breeding ground for incurable degenerates. Thus, in his asylum, patients are not so much treated, as merely segregated from society. Dr Seward, however, does not see his role as being merely the custodian of the insane; rather he believes the alienist can be a healer of the mind. He seeks to understand the inner workings of the diseased mind.

Dr Willis, famous for his successful treatment of his majesty, King George III, believed in removing the patient from his present "maddening" surroundings and placing him in a pleasant and restorative environment. This pleasant environment was usually his own modest (though costly for patients) farm in North Yorkshire. Here the mad were distracted from themselves with hard work. This would keep their hands busy, rather than their minds. Dr Willis believed that the mad spend too much time thinking of themselves. John Conolly, longstanding, former super-intendent of Colney Hatch Asylum, likewise stressed the importance of hard work to keep patients' minds and hands occupied. This method of treating the insane, called "moral management," was based on the assumption that the insane were in need of moral supervision and training. This supervision and training was attended to personally by the physician-superintendent who came to regard his patients as part of his family.

Dr Willis claimed a high cure rate, but the reality is that the insane are, and have been, an ever increasing segment of our society. The once paternally run asylum has become a warehouse where no treatment is offered at all. Much effort has been expended for the last four decades to find a cure for insanity. However, not only has a cure not been found, but the plight of the mad has not improved. In fact, moral management has been abandoned, and shackles and straight-waistcoats, thought to be obsolete instruments of the past, have returned. This is because madness is now accepted by most to be incurable.

The view on how to treat the insane has changed considerably since the advent of the moral treatment of Dr Willis. Dr Seward bristles when his detractors suggest that his unorthodox views are merely clinging to the past. "It is now known that insanity is determined by heredity and not by environment," says Dr Maudsley who is now the superintendent of Colney Hatch. It has been suggested that if Dr Seward had studied here in England, he would know insanity is incurable. Even the Austrian alienist, Dr Sigmund Freud, despite his success with cases of hysteria, also contends that madness is not treatable. Dr Seward, however, believes that there are clues in the ranting of the insane and that these hold the key to the origin of madness. "Finding the source," Dr Seward states, "will lead us to the cure. ... I listen very carefully to the patient and take notes. When I have amassed enough discourse from one patient, I can begin to piece together the puzzle."

Widespread disillusionment in finding a cure for madness is not the only barrier to Dr Seward's efforts.

Madness, it seems, has many forms, making it extremely difficult to study from a medical point of view.

The various forms of insanity each respond to treatment differently. The most curable form of madness is that brought on by sudden shock. The mind cannot absorb the blow and for a time reels from it. However, just as one slowly regains one's balance after spinning until one is dizzy, the mind collects itself over time.

Less understandable, and thus less curable, are the conditions known as melancholia and dementia praecox. The first is unreasonable and lengthy sadness. The melancholic patient is listless and moody. This condition may last for years and often results in suicide. Dementia praecox is the name the alienist uses for what we laymen think of as madness. The person stricken with this condition sees or hears things that are not there. They may become agitated or even violent. The alienist takes age into consideration in cases of dementia praecox for it has long been noted that the age of the patient at the onset of the condition will likely determine the outcome of treatment. Those stricken between the ages of 16 and 30 are least likely to recover. Those younger and older respond to treatment more readily.

Using examples like the one above, Dr Seward intends to study in depth the origins of an insane patient's fancy. Here he will look for clues to the inner workings of the mind. He has chosen one patient with which to begin his study. This patient suffered a late onset to his condition and thus is likely to respond to treatment. The patient is a seemingly pleasant and well mannered man in his fifties. In outward appearance he is neat and respectable; one might even take him for a sane man.

Behind this façade, however, lurks a homicidal maniac. Once, after tearing up his room, the patient was asked to remove himself to a quiet room. Rather than comply peacefully, the patient struck a warder in the chest so violently that he bruised the man's ribs. It took two strong men to get him under control.

Dr Seward seeks to find the motivation for the man's behaviour, not merely suppress it. To achieve this end, Dr Seward encourages the patient to talk of himself in hope that the patient may, perhaps inadvertently, reveal clues to the cause of his illness. He then records his findings by speaking them into a phonograph. This modern device, the doctor says, will relieve doctors of the tedium of recording their observations by writing. The cylinders are easily stored and retrieved when needed, says the doctor. As the doctor begins to understand the content of the patient's dialogue, he can refer back to earlier conversations and recreate the world of the mad.

With Dr Seward's gentle guidance, this patient has developed an unusual hobby to keep himself occupied. He makes careful drawings and observations of insects, spiders, and birds. Though an unlikely place for a naturalist, the asylum has afforded him the time and space to exercise his intellect. His body may be restricted, but his mind is not.

RENFIELD'S POCKET-BOOK

(*At this point in his notebook, Renfield now fills the left pages, which were reserved for drawings, with lists of numbers. G.D.*)

7 July.— The sparrow is indeed a boon to my studies. My overpopulation problems are solved for the sparrow eats constantly and is greedy for more. It is impossible to make a precise measurement without scales, but I estimate the sparrow can eat over twice its own weight in one day. The small beak of the sparrow can open quite wide and thus it swallows its prey whole—even large spiders. Spiders that are too large, it tosses away only to hop to the cast away meal and peck at it again. Perhaps the bird is trying to break the spider into smaller pieces.

Sparrows

Flies

Spiders

8 July.— Today, Amos, as I now call the sparrow, ventured to sit upon my forefinger. My method of befriending him was simple: I held out a spider with my left hand and extended my right forefinger to create a perch at a comfortable distance from the spider. And with

the spider-box close at hand, I fed Amos until he was sated—five spiders in all were greedily consumed at this first contact. I added a new tally to this book as the reader will observe on the facing page. This account records the number of spiders I observe Amos to eat each day.

RENFIELD'S JOURNAL

9 July.— To-day I was taken to the common room for the first time. When George came for me this morning he did not tell me where he was taking me. This is typical of George. I went along in a polite manner, of course, for I do not like to upset George. As he led me to the main corridor, he pictured the common room clearly in his mind so I was not surprised when he brought me there.

His picture of the room was a good match for the genuine article. Seven large windows comprised the outer wall. The floor tiles, set in a wide alternating black and white pattern, stood largely empty. The patients, like still figures, raggedly circled the perimeter as though taken pieces in some weird, life-size chess match. The only item he had forgotten, or neglected to notice, was that there were large paintings on three walls, each depicting a hunting scene comprised of slim riders in scarlet and smart, black, top hats. The scenes showed a foxhunt in progression. First the chase, then capture and finally, the kill.

The inmates, however, he pictured quite accurately —specifically where they would be located in the room. Tom paced quickly at the far end of the room. (I cannot fault him for this, for recently I find that I am pacing, myself.) He had pictured Mary in the far left corner, furthest from the windows, with her head bowed and eyes melancholy. To my astonishment this was exactly how she was situated when we entered. Even I cannot see through walls! How did he know how she was situated—even to what she was wearing?

The others I did not know. A man (who seemed quite normal enough) was sitting at a small table near the centre window. He had books but he was not reading; he was watching me. Another young man, a boy really, huddled in his own arms, paid no notice to my entrance, but stared with rapt attention at the pattern of the floor tiles. George departed closing the door behind him.

At that moment, another warder, whom I had seen before, looked up from behind his newspaper where he was seated in the right corner by the windows. His look spoke a language I have learned well in my short stay here, "Don't make any trouble—I'm watching you."

I looked right, then left. The only sound was the muttering of Tom and his shoes scuffing on the floor. Behind him sprawled the other agitated patients, fidgeting nervously. None looked up, but they were watching me all the same. To the left the melancholy patients sat in total silence. Mary sat with her legs drawn up to her, hugging them. Her bare toes peeked out from beneath her frock and lined up neatly with the edge of the chair. It seems the patients had separated themselves into two groups: manic and melancholic.

I stood in the middle. I was to choose. It was a long uncomfortable moment for I do not feel I belong to either group. Then I again noticed the well-dressed man sitting with his books. So tempting. His look was studying, neither congenial nor aloof. He had not yet sized me up and was reserving judgment. Not wanting to appear forward, I did not approach but opened out my palms and gave him the sparest of nods. This he returned, thus giving me all the acknowledgement I needed.

The warder's newspaper rustled as he again brought it up before him. I was quite aware from his gaze that these first introductions do not always go well. Introductions! Did I actually use that word? Formal introductions are totally absent here though they are most needed. Why must we inmates always have to fend for ourselves, disoriented and alone? Our ancestors created manners, like introductions, to increase our comfort with our fellows. Simple manners are the warp of the fabric of our society. Thrusting a newcomer into a group, even a group such as we are, is a blow to one's sense of worth and each blow strips one of another thread of one's humanity. But I digress.

The gentleman gestured me to sit. I did. His eyes betrayed him as he smiled his hello; they glanced down sad and ashamed.

"Renfield," I said, as I extended my hand. (I neglected using my title lest I bring shame upon my profession.)

"Jamison," he admitted as he half-rose to meet my hand. His eyes did not meet mine. I volunteered nothing personal. No use getting off on the wrong foot talking of my troubles. Instead the subject was books. Before him he patted a short pile. Keats, he was reading, enjoying how the poet had "read his mind." Byron's epic poem *Manfred* was his favourite and he absently held the volume to his heart as he spoke of the poor, misunderstood and hated Manfred. Presently he was reading *Bleak House*. He asks his family to bring him Dickens novels because they are invariably long and can take months to read. That way he can fill the time between their infrequent visits without appearing to be asking too much. Indeed, asking for one large book is nothing compared to asking for several small ones. With Dickens, he likes to read only one short chapter a day, in serial fashion, the way they were first published. Then he places himself in the scene—a fly on the wall so to speak—and has all the characters come alive in his mind to act it out.

Our talk was interrupted when George returned and announced dinner. He did me the honour of taking me first and led me to the door. The moment he did so my head became filled as if water had suddenly been pumped into my skull. The pressure was so terrific I clasped my head with both palms, pushing inward lest the force from within cause my head to explode. A loud piercing shriek hurt my ears and frightened me beyond belief. Jerking my elbow away from George, I searched for the source of the sound. The sound stopped and I found that it was I, myself, mouth still ajar, that was the source of the screaming.

When George had taken my arm, my mind instantly became one with each inmate in the room. All eyes and thoughts focused on me. Each cried with some inner turmoil: George's anger, Mary's fear, Tom's anxiety, Mr Jamison's despair. I turned in place matching each inmate with their respective thoughts, hoping to alleviate— eliminate—subtract those thoughts from my mind but to no avail. Again, without realising it, I began to scream.

George, quicker than one could believe possible, whisked me out the door and in no time I was secured in my room.

Distance abated the other's thoughts somewhat, but still left fragments of jumbled phases, pictures, sounds, and feelings whirling in my mind. Gulping for breath, I remained helpless until finally my heart slowed and gradually my breathing became even again. I did not need to look up to know George had quietly returned and was observing me through the trap. I pretended not to notice him as I wiped the tears from my face. It is the third time since my incarceration that I have wept.

Because of this incident I will miss having dinner with the others. George has placed a plate by the door, but I cannot eat this food. Another meal not eaten, yet I am unconcerned, for I will find my own nourishment. What does concern me is why the others were so jealous of my getting to the dining table first. My only guess is that boredom has blown the importance of mealtime out of proportion for these poor souls. What they need is something to occupy their minds and hands, a job or a hobby. Idleness, and forced idleness at that, is indeed an invitation to the devil.

Chapter 5

GLUTTONY

RENFIELD'S JOURNAL

(*Continued*)

11 July.—A tiny fly, no bigger than a speck, touched down on the volcano of mashed potatoes. Immediately its wings adhered to the hot lava flow of gravy—dreadfully wonderful way to go!

As I sit watching the flies circle my supper, I listen for the sparrows that will soon fly to my window, one by one, in search of spiders. Amos was the bravest, but now his friends come to me as well. This has caused a stress in the balance of nature here in my room. The sparrows are endlessly ravenous and there is much fighting over the now meagre supply of spiders. The window casements of the common room are now bereft of livestock and the others' rooms are forbidden to me. So to replenish my spider population, I sneak downstairs to the basement; the damp corners there yield an abundance of spiders. Still, this supply will not last if the sparrow population continues to increase. Each day I journey farther down the tunnels to catch prey, yet food remains in short supply.

In my search for spiders I have learned much about the hospital or "house" as Dr Seward calls it. Across from our rooms are three doors. The first I found locked, but, the two doors set close together before the tub room were not. The first was a linen closet. No spiders there. The second was labelled Janitor. I opened it without hesitation and found to my surprise, George sitting upright in a chair. Startled though I was, it took only a moment to realise he was fast asleep. An acrid smell hurt my eyes; beside him was a makeshift shelf holding the nub of a candle and a small bowl overflowing with the stubs of "coffin nails," as George calls them. I quietly closed the door and quickly made my way downstairs, fleeing the choking stench of spent tobacco more than fearing being caught.

The basement is very large for there are tunnels that extend to the annexes behind the main building. Under the west wing is the laundry. There is too much activity here, so it must be avoided lest I be caught out of bounds. One section under the main building, where the incurables are housed, is for storage and the doors of the storage compartments are locked. The rest are filled to capacity with coal bins, treatment rooms, and yes, cells. One would not call them rooms for it is more like a prison than a hospital here.

There is something uncomfortable, yet familiar here that I cannot place. Overcome, I made my way back upstairs. Though I am fearful, my duty to carry out my experiments is of the utmost importance. I shall return here later.

Back in the common room, Tom, who now has forgiven me for the flies, joined in the search for spiders and has proved an excellent hunter. He sat with me for a long while. Tom, when not belligerent, has an endearing charm. He speaks with the native wile so often possessed by Irishmen. He confided that his initial fear of me was prompted by my initials R M on the door of my room. Apparently, he had more than one encounter with the Rural Magistrate back in Tipperary. Yet, it seems his troubles began when he moved his family here to London. His story is a sad one. Most importantly, he stresses his wish to conquer the "evil brew" and return to his life outside.

"The craving never stops. If I could have just one sip. One sip to stop the pain, a pain so overwhelming it stops me from moving, altogether. I'm helpless, you see. I can't move. There I sit, hour after hour, day after day, until I can't hardly even blink. Thoughts slip into my mind, bad thoughts, terrible thoughts. All I can do is think, think of what I've done and what I've become, and most of all, what I might have been. And that's the worst of it—what might have been. It drives me out of my mind, entirely. It drives me to distraction.

"When distracted I begin to shake. Sometimes it's like my hands are unsteady. Sometimes it's much worse, and my elbows and knees shake, too. The shaking upsets people. Do you know what I'm saying? I am deserted and left all alone. I don't like being alone at all, at all. When I'm alone all I want is a drink. I drink to fill the emptiness inside that pulls the flesh in towards my heart as if it will cave in. You know what I mean? My insides burn, burn with the pain of Hell itself.

"The drink, now the drink stops all that, you see. Warm and thick, I feel it flow slowly down my throat into my stomach. 'Tis here, where I feel it." He showed where he felt it running his finger up and down the front of his neck. "The voices stop, the memories stop, the flashing pictures from the past stop. The world comes into focus again. My nerves calm and relax. Friends gather 'round me bringing comfort and companionship. No better camaraderie have you ever seen. We gather together and go have a drink. Sometimes we drink away into the night, telling stories and jokes, talking politics and making plans.

"Then I wake with my head on fire. My mouth is dry, but I'm so full of water I could fill the Thames. There is a buzzing between my ears and a pain. A pain that shudders my whole body. A pain that won't go away."

George, seeing that Tom was too weary to remain in the common room, began to lead him back to his room. And, just before he disappeared out the door Tom turned and said, "Flies!, buzz buzz."

Poor Tom, what will become of him?

The sparrows have arrived. George has arrived too and has snatched my plate away, which he will take with him to the closet. Each evening he feels the need to help me finish my meal. His appetite is insatiable.

RENFIELD'S POCKET-BOOK

15 July.— Sparrows, surprisingly enough, are quite diverse in markings, call, and behaviour. Are these distinctions noticeable to others? Have we just never taken the time to notice? Or perhaps it is the gift that allows me to see that here the striping is darker, there the hopping more agitated.

Naming my little friends is a delicate art. First, a distinguishing feature must be found. Then, I consult the Old Testament for a name that suits that characteristic. If the number of sparrows continues to increase at this pace, I shall have to consult the New Testament as well.

17 July.— Sparrows do not walk, but rather hop with both feet together. Sometimes they fly low to the ground. They amass in groups of 30 to 40 on the ground or in the trees. Once one begins to chirp the others join in, in a monotonous chorus. Soon they lose the meter and divide into syncopated groups so they are as a Greek chorus, more percussion birds than song birds. At times, a young bird may chirp in a quicker cadence, hunching low to the ground and vibrating its wings. A parent will peck up spiders for them and insert the morsel into the eager maw.

My earlier estimate was clearly too conservative —sparrows can eat at least three times their own weight each day. I must find a way to diminish their number.

PATIENT LOG
(Entries kept by warder, George Simmons.)

Patient: R. M. Renfield

4 July. 9:00 a.m.— quiet—birds in room —eating.

5 July. 9:30 a.m.— Patient feeding bugs to birds.

6 July. 9:00 a.m.— Patient quiet writing.

7 July. 10:00 a.m.— Sparrows in room all day.

8 July. 9:30 a.m.— Has some tamed sparrows. Patients complaining of noise.

9 July. 9:30 a.m.— Patient good and ready to go to dayroom.

7:15 p.m.— Patient misbehaving. He set to screaming after I merely touched him in the common area.

REPORT FROM PATRICK HENNESSEY, M.D., M.R.C.S., L.K.Q.C.P.I., ETC., ETC., TO JOHN SEWARD, M.D.

"12 July.
"My dear Sir, –

"Here is the report you asked for, and, in compliance with your wishes... The patient Renfield has been carefully watched and observed. His first visit to the dayroom was, for the most part, a success; he sat quietly with Mr Jamison the entire time and composed himself properly. However, at the dinner bell he began to scream uncontrollably. Apparently, the bell frightened him and he had to be removed to his room immediately. For now, I have instructed George to return Mr Renfield to his room before dinner, where he may take his meals alone undisrupted.

Mr Renfield exhibited peculiar behaviour in the dayroom to-day as well. Crawling on his hands and knees, he inserted himself under the chairs and into the corners. This was permitted by some patients, but Mr Tooley and other more discomposed patients like himself, were led to activity of their own. Mr Tooley began to imitate Mr Renfield and then Miss Smithe joined in. They set to crawling about the floor, thus disturbing Robbie, as you can well guess, and rooted every patient from his or her seat including Mary. The object of Mr Renfield's search was to find spiders; with great delight, he showed me a tangled pocketful of them and explained that he needed them. I was much distressed by the way he said "needed." Elwood, who as you know is slow to anger, was forced to intervene. Thus, Mr Tooley, Mr Renfield, and Miss Smithe were removed to their rooms early, lest more commotion ensue. Simmons, who as you know is the most kind and gentle of warders, took Mr Renfield personally back to his room.

"Believe me, dear Sir,

"Yours faithfully,

"Patrick Hennessey."

RENFIELD'S JOURNAL

12 July.— There is no sense in going to the common room anymore. Even when there is prey, I cannot get at it. The others have become annoyed with my need to look under chairs or use their chairs to stand on. And it is useless to capture flies there. Flies, no matter how careful I am, crush in my pockets and the spiders will have none of them.

Also, there was some trouble again today. Robbie is given to many peculiar habits. Though at least eighteen, he acts and appears much younger. Robbie, as he apparently often does, set to counting. It was the floor tiles, which was not surprising for these fascinate him, that he was counting this time. As he counted he repeated "shhhh shhhh, clunk clunk." Burly ignored this at first for

Robbie had started in the unoccupied centre of the floor. Round and round he went until he came to Tom.

Tom, observing the boy's need to touch each tile as he counted, had deliberately stepped directly in his path and taunted, "Robbie Smells, Robbie Smells."

Robbie showed no sign of offence or even awareness of these words.

"You think you can get what you need? You think you can get where you're going?" Tom asked Robbie trying to inform him and knowing he would get no answer.

Robbie did not look up or say anything, or do anything for that matter, but fidget—his mind fixed on his simple self-ordained task. Robbie Smalls is not deaf, he only appears that way. Tom loomed but was careful to stay just out of reach. Robbie began to rock himself back and forth and the rest of us became absolutely still and held our breath. Finally, when Burly set his illustrated papers down in a huff, Tom gave ground. Everyone must give ground, for Robbie is given to paroxysms if his intentions are thwarted and sometimes at merely being touched.

Tom knew he would get nowhere and would perhaps even be attacked, but his perverse nature thrives on trouble. He cannot help himself. His mind is full of wants and these wants circle in his mind endlessly. Robbie's mind is the most fascinating I have encountered and perhaps ever will. Numbers, dates, and facts from his past race through his thoughts so quickly there is scarcely time to realise them. When I touch his thoughts I get an attack of dizziness after only a few seconds. Yet we are much alike, this lonely child and I; we must fill our heads with busy thoughts. For me it is to keep out others' thoughts and for him, well... I may never know. As for Tom, in Robbie's mind, he does not exist.

I am angered that I could not assist Robbie, but I can afford no more trouble. Yesterday, Tom and I were returned to our rooms after he and Angie tried to help me catch spiders. Tom, of course, was looking more for a diversion than prey, and got us into hot water with his zealousness.

George heard the commotion and entered the common room. With barely concealed rage, he immediately crossed to Tom. As George passed, Angie, in her most girlish and prissy voice sang out, "Georgie, porgie big and stout. Thick within and thick without." The simple tune –- dah te, dah te, ta ta ta—arrested George in midstride. He turned slowly daring her to continue, his face hard and his fists clenched. She, by contrast, simply smiled back as if expecting kudos for her contribution. She waved bye-bye at him suppressing a giggle. He would not attempt retribution while we looked on. Composing himself, he turned, placing his eye on me. I must learn to shield, nay conceal, my emotions. Detecting guilt, he fixed his ire on me.

George took this chance to drag me out of the common room, yet again. And there, in the vacant corridor, he jabbed me in the ribs. This opportunity has held the focus of his thoughts for weeks now. He did not strike me again though he thought about it during the whole time he walked me to my room. He pictured me receiving blow after blow and begging for mercy. Once he was satisfied that I was contrite, the story began again from the beginning. I miraculously returned to health, and though the scenario was the same, the details of which blows knocked me down and the wording of my pleas for mercy changed each time. The pictures of this repeated throttling faded finally when George left the ward.

Therefore, while in the common room, I will not search unless the prey makes itself readily available. If I cannot search the common room, then the basement is the only good source of spiders left for me.

13 July.— Desperate for spiders, I venture to the basement corridor under the East Wing where the general men's ward is located. It is cool in the basement. A draft? Here it is dimly lit and I must make use of my keen eyesight. Crawling on the floor, I see the world much as a cat must: colours are diminished and objects appear strongly outlined with the soft yellow light of the gas lamps. Spiders like damp corners, and here there are many. When they are still, they blend into the rough hewn stone of the wall or floor, but in motion, they are silhouetted against the background and easily spotted.

It took a bit of trial and error to get the spiders to move from their hiding places. Superior intellect, however, as I of course have over spiders, yielded a solution to this problem. I used deductive reasoning. If a running spider is hiding, he must be hiding for a reason. Hiding from predators? No, this cannot be—until I befriended Amos they had none. More likely, I reasoned, they are patiently awaiting prey to come to them like their "sleeper" cousins. And how is the runner alerted to the approaching prey? (I will tell you for you could never guess. You cannot see, and hear, and smell as I do!) They hear them. Tiny membranes on either side of their abdomens vibrate like ear drums, only they can detect more vibrations than just sound. The spiders hear (or should I say feel) the vibration of the beetle's feet as they trundle past. Cockroaches are the loudest and seem to actually click their heels to provoke their would-be predators. They are quick and dart off at the tiniest motion. Cockroaches have a most powerful predator warning system: they can feel the "wind" of the predator's movement.

I tap my fingernails on the floor imitating the sound of a beetle's gait. I have let my nails grow long for just this purpose. And since I now find they grow very quickly, I need spend less time trimming them. The runners, hearing this sound, dart out like sprinters at the start of a race. The fastest of them is laughably slow. Once spotted, I merely pick them up and begin tapping for another.

(The initials G.P.I. mentioned in the entry below stand for General Paralysis of the Insane, a common form of dementia at that time. Some thirty years after this journal was written, it was discovered that G.P.I. was, in fact, the final stage of syphilis. G.D.)

14 July.— Regrettably, I am restricted to quarters again. This morning in desperation for bird food, I returned to the nether reaches of the main basement. The incurable ward has always made me feel uneasy for the sights, sounds, and smells provoke unpleasant thoughts—and it is now clear why. Yes, there can be no mistake. Though most of the cells are occupied by those whose brain fever has left them raving or totally immobile, one is reserved

as the "quiet room." Here I spent two nights of unspeakable misery.

The cell stood empty, yet I dared not enter. A fear that the door would shut behind me of its own accord, trapping me there, kept me from searching it for spiders. I lingered there too long. The visions of spattering blood, much like the ones I had when shut in that cell, returned. Great sprays, thick and red, struck with such force they made the sound of rain. I heard the splashes inside me—outside me, the corridor was dead quiet. Soon all around me, the walls, the ceiling, the floor, was streaked with red. (The surfaces were all covered with cloth. Odd, perhaps it is paint that I see, falling on drop cloths.)

I hurried on as quickly as I could, more to reduce the hold of those hideous thoughts, than to reach my destination. As I remembered, there is a washroom at the end of the corridor. The smell of urine and waste and water led me to it instantly. (With water, it is not so much a smell, as a sensitivity of the nostrils for detecting slight variations in humidity.) I did not have to guess it was full of livestock—spiders like damp places.

Spiders, though tenacious at times, are quite docile in captivity. Placed live in my pockets, they curl themselves up and do not try to climb out. Spiders have a talent for getting free rides. Perhaps... no, how could they know.

On returning down the corridor—with a copious supply of crawly things—I was startled by the patient who had been my neighbour during my time in the quiet room. He had begun singing *Titwillow* (from *The Mikado* I believe) at the precise moment I passed his door. Now, here's a howdy do. I was quite startled. His presence loomed, unseen, behind the thick door tacked G.P.I.

Tempted as I was to open the trap so we could see each other, I did not. We both knew the other was there but did nothing.

He addressed me with a weak, but surprisingly youthful and genteel voice. "Do you like women?" He was speaking to me through the door.

I could not deny I had heard him, but I was reluctant to answer him. "Women," I said, "oh, yes." I did not want to stay on this subject—I have had so little experience.

"I don't, not one bit!" I was shocked at his tone of voice. "I like you though," he said, his anger suddenly abated.

"Thank-you," I choked but regretted it, for he misunderstood, I am sure.

The door of his cell creaked as he leaned against it. Instinctively, I reached to brace it against his weight. His thoughts became mine.

He pictured three fine young lads, clearly undergraduate students from their dress, making merry together in a room with a blazing hearth. They laughed and swatted one another and he began to tell me of his college days—not in spoken words, mind you—but in words pronounced only in thought. The three were roommates. Their rooms clustered around a large parlour with adjoining servant's quarters. A fine ginger cat circled each, begging attention only to snub one generous youth to beg from the next; and so circled the room in an endless, orbiting game of hard-to-get.

They were fair and slender—too "pretty" really, not rugged, as the cricket bats and sculling oars that decorated the walls were to suggest. They were not unlike the Cambridge men of my day. We Oxonians are, by nature, more robust.

One youth, with captivating eyes, picked up a book. The others became attentive and the one who was standing, sat. The book open, a recitation began. A poem by Shelly was announced and then begun in a clear resonant voice. Recited beautifully and with ardour, I heard the words. I realised at its completion that since these were his memories, he must have memorised the poem as well as remembered the day he recited it. (This was only one of many poems and songs that live in his mind.) He then announced an original poem. Though the verse was competent, it conveyed youthful silliness rather than heartfelt emotion. Naughty and playful at first, it then became violent—more slap than tickle. This mental discourse ended suddenly when the scenes of blood returned.

I dread the quiet room. It must be haunted, for a fog, moist and heavy, surrounded me, and scenes of blood filled my head. What was worse was that this time, the blood was unmistakably spattering on a woman's skirts. In the vision, a small, dirty woman looked up smiling at him revealing missing teeth. She tottered from one foot to the other, a bit wobbly from drink. Though unsteady, she lifted herself up on her toes to meet him face to face. In chilling silence, the smile changed to sudden horror and fell away. As I pulled my hand away from the door, he whispered to me.

"You feel him too, don't you?" His voice betrayed his illness of both body and mind. It was a voice close to death and certain in its conviction, of which the latter was the more disturbing. Then he began to scream, in terror or delight, I cannot be certain.

Echoes of the warders' quick footsteps filled the corridor with fear and all who were able joined in by screaming, stomping, and banging their fists against the doors of their cells. The warders halted before me very curious as to what I was doing outside that particular door. This curiosity seemed to spread down the corridor silencing the patients one by one, until the only sound was the inmates shuffling at their doors trying to hear and see through the trap doors of their cells.

George took hold of me while the one I call "Burly" looked into the cell marked G.P.I.

"Quiet now, Mr S., I'll 'ave a nice sup" for ye soon. Warm enough? That's a good fella," Burly said through the trap trying to soothe him. I saw Mr S., or perhaps just the thought of him, in Burly's mind. He was quiet but still agitated. The padded walls were covered with filth, yet even George did not seem concerned or angry about it. Also unusual, was the deference Mr S. was paid. George was actually courteous, yet his fear of Mr S. was profound—fear of contagion. George will not even open the trap to view Mr S.

"Who's this then?" George asked. I could see him squinting at me in the flickering gas light. He reached up and turned the screw to increase the flame. On recognising me he said, "Someone's far from 'ome, ain't 'e." And with the simple order, "West wing," George turned, and I must say fled, for his retreat was most sudden. Burly escorted me back to my room, my feet rarely touching the floor the entire journey.

Mary is now sharing my thoughts. She is telling me of Patient S. A "swell" apparently enough, they call him Patient S. for his name is not to be revealed. There is little sympathy for him here in Ward D. Perhaps if they had seen him through his memories as I had, youthful and spirited, they might reconsider. The piteous view from George's mind, thin, pale, and naked, showed Patient S. no longer appears in reality the way he does in his thoughts. Only his eyes, gifted with verse heard yet unsaid, have remained unchanged.

15 July.— I am tired. I could get no sleep last night after the fright I had in the basement. While restricted to my room, I will spend the time continuing my experiments. To-day I will continue with my sparrow sketches depicting the variations in marking—my drawing ability has much improved.

Each day there are more sparrows on my windowsill. They make quite a noise. It seems Amos has many friends and now they will be my friends, too. Though they are playful and gay, they cannot lighten my mood. I wonder how my flock is doing without me back in Whitby. They perhaps do not miss me at all. Is there anyone left after the fire?

I remember that day, the day of my most terrible vision. The sexton, being indisposed, left me in charge of communion for St Mary. Not having set up the bread and cup before, I had no idea how much bread and wine to set out and greatly overestimated how much would be needed. After the service, I quickly consumed the excess in the sacristy to hide my error.

That evening, during my service at St Ann, I saw the beacon of death shine on my congregation. Are these events somehow linked? Could I have had too much? That is what Ham believed.

I miss Ham. He was the best friend I had during my siege. He was so irreverent he stepped on the pages of the Bible as I tried to read. He liked to gnaw on book corners as if sharpening his teeth. Our favourite game was "nibble." He would stand on his hind legs to receive the bits that I fed him one at a time. Sometimes he would nip at my fingers, but then he would lick them as if to apologise. It is these once annoying habits that I miss the most. I am no longer angry with him, how could I be?

16 July.— I will fill the lonely hours with writing. Writing, which requires a good deal of concentration, helps my mind block out others' thoughts. So I will write to keep my mind occupied.

It was a very hot day like to-day, that I said good-bye to the people in the village. In Zambezia, January is the hottest month of the year. Despite the heat, however, a feast was prepared. The other Englishmen and I played cricket. And for three days all activity was stopped save sporting, dancing, eating, and drinking.

Beer is the one colonial item that King Lobengula took to immediately. Though admonished that his beer consumption had exacerbated or even caused his gout and lumbago, Lobengula still drank large quantities every day. And though he had for a time sported western clothing, the king had reverted to wearing a simple monkey-skin funnel over his loins. His ever increasing girth had no doubt precipitated the change. At over six feet tall and 21 stone he was, as they said, "every inch a king."

The last night before my departure the king invited me to his fire. A great honour. We stayed up long into the night talking and confiding. An ivory trader (I do not remember his name) who had served the crown in the Boer War back in '52, regaled us with war stories. He had survived unscathed through that whole affair and even seemed quite cheery about it in retrospect. He entertained us with an endless list of "dreadful Boer" jokes and I laughed more heartily than I ever have in my life until tears rolled down my cheeks. He planned to settle in Mafeking now that it was safely under British control.

Just before dawn, Lobengula, now solemn, confided his thoughts to us. "Did you ever see a chameleon catch a fly? ... The chameleon gets behind the fly and remains motionless for some time; then he advances very slowly and gently, first putting forward one leg and then the other. At last, when well within reach, he darts his tongue and the fly disappears. England is the chameleon and I am that fly."

That, of course, was the last time I ever saw King Lobengula or the people of my village. There is a darkness inside my heart. It came when I was asked to leave Africa. My work was incomplete and yet I was being replaced—most likely by someone younger and stronger.

The details were made clear to me in the letter from the London Missionary Society. My mission in Matabaland was to be abandoned and I was to return home to England. I was to take over as vicar of a small parish in Yorkshire. The vicarage would be at my disposal and a living provided. When the letter arrived, it was handed to me by a uniformed soldier from South Africa, in a blazing red tunic. It does seem odd to me now that the messenger would come all that way to deliver the letter; you would think I was Livingston, himself. I felt at that moment that I was about to receive God's bounty.

My return to England was a shock and a disappointment. The shock was due to the instant onslaught of abuse I received the day of my return. After six weeks at sea, I became quite nervous. The need to feel the earth beneath me nagged endlessly. I stood on deck as we pulled into port longing for the first glimpse of home. The squalid pier was a sorry sight. Several seamen ran down the long ramp to the dock as soon as it was put into place. Yet, they did not go far, for there on the docks was a line of drinking establishments. By the time I had collected my things, they were already drunk and carousing.

The docks thronged with all manner of ruffians, thieves, urchins and harlots. I was jostled, sneered at, and pushed, with no regard to my clerical collar—or perhaps, on later thought, because of it. A harlot offered me her services and on my decline, raised her nose in the air and gave a sniff. Soon after, I was engaged by a small, filthy, blonde child who asked for some assistance. Of course, I was only too glad to help. When asked about her family and how she got along, she said she was twelve and lived on her own. I was horrified.

"I don't need no parents, ain't none of 'em any good, anyhow. Besides, we might all be dead tomorrow," she added matter-of-factly. Then the child insisted on the immediate "forking over" of a shilling. And when I was not quick enough, fumbling in my pockets trying to acquiesce, she assumed a posture as if given the most severe of slights. Then, as I offered her fourpence, she smiled, daintily lifted both sides of her skirts slightly as if to curtsy, and then dealt me a mean kick to the shin.

No one seemed to know where the train station was. One man, slow and stout, scratched his head, his eyes rolling up into his skull as if to look inside it for the answer. I grew impatient for the harlots were now giving me sidelong glances. Giving up, I turned and moved on to ask someone else. At this, the man jumped to his feet—perhaps it is only his mind that works slowly—and angrily shouted, "I don't like your kind."

It was then I realised that my back pocket felt empty. No doubt, during the jostling, someone had stolen my prayer book thinking it my purse. This is easily understandable for it folds into a leather case that snaps shut, not dissimilar to a gentleman's pocket-book.

I was about to ask around for it when a great swell in the crowd pushed me forward. Women fell into clumsy curtsies and men gave half bows. I was shoved aside by two men making way for the personage for whom this homage was being paid. A tall, dashing figure in a long, black cape with a high collar and vivid scarlet lining, waved regally. He was pale and slim. His eyes, framed between bushy eyebrows and an arched nose, held mine. He smiled at me as if he knew me. But it was a false assumption on my part, for he then smiled and glanced at others in just the same way.

The crowd, pushing and pulling me along, moved quickly down a passage between two large buildings. And to my delight, we emerged onto a main

124

thoroughfare, and from there, I heard the chugging hiss of steam and the blast of a train whistle. I was later informed that the man in the cape was none other than Irving, the celebrated actor.

Yes, the England that greeted me upon my return from Africa was a far cry from the England I had left thirty years before. People were then more devout, honest, and helpful. The smallest crime would render all onlookers aghast, but no more. Now, everyone hurries about in their own world, oblivious to other's pains and pleasures. I vowed to repent sinners, encourage the hopeless, and give solace to the downhearted. Yet, upon my return, I have found that not only can I not help anyone, I cannot help myself any longer. I am pitied by paupers and looked at askance by harlots. This new world, populated by condescending morons, twelve-year-old nihilists, and idolised actors leaves me utterly confounded.

PATIENT LOG
(Entries kept by warder, George Simmons.)

Patient: R. M. Renfield

11 July. 9:15 a.m.—quiet—behaved hiself in dayroom which is uncommon.

12 July. 9:00 a.m. .— Pat. crawling about disturbing other patients in the dayroom.

13 July. 10:00 a.m.— Other patients complaining about birds.

14 July. 10:15 a.m.— Found patient in incurable ward bothering Patient S. Rec: secure in room.

15 July. 9:30 a.m.— Restricted to room. Patient
up all night riting in the dark, says he can
see by moonlight.

16 July. 9:30 a.m.— Restricted — patient riting
alot again. Agitated. Still not sleeping
much.

17 July. 9:15 a.m.—Restricted to room. Patient
nervous, wants to see Dr Seward.

RENFIELD'S JOURNAL

17 July.— I can no longer feed my sparrows. Though the
sparrows could fend for themselves outside, they
stubbornly stay in my room begging. As the food
diminishes, their chattering becomes more insistent. I
have almost no more food and only the largest spiders
left. Surely, I will not feed Samson to the birds—he is far
too dear to me.

Dr Seward has not visited in a week and I need his
help. Only he can return my privileges. When he is in, I
focus on his thoughts: train schedules. He divides his time
between pursuing Lucy and writing the "definitive book
on psychiatry." Thus, he must travel between Whitby and
London frequently. If he would remain here more often,
then I could understand him better.

I do know his book will be tainted by his melancholy.
He has had a great loss, and this will colour his
perception; he will see others as the progeny of loss.
Preachers are prone to this. I knew one minister at _____
whose every sermon dwelt on guilt, for he himself felt
guilty about everything. It is a foible to be cautioned
against. Dr Seward has no bishop, however, to answer to.

And what is more, his "congregation" cannot reproach him at fellowship hour after services. There is no rebuttal, for the alienist wields absolute power.

I can only carry on my experiments with his consent. Still, his whim may allow me to leave my room again. When I do see him he does not understand—he does not listen. If I do not leave my room soon and find more spiders, my experiment will end before I have enough data to understand the feeding rates of sparrows. But wait, perhaps it is time to bring my study to the next step. I must ask Dr Seward to aid me. Yes, I am ready.

PATIENT LOG
(Entries kept by warder, George Simmons.)

Patient: R. M. Renfield

19 July. 10:00 a.m.— Patient wants to see the doctor, wants cat—bad idea pets. Best that doctors don't give him none.

20 July. 9:00 a.m.— Careful watch ordered by Dr Seward. Patient happy enough not eating nothing.

11:15 a.m. .— When I come into the room I saw right off something were different. He sits riting but I could tell something happened. I thought to meself he sits there quiet but hes up to something. Room quiet now cause his birds is gone. Then hes sick and vomited. Saw feathers in it. Called Dr S. Dosed.

21 July. 9:15 a.m.— patient groggy. Says his food is louder than usual and the sun is too bright.

4:30 p.m.— Patient has stomach pains—
got gas.

8:30 p.m. .— Pat. howling like wolf—
keeps waking up. Double-dose.

22 July. 9:00 a.m.— patient awoke. Double-dose.

23 July. 10:00 a.m.— patient sleeping good.

REPORT OF DR PATRICK HENNESSEY

24 July.— Patient Renfield's behaviour changed
suddenly from that of calm compliance to enraged
obstinacy. Though his mood has been temperamental at
times, this is the first major shift I have detected over the
last month. This shift, though long in coming, was not
unexpected. The patient has become too dependent on his
doctor. Thus, Renfield, thwarted by Dr Seward, reacted as
same to the same situation. The details of the situation I
will now unfold. The patient is becoming a sort of pet
study of Dr Seward. Thus, when Renfield began raising
sparrows in his room, Dr Seward did not intercede, but
rather fostered this activity. This hobby satisfied
Renfield's needs for a time. This week, however,
Renfield became obsessed with acquiring another pet and
called the doctor to his room. (The patient has been
restricted to quarters for having left the ward without
permission.) He then asked the doctor for a kitten making
every effort to show the doctor his appreciation. This was
not an unreasonable request for paying patients are
allowed pets within reason. The doctor, however, in line
with his authority, said that he could not have a cat at this
time.

At first, I was surprised to hear that Dr Seward refused Mr Renfield's request for a kitten. Mr Renfield, per order of the Bishop Fairfax, is to be treated as a guest and all his requests, within reason, are to be granted. I find that patients respond well to the stimulus of animals, dogs and cats especially. Animals have a calming and elevating effect on the patient's spirits, sometimes even eliciting a cure to the patient's ills. Dr Seward, however, suspected the cat might eat the sparrows. Renfield said nothing in his defence except that he "must have a cat," but finally acceded to the doctor's will. Yet this was not the end of the matter. Renfield sank into melancholy and could not be consoled. Simmons informed Dr Seward of the patient's unhappiness and the latter returned later that night to check in on the patient. Renfield begged and pleaded again for a cat as if his life depended on it. Dr Seward remained firm neither giving in nor giving a reason for his decision.

Simmons informs me that Renfield was wakeful in the night which is usual for him, being that he is an insomniac. This morning brought another sudden change. Renfield was in fine spirits and no trace of the melancholy or lack of sleep were visible. His sparrows had gone, leaving only a few feathers. Later, as Simmons was changing the chamber pot, he noticed bird feathers and bones in Renfield's vomitus. Renfield, after he showed much compassion and loving attention to his many sparrows, has most likely eaten them. There had been many sparrows, perhaps 20 or more, and now there is not one left. Simmons believes Renfield ate the sparrows raw sometime before 6 a.m.

My conclusions, drawn from the descriptions from Simmons mentioned above, are as follows: Renfield has cancelled the raising of sparrows on the denial of his request for a cat by Dr Seward. It is my belief that fixated on the need for a new pet; the patient became obsessed with the subject of denial, i.e. Dr Seward. No doubt, since Renfield's nature studies are of great interest to the doctor, the sudden ending of those studies was meant to gain attention. Moreover, Renfield has chosen to punish Dr Seward by eating the sparrows. Renfield is the most gentle of souls between these fits. Therefore, it is my conclusion that the patient is suffering from a cyclical disorder, characterised by profound and sudden swings in mood.

Recommendation: Patient Renfield to be committed and remain in hospital indefinitely.

Chapter 6

WRATH

RENFIELD'S JOURNAL

19 July.— To-day I made but a small request of the doctor. At first he seemed receptive, but soon showed his true intentions. He was toying with me. How did he know what I wanted before I had a chance to ask?

What is strange is that Dr Seward seems to read my mind as I read his. The doctor controls my mood as The Lord controls my appetites. It is a testament to my stability that I can be calm while confined with raving maniacs and treated shabbily by those who would be my inferiors on the outside.

The business of the mad-doctor is invasive. Clearly the techniques of talking therapy were developed by someone with no sense of propriety or personal privacy. This mental voyeur would have us believe he is helping me. Yet, it is not the doctor's persuasive manner that holds me here—it is the locked doors!

I dare not show my anger to the doctor for fear of being punished. Only they do not call it punishment. If you are bad, you get "treatment." If you are later good, they will claim the treatment worked! I feel helpless. I raise my arm in defence, but I dare not strike out. They are free to defend themselves—I am not!

20 July.— George has finally left; he had been standing at my door all morning. I am not feeling well to-day. I cannot keep anything down. Dr Seward and George are talking in his office upstairs. They do not know I can hear them. George is getting dressed down by the doctor. Odd, the doctor is usually so lenient with the warders.

"But sir, I have to sleep sometime," says George, "He seemed so happy—I never suspected."

"That is precisely the point!" says the doctor, "All the signs were there for you to see. Had you been attentive you would have seen it coming. Now out of my sight with you."

I wonder what they are talking about. Their minds are full of memories, incidents just such as this one, but from the past. Oh, now George is coming down the stairs—stomping harder than usual. Angie calls out, "Lov-er-ly day, ain't it?" but he continues without reply. Angie is pleased with the result of her "greeting."

Oh, he is right outside my door. He is picturing me—me in horror looking up at him. I hear the keys...

Rescued! Tom is now taunting him and this has distracted George from me.

"George! Come quick. I've spilled my pot again. Come clean it up. Hurry!" Tom knows this will not sit well with George. Why does he say it? "Hurry, hurry." But George is going the other way. Victory! George has gone off in a huff. The whole ward is laughing and rejoicing.

Suddenly there is silence. The matron has entered the ward.

Now that things are calm again I will continue with my experiments. Since my last account failed to reach conclusion, I have begun the experiment again. This morning I caught six flies which I am feeding to Samson one by one. Samson is my only spider now and I will have to find others to...

George is back! He pictures Tom clearly in his mind. Rage. God have mercy—he has brought the stick.

Later.— I cannot work. The excitement of a new beginning is now just nervousness. Each day it begins a few minutes earlier, a thought that tugs at my mind. My past haunts me. A list of disappointments and unfinished goals dominates my thoughts. Each disappointment is as a blow, striking out any hope of redemption. I am all at sea. Yes, I could describe myself as a ship's engine under a full head of steam, spinning fast only to make slow progress through the churning waters.

My sense of time is still that of a man living in the bush. My failure to arrive at Whitby when expected was due to this. The Bishop was most put off and did not let me explain my delay. Yes, it is clear now that this is what had upset him so. It was not the chapel roof or even the asking for money. It was leaving him waiting at the train station the day of my arrival. How could I have forgotten this? My mind had buried the entire incident. I simply wanted to pay a call on an old college mate of mine, William H. Monk.

The day was cool and there being no reason to delay in the bustling, dirty city, I wired ahead to inform Bishop Fairfax of my departure for Whitby. I had detrained in London and had some hours before my connection to York. Then, it occurred to me that I had plenty of time to bung over and visit Monk, my friend the organist and composer. I found his mother there. Monk, whom I had admired greatly for his compositions, had passed away in 1890. Now we shall never meet again. His immortal music will be remembered long after that Irving fellow is forgotten.

Mrs Monk was most gracious and insisted I sit, chat and have a spot of tea. She also insisted I take the many books and science journals I had given Monk on my departure for Africa. After our repast she lead me into an adjoining room, and there, covering one entire wall, was my oriental collection of statues, vases and enamelled boxes. All were carefully arranged and free of damage and dust. My heart swelled. We arranged to have them shipped to Whitby without delay.

She asked if I would visit his grave before I departed. He was buried at Kingstead Cemetery. Kingstead, being just north of London, was not far out of my way, so I agreed to stop and pay my respects. Though I was already expected at Whitby, I took the first train to Kingstead and planned to continue on with a later train.

The cemetery, large and growing, lies just outside the village centre, past the Literary and Philosophical Society. It is divided into two sections by Swain's Lane: the new east section and the old west section. A beautiful chapel nestles up against the more fashionable west section. The grounds are extensive with many levels and rows of grey, granite mausoleums.

The sun was bright that spring afternoon. The caretaker invited me to view the Anglican side of the chapel. The caretaker's wife, a plainly dressed but pretty woman, accompanied me. A vestibule in the centre divided the Anglican from the Dissenter's chapels. As I perused the architecture she gave me a history of the cemetery which was one of a series built 50 years ago to relieve overcrowding and grave robbing in the London cemeteries. In its hey-day there were 70 grounds men alone. Now, the graves were becoming overgrown with ivy and other trailing vines. She gave a list of important figures who were buried there, including R. Gardener Hill and Michael Faraday. She said that George Eliot was buried there and offered to show me her grave site. (Kingstead is "literary" and boasts a Bohemian lot of writers and thinkers. Female novelists—what is the world coming to?)

The chapel itself is most surprising. Small, but wonderfully detailed. The vaulted wooden ceiling reaches up two stories, making the room taller than it is wide. The sun filters in through leaded glass as fine as that found in any cathedral. Above the altar the ceiling is inlaid with multihued blue and gold tiles that draw the eyes heavenward and do not release them.

I should not have lingered so long in the chapel. How could I have forgotten the volatility of English weather? I heard the first thunder clap as I left the chapel. A mist appeared and I readied my umbrella. Across the street the caretaker was waiting at the east gate. There was a second clap. Reluctant to risk getting wet, the caretaker gave only terse directions and I was sent off on my own to find the grave.

"Go all the way to the back gate and turn right."

At that moment the mist turned to rain and I hurried off thinking the grave cannot be difficult to find—better to make it quick before the heavier rain comes.

The path was wide and sloped gently downward. A red-throated robin flew low overhead, chirping its song. It too has just returned from its journey abroad. Ten minutes passed before I met the aforementioned gate. Following the path to the right, which narrowed significantly, I found I was out of directions. As I quickly read the names on the headstones, the rain turned to sleet—not the usual hard ice pellets, but light fluffy spheres that bounced happily from my umbrella making white patterns on the grass.

Soon the path became muddy. I hurried as fast as I could from grave to grave along the back fence looking for the dear man. Reluctant to give in and with only fifteen minutes until closing, I became more daring and left the path. The graves were set so close together it was necessary to step on the edgings between them to move down a row. What was I doing—risking stepping on and thus defiling graves to make my humble tribute?

I had lost all sense of time; the train to Whitby would leave soon. I had to run to reach the main gate before the night closing. The path seemed steeper than I remembered. My legs ached and I had to pause to catch my breath. The wet graves glistened. It was quite a beautiful scene: the weeping angels, Egyptian obelisks, and half draped urns rained down upon by tiny snowballs from heaven.

At the gate, the attendant assured me he could help me find the site the next day. With that, he hurried me out and pushed the high, heavy metal gate closed behind me nearly crushing me in the process.

I hesitated there wishing to explain that I would not be back on the morrow. I caught his attention through the narrow bars and said, "It's a marvellous thing, these 'snowballs.'" I tried to point out the wonder of it—I had not seen snow in thirty years—and on a spring day! He would have none of it.

"Hail," he said turning away, as if it had no significance.

21 July.— The carrot stick I was given this lunch is astonishing. Crunch loud and crisp the biscuits go crunch too—very much enjoyed it. Never heard it before. Cannot write anymore—It is too bright in here this morning—too bright.

Later.— God is nearer. I feel him. Each day he is close to me. He is speaking to me. I hear him. God hath spake unto me and said, "I will come to separate the sheep from the wolves."

(*Though carefully reproduced, several lines in this journal entry are missing, this editor finding them illegible. G.D.*)

24 July.— I felt sane. Indeed, I had never felt saner in my life. Surely I could not be under delusions and think so clearly. I am aware and cognisant of my surroundings—at least more so than the other patients who now come to me for all manner of information and advice. Yet, after a short talk with Dr Hennessey, I begin to doubt my sanity. [...] Many subjects I do not dare to broach. I cannot speak of the Bishop, or even the parish in general, without the sense that he knows something I do not. And even after I repeatedly ask him if I am not right, he answers me with

yet another question such as: "Do you think so?" or "Aren't you sure?" with a covered but detectable arrogance that wears on the nerves. He is playing innocent with me, "protecting" me from knowledge he believes will upset me. He gives names I do not understand to all my moods and attitudes. Thus, reading his thoughts leaves me more befuddled than without. What does "cyclothymia" mean?

Angie recommends giving them _____. Which is to say, one should retaliate. There is no sense appealing to their good side because a bully will not take your kindness and consideration into account. The bullying, in fact, she contends, will actually increase if you do not "show them a bit of teeth."

No one in their right mind would commit themselves. The mildly insane would be better off to remain in their attics than to seek shelter in the asylum of to-day. [...] I have developed a hatred for all the so-called medical science that put me here, my own personal *odium medicum*. The science of the alienist is no science at all. Dr Hennessey believes I am a lunatic which literally means soft on the brain and thus susceptible to the moon's forces. But it is not the moon that influences me. It is at moonrise that I feel most at peace. It is a divine influence. Oh, I know they all think I am mad. It is the natural reaction of those who do not understand, stemming from fear of the unknown. I will not ask so much as to insist they believe me. It is enough that I know that I am here for a purpose and I know that that purpose will be revealed to me in God's good time.

Dr Seward is no better. He has come to my room in my absence. The smell of his hands was on my pocket-book. If he really was interested in my experiments why would he not give me a cat—even a kitten—a little one? [...] This irritated me so much that I became angry and insisted he listen to me. His response was to be even more placid in demeanour.

Undaunted, I insisted he help me. I will not be intimidated by this scamp who is still wet behind the ears. I have firmly decided to not answer one more question of his until he answers mine. I asked him, interrupting his stream of effluvium, "When will I have permission to leave my room again? When?" To this direct question he said, "You are to be looked after, with gentle kindness." I am sure, however, that kindness is not the doctor's strong suit. Oh, I was too weak. He needs a stronger hand. No more asking—it is time for telling. I will not answer [...] Dr Seward then left without even the most perfunctory of good-byes, which leaves me no doubt this overeducated "poop" has simply no sense of etiquette.

Two can play at this game! If he will not grant my requests, I will give him nothing. To his questions I will return silence, to his visits I will give stillness. I will not be the plaything of this godless man.

28 July.— It seems that I am not the only one who is not speaking to the doctor. His love, his Lucy, has ceased correspondence with him. I had been confiding my small knowledge of the doctor's "lost love" to Jamison when Tom joined us. Clearly he had overheard most of our conversation. He had been listening from a short distance away, but hearing the name "Lucy Westenra" had piqued his interest.

Tom loves names and is very playful with them. He said the name out loud as he thought over the rhymes and connections. "West End, eh?" he said, so the pun and the puzzle were one in the same. He pondered the possibilities with delighted concentration, his eyes rolling to and fro as if seeing the words hover above him. Then he smiled with triumph as an idea struck him, and, poising himself with an air of condescension, stated, "West End, ha! It is a charade. She would fool us."

And thus, ensued Tom's well studied and well rehearsed mimic of Dr Hennessey. "This pretender, this harlot, she is from the "East End" as so obvious a pseudonym would imply." (To the doctor, every clue leads to the opposite—if you miss your home he believes you hate your home. If you loved your mother he believes you hated your mother and it is your father you loved.)

Tom stroked his hair back from his forehead exactly three times as Dr Hennessey so often does and continued. "Let us consider the name Lucy—a simple childhood name on the surface, but let us not be so easily fooled, gentleman, so easily drawn into the trusting, fawning, state of a would-be suitor. No! let us instead examine the facts, in a logical manner. Yes, let us examine only the facts!" We all laughed. (This is a joke for Dr Hennessey has a talent for finding clues that bear no meaning to the matter. In fact, little of what either of the doctors says makes any sense at all to us.) "'Lucy,' my good friend, is short for 'Luci-fer' and is nothing short of a declaration of the embodiment of wilful perdition. She is the devil that draws the unsuspecting man from the haven of bachelorhood into the den of matrimonial hellfire. No man is safe from such an one! Beware, Beware!"

"Lucy," to me, means "light" as I recall clearly from my Latin days. And, such an "apt-nomer" was never given; yet how could her parents know when she was just a few hours old that her later radiance and fair beauty would warrant such a name?

Tom has conveyed a great deal of information about Dr Hennessey to me. He has been here longer and has seen and heard more than I. Dr Hennessey is a misogynist, he contends, for why else would he spend his entire day here and rarely return home to his wife and son before bedtime. "He may be a devoted doctor, but in truth, Dr Hennessey is not a dutiful husband." Perhaps Tom's words are too harsh for it is "Mother Hen" who belittles the love Tom has for his wife. Yet, I suspect there is a deeper reason for the doctor's dedication that I did not share with Tom.

Tom delights in his naming game. I must admit I was quite put out when I found he thinks of me as "Old Peculiar"— his favourite drink—or, even worse, "Ravenous Renfield." Still, there is no malice in his thoughts, and of course, he does not call me these things to my face. Angie objects for she dislikes Tom's name for her intensely. Tom calls her "Angie Quicksand" because men are ever so slowly drawn down into her seductive trap. (And that she was a resident of Chicksand Road in Whitechapel, no doubt, prompted this connection.)

"Yes, chicksand," Tom explains, "is a sort of snare for unsuspecting goody-goodies who the wicked wanton women of Whitechapel wield with great wile! Surely no man would wander those forbidding streets unless he were lost or misguided. The trap is set for the do-gooders and gawkers who only enter that den of inequity to proselytise or ask directions," he says with wide-eyed credulity that quickly melts into a knowing wink directed at me. I was tempted to say I would not be the sort to wander so, but thought better of it.

Angie did indeed inhabit Whitechapel with her "fella" who worked nearby in the slaughterhouse. "Abattoir" she likes to say; perhaps she believes the word sounds more "posh" as well as less gruesome.

Angie's presence here is somewhat of a mystery, for she cannot have the means to provide for the private accommodations. Tom has warned me never to broach the subject for it "brings out the worst in her." Yet, Angie has confided in me that she has a sponsor of sorts, and, of course, has great expectations. It seems a local artist, who has many wealthy and influential friends, has made a habit of setting up professional women such as herself. She had every reason to believe that she would be next.

Tom calls the artist "Sick-heart" for he is forever pining for his lost models, three of them having been killed, so the authorities claim, by the Ripper—so much for names.

PATIENT LOG
(Entries kept by warder, George Simmons.)

Patient: R. M. Renfield

26 July.—10:00 a.m.—Patient wont talk none. Pretends like I'm not there sometimes.

27 July.—10:00 a.m.—Patient still not saying nothing to me or Drs in the dayroom.

28 July.—9:12—Patient causing trouble in the dayroom. Laughing with other patients but

stopping when warders are around. Reported to Dr Hen. his secretive behaviour.

29 July.—10:00 a.m.— Patient sick again wont eat food only bugs. Wont tell me what he ate.

30 July.—9:45 a.m.—Patient not obeying orders. Says he will help the doctor with his problems. Teaching the other patients things.

31 July.—8:30 a.m. —Patient found howling like a wolf disturbing other patients.

REPORT OF DR PATRICK HENNESSEY

31 July.— Mr Renfield has become difficult to manage. He staunchly refuses to speak to doctors and warders and has evaded interview. When, on rare occasions, he does interact, he evades direct questions or answers with enigmatic declarations or quotations from the Bible. Displaying mild manic excitement, often a flood of ideas pour forth, but no substance can be fathomed from them; then, in contrast, he slips into sullen silence.

Patient is careful to evade questions about his delusions. He indirectly challenges my professional authority by questioning how I should know who is sane and who is insane. When I do not answer his questions to his satisfaction, he reacts with sullen silence or in triumphant bursts of "Ah-ha," and then lifts his head in a regal air. This is in contrast to his usual servile attitude.

31 July.— Life is becoming routine. Each afternoon I sit with Jamison at the little table in the common room where we talk about books. Jamison perks up when we talk about books. He can be frightfully gloomy. "What is the purpose?" he says. "I sweep the floor and no matter how well I do it, it will still be dirty again by to-morrow. Life is nothing but work and misery. We are born, work, have children, and the cycle continues, on and on."

Jamison is a painter. He is self-educated and widely read. People liked his work. However, he could not support his family on his meagre earnings. Poverty forced him to work days in an assurance bureau and paint only at night. This frustrated him for there was not enough light to paint by. Soon his work at the office drained him so, that he was not able to continue to paint. He became downhearted.

He spoke to me of his trials.

"After the low period there is a period of heightened energy. During this time I can work for hours without tiring—without eating. This is when my best work comes. My best painting, "Cathedral at Night," was completed in one long stretch—twenty straight hours without stopping. When I was done, my legs had cramped from standing so long in front of the canvas. I could hardly walk, yet I did not care. I knew the picture was good before I even finished it, and as I worked, I became more and more confident. There was a hint of fear for I knew it wouldn't last—the energy I mean. It never does.

"Then the sadness comes and that is useful too. While in the *slow* times, I arrange for the sale of my work, refine and fix work that is too frenzied or too rough. This period must not last too long for I must work. If I cannot work I become heavyhearted. I fear that the sadness will last longer than I can stand it. I fear it will never end.

"I thought the sadness was sickness and longed to be cured. Doctor after doctor, I visited. My wife insisted on it. None could help me. That's why I came here. I don't trust myself anymore. If only I could work, then I could be happy."

I told Jamison that, during such times, I write poems to focus my feelings and gain understanding of a situation. Perhaps he may benefit from this advice.

Letter, Mrs Johnston to Rev Renfield

"Whitby, 6 August.
"Dear Rev Renfield,

"Just a short note to let you know that your affairs here in Whitby are being attended to. I dusted and aired out Hollow's Den. I, of course, took special care when dusting your Chinese vases.

"It is a shame you were not here to meet two splendid new members of our congregation, Lucy Westenra and Mina Murray. They will spend the rest of their summer here and are lodged near my aunt at the Crescent. Rev Jenna paid a call on the young ladies on your behalf.

"Ham, the brave little soldier, carries on your good work in his own shy way. He spends his time diligently watching over these two. They enjoy sitting by the sea near the Abbey and also take long walks along the cliffs. When they approach Hollow's Den, Ham watches them with much excitement, so unlike his usual, composed self. Then he follows a polite distance behind. He even followed them across Mr Dell's cow field! After that incident with the pitchfork you would think Ham might think twice before going there. How the silly man could possibly think that Ham's presence upsets his cows, I'll never know.

"You needn't worry about Ham, an extra-large dish of milk is left for him every night. He must be very thirsty for he is constantly perched by the bird bath. We never see him drink the milk, but he must be well fed for he is becoming stout.

"Yours,

"Mrs Johnston.

"P.S. The weather continues fine."

RENFIELD'S JOURNAL

7 August.— I cannot sleep though I tried. The air is warm and moist; it is too hot to sleep. Anxious and wide awake, I tossed in my bed hoping for slumber so that I might awake early to my work. No use, I will write to busy myself.

I am filled with anticipation. Something is coming. The wind plays the hills as if they were an organ, the pitch rising as the wind blows harder. The short, fervent blasts convey an urgency rattling the windows like a messenger knocking with bad news. The wind invades my room through the open window and caresses me. Its cold tentacles curl around my limbs relieving me from the thick, damp heat of the summer evening.

The clouded night sky is oddly bright as if lit from behind. The stars are hidden there. In this dim world I write without the aid of a candle for my eyes can now adjust to the low light. Samson is staring at me in the dark. His six smaller eyes give off a greenish glow like a cat's. My ears hear the high whine of the moths' wings fluttering in the hallway and the low rumble of carriage wheels on a distant street.

This afternoon, I could smell the storm coming. And what is more, I could feel the fall in barometric pressure. The ease with which I passed through the air was noticeably increased. I am the glass and the approaching storm, rising and falling, grips and releases me. Do cats perceive this, too? Ham always seemed to know when a storm was coming.

Pain shoots through my head. Unexpected shrieks tear at my ear drums. Two inmates shout obscenities at each other. They are resigned to fight it out. I am trying to block out this noise, but it has gone too far; the tone of their voices indicates murder.

I stepped toward the door to take a glimpse through the trap, but thought better of getting too close when I heard the stern voices were just outside. It was Angie and Tom.

"He's comin' for you. He's goin' to get you!" Tom teased and then released a hideous laugh enjoying how it echoed in the hallway. "Jack is comin'."

"'Is name's not Jack!" Angie insisted unable to stop a fit of temper.

"He's just comin' for a wee visit with his lass."

She shook her head back and forth. "No, no, no!" she cried, her eyes half closed with anger and fear. With just a glimpse of it through the trap, I could see her face was flushed even in the dim flicking gas light. She wiped the sweat and tears from her eyes into her loose, dishevelled hair with the back of her hands.

He wiggled taunting fingers at her and continued his bellowing laugh.

"Stop it. Stop it!" she cried over and over, but Tom kept on. It was as if he had to—he could not help himself.

We all froze when we heard the quick steps of Matron on the stairs. Burly and George soon followed. Separated, the two quarrellers cursed each other all the way down stairs, their voices growing fainter, until they stopped abruptly at the distant slamming of a door.

Now there is silence only for the sound of the wind. It is curious how the wind in the trees sounds much like rushing water dashing against a rocky coast. I sit watching the night. The music of the wind grows louder as it draws closer. The trees wave a frenzied warning of the impending storm.

Something scurries in a wide circle in the corner of the yard. It stops and starts, like a mouse evading an owl, but it is no mouse. It is not alive at all. It is just a large dried leaf caught in the changing winds between the stark angles of two adjoining buildings. The similarity in the motion and sound has revealed a harmony of nature I never realised before. Could it be that a mouse can imitate the movement of windblown leaves to evade capture?

(This storm travelled the east coast of England and was reported in the London news as the most severe storm in seven years. G.D.)

Later. — I must have dozed. I do not know how long I slept but it is now past midnight. The storm is picking up and the first drops of rain are beginning to fall.

I had the most curious dream. It was set in a place I have never seen, but in the dream I felt I knew the place well and was there for a purpose.

It was an alley, perhaps in London, but surely in the city for the air was foul with coal dust. The sun was rising and the fog was fast being burnt away. The cobblestones were wet—perhaps the early morning street cleaners had just been by. A sense of urgency pulled me further down the alley.

As I walk the view does not change—all is grey. The wet bricks, the wet stones and the wet granite blend together to form a sad, lonely passage where all is still.

Finally, I come to the spot I am looking for: the entrance to an arcade that affords a view of the alley. Here an observer can watch the goings-on in secret. Across the alley, a metal door, about three feet above the ground, like that of a dumbwaiter, fits flush into a recess in the brick wall. A feeling of knowing confidence surrounds me as I wait in the shelter of the archway. I wait, but for what?

After a short time, a woman walks slowly down the narrow way carrying a bundle in her arms. She steps up to the door. Unexpectedly, the door swings outward turning on an axis in the middle. It is a revolving door with a shelf on the back on which stands a metal box. It is much like a bread box, only larger, but with the familiar circular pattern of punctures that decorate and aerate it. Her face is hidden by the folds of her shawl which she wears far forward like a monk. Though she must lift the shawl to glance both ways down the street, her back is to me so I cannot see her face.

Satisfied that she is alone, she lifts the bundle from the cloth that is slung around her shoulders and places it in the box. The bundle begins to cry, but she turns and hurries off not looking back. Slowly, the revolving door turns until the flat door is again flush with the wall. The baby's cries have stopped.

I have never had such a dream before. It has shaken me. And though I do not know what it meant, I know that I am now somehow changed.

The long awaited rain has come, and with it, darkness. It will be a magnificent storm. The other inmates grow restless, but their moans and shouts are muffled by the rain drumming on the roof and the wind pounding on the window panes. Thousands of geysers spring to life covering all horizontal surfaces with crystal florets that shine by some hidden light source. The air, though damp, smells clean and cool.

The rain cleans the air of its fairy dust and adds it to the dirt. The rain washes the grey dust from the brown buildings and the brown soil from the grey streets sharpening the straight lines of the man-made world. The rain makes the streets appear clean and the buildings dirty. The rain sweeps the tramps and the whores from the street as well so they now appear innocent, though barren; no traces of its recent teaming with life are left.

Not a cat or a dog or a mouse or an insect will stand in the rain and be washed clean. I have.

Chapter 7

LUST

RENFIELD'S JOURNAL

(*Continued*)

11 August. a.m.— Another dream. There is the taste of blood in my mouth and my body is trembling. I will write to calm myself.

In my dream I stood with a beautiful woman under a clear starry sky. We were in Whitby. I know this because we walked through the ruins of Whitby Abbey by moonlight. And there, in the cliff-side graveyard, she sat on a bench by the sea. The dream was so real. I could smell the salt spray and feel the night air. We were alone and I stood behind her as she gazed over the moon-glazed waves. A gentle touch asked if I might hold her. She answered, silently turning ever so slightly to brush her shoulder against me, filling me with joy. I leaned over to kiss her, a long lingering kiss on the neck.

Then we were startled by someone watching us from the west cliff. Though far off, in my dream I saw a woman clearly. She peered at us from across the mouth of the Esk, her flowing garment moved with the wind creating a dancing silhouette around her as she stood stock still. This awoke me with a start and shattered my serenity.

It is not just in my dreams; of late my mind is filled with memories of Whitby. No wonder I should dream of being there. I have had no word and I despair of ever seeing my cherished congregation again. Here, no one gives me solace on these lonely nights of doubt. Ham was a comfort to me back in Whitby. One could never be alone with a companion such as he. Until now, I never wondered at the change in him.

Ham was one of three ship's cats that washed up on the shores of Kettleness. It was at the end of the very rainy spring we had last year. A storm had dashed yet another ship against the sea breaks that guard the mouth of the River Esk. All hands were lost. The only survivors were these three. Cold, scared, and soaked to the skin with brine, it is no wonder the cats were skittish and reluctant to be handled. Widow Johnston, Rebecca, armed with only a dish of fresh water, waited patiently for them to come to her. With her gentle hands, she wrapped each in a towel and brought them home. Ham was the biggest and strongest of the three and had an appetite to match. After a few weeks of recovery the other two, Shem and Japheth as I named them, found employment on Capt. Colbert's fishing boat. Ham, however, had attached himself to me and I had no trouble deciding to share my living with him. It seemed fitting that he, with his shiny black coat and I, with my black liturgical robes, should share my cottage. We were a pair.

Ham soon became an important part of our daily lives. He was the silliest cat; surely he thought he was human. Yet he was more personable than a person, as cats generally are. He visited me in the mornings and would lick my eyelids, the raspy sound of his tongue echoing in my head. He was a most reliable alarm clock, for he did not stop until he knew I was awake and was ready to rise. This task completed, he romped happily to the kitchen where Mrs Stimpson would be preparing breakfast. He nestled her legs in a figure eight pattern until he got his saucer of milk. She could not dissuade him from this. So eager was he that Mrs Stimpson could hardly walk to the cupboard to fetch a dish, which only delayed his getting his breakfast. So anxious was he that he would nudge her hand as she stooped to place the dish on the floor, sometimes causing her to spill. No matter how she scolded, he never changed in these habits for he was not obedient to anyone.

A faithful companion, Ham stayed by my side as I moved from task to task, going out as I went out and coming in as I came in. Ham was aware of my usual bedtime and was already curled up at the foot of my bed, snuggled deep into the coverlet, when I retired. I cherished this company, but when I sat at my work his doting became a nuisance. He was a most overt supporter of my sermons, showing his enthusiasm by rolling on the pages as I wrote, ending up on his back with his paws up in the air gently resting and his tail swishing back and forth slowly, making swirling streaks of ink across the pages.

I always talked with Ham, but in the beginning his communication was the simple *miaus* and body movements of a cat. I could clearly tell, as most cat-fanciers can, when he wanted to eat, go out, or be petted. Later his communication became more—subtle. It was not so much his speaking then, but my sensing of his thoughts. I was able to feel his pleasure much as I can sense Mary's sadness now. At first I thought it was our relationship that allowed this and thought nothing of it. I simply prided myself as very receptive to my fellow creature. But, when he started to speak, I accepted it as part of my new vision, or in this case "hearing." Oh, his mouth did not move, but his thoughts formed in my head. I am not sure how, but I knew when he wanted me to open the door or put out food. Where before he had to *miau* and paw at an object, now he merely needed to get my attention for me to understand. Mrs Stimpson did not share this rapport and was unaware of our developing discourse.

In retrospect, it was odd that I should have neglected to recognise such a miraculous phenomenon as a talking cat. It was as though Ham did not want me to know it was odd. *Horresco referens*, it is only now that I am away from him, that I have realised that the situation was unusual, let alone fantastic. I must try to remember when his communication changed from my understanding his needs and feelings to his understanding mine.

I should have known something had changed when he stopped sleeping at the foot of my bed. I should have known that something was amiss when he lost his fondness for milk. I should have known that something had gone horribly wrong when he attacked Mrs Stimpson.

Oh yes, I remember that night well. In the tumult that followed the candle went out and poor Mrs Stimpson screamed in the dark until I came. I was already in bed and had to take a moment to secure my robe. When I entered the hall, my candle lighting the way before me, the commotion suddenly stopped.

"The cat, the cat!" she cried.

I lifted the candle and slowly searched the floor. Ham was not there.

"I do apologise, Sir," she said. "It's nothing. The poor creature must have been frightened by my skirts. I probably scared him more than he scared me." With that she lifted her skirt just above the ankle to observe the wound. The bite was deeper than either of us expected. I had never seen a cat bite before. There were two marks about an inch and a half apart. This seemed odd at first, but then I realised he must have caught the muscle at an angle, leaving one mark from an upper canine and one from a lower. Blood trickled down from both. Mrs Stimpson gasped at the sight and pulled her skirts higher—no doubt to prevent them from getting bloodstained.

Struck, my eyes lingered on her limb. A mixed feeling of dread, fear, and longing came over me. I had to turn my face away lest she notice me staring. My eyes were now looking at my shoes, yet I could still see the image of her limb in my mind's eye. I hid my face from her, though I was afraid that she might think I did not sympathise with her for her injury.

With a curt excuse I turned to leave the hallway. Ham was there. Perhaps he had been behind me the whole time. He gently licked his paw and rubbed his face with it. I know now that he was only acting innocent, for it soon came to pass that he could not be left alone in the cottage with Mrs Stimpson without incident.

Letters from Mrs Johnston to Rev Renfield

(These letters were found in the possession of Mrs Aptgate, grandniece to Mrs Johnston. Though how they came to be in her possession is unclear, it was said that they had been returned unopened to Mrs Johnston some two years after the death of Bishop Fairfax. G.D.)

"Whitby, 12 August,
"Dear Rev Renfield,

"There was a dreadful storm last week. It was even worse than last year's gale. The chapel flooded yet again, but have no fear, the ladies of the Philosophical and Dramatic Society pitched in and we made the nave ship-shape for Sunday services.

"A most terrible shipwreck occurred in the storm. The only survivor of the wreck was a large, black dog who many thought looked more like a wolf. The S.P.C.A. tried to help him, but he has run off and we cannot find him. He could be hiding anywhere. The two young ladies who summer here, Lucy Westenra and her friend Mina Murray were frightened by a large animal the very next day. We believe it must have been this dog but we cannot be sure.

"Rev Jenner, the new curate, comes once a week to preach in your absence. He stayed only one night at Hollow's Den, saying he found it disagreeable. Mrs Weakes much prefers your encouraging sermons to his which dwell on a "repent ye sinners or be damned" vein. She instructed me to say that her preference is in no way based on the length of the respective sermons—yours being shorter—and I must add more to the point. Still, he is young, and perhaps his sermons are directed toward the young tourists. It is the young, I fear, whose moral strength is more often tested.

"Yours,
"Mrs Johnston"

"Whitby, 17 August,
"Dear Rev Renfield,

"I am sorry to report that dear Ham has gone missing. When we arrived this morning, he was nowhere to be seen. You need not concern yourself too much, however. Mother and I have made sure a fresh saucer of milk will be left on the doorstep each morning awaiting his return. If he is lost his stoutness will keep him in good stead until his homecoming. Cats are very good at finding their way and Ham will surely find his way back to his beloved master.

"Yours,
"Mrs Johnston"

RENFIELD'S JOURNAL

11 August. (*Later the same day*)—I found a big hairy jumper much the same as Samson, only he is not nearly as large. He will go into the special box with Samson to be his new companion...

What is this? A bang from upstairs. The doctor has returned or someone is in his room. I will reach out to touch his thoughts.

Dr Seward has returned from Whitby and I sense him in his lonely room, drained and sullen. There is something unusual in his manner. His step is heavy and his movement slow. Perhaps he is drinking again. There, there are his thoughts. No, now I am not sure. A thought of Lucy came and departed. Yes, I have it now and to my shock, I have stumbled upon the doctor's most private fancies. Remorse, guilt, hatred—it is more than words I perceive, it is emotions. He begs himself not to weep. "Be strong," he repeats to himself.

This plea is becoming more urgent. He is trying to screen out thoughts. The thoughts are of Lucy. She said she wanted him, desired him. "But you belong to another," he cries in his mind.

The strangest thing has just happened. The doctor's thoughts have melted! The once steady, controlled stream of thought has turned onto itself. The ebb and flow of his thoughts splashes bits of ideas and memories at random. He is laughing. I hear him laughing. He is euphoric and is dancing at a ball. "I will dance with all of you, my dears," he declares to a group of young ladies. "They all want me," he says to himself.

"George," the doctor thinks, embarrassed, waking from his reverie. "He will know!" George is now in the room with the doctor. Dr Seward is trying to distract George from looking at his desk.

"No, I won't be needing anything, George." He is resisting.

"He has seen the syringe," the doctor thinks, his mind trying to focus on his conversation.

"George, I'll be right in the morning," the doctor says aloud, yet inwardly scolding himself for being "caught."

"Yes, Sir," George says as I hear him leave the room.

Thoughts of Lucy dance back into Dr Seward's mind and her earlier protests have ceased...

This is odd. As I write Samson and his new friend have scrambled out of their box. They have stopped, faced off, and are now staring at each other. How marvellous, the smaller one is starting to dance. He moves from side to side waving his two long front legs. Samson, motionless, watches this ballet.

The smaller spider slowly circles Samson who turns so he is always facing his partner. Now the smaller is tapping his tiny "feeder" legs on the desk. These, I have just noticed, are longer than Samson's and have furry black muffs on their ends. Could he be drumming a war signal? His body vibrates as if struck by a chill. Then, suddenly, he stops and stands motionless, waiting for Samson's reaction.

This stand-off lasted some minutes and then he began his routine again, repeating each step as before. Samson watches, his cold eyes fixed.

After a long pause, Samson is now waving back. The little one is inching his way closer. They have begun tussling! The smaller backs up on tiptoes and then charges toward Samson. Samson stands his ground and rears up his four front legs. On impact, Samson grasps the smaller by the head between his two powerful jaws. Bravely, the smaller continues to strike at Samson's abdomen with his feeder legs. He is hitting below the belt. (What the Marquis of Queensbury would make of that!)

Samson and his new friend have been tussling for quite some time now. Though Samson surely could kill the smaller spider, the latter will not be dissuaded. When Samson released him he did not go far. He only rested a while and then returned for another round. Finally, Samson, with a menacing lunge, frightened his attacker away who escaped out the window aided by his thread-line. I watched him crawl down the side of the building to freedom. Perhaps there is a natural animosity between members of this species of spiders.

Companionless, Samson returned to his box. There, seemingly undaunted by the scuffle, he tends the silk lining which he set down not long ago. The man upstairs in his lonely room could use a companion himself.

August 12.— Samson is acting very strange indeed. This morning he has a paper ball, as big as a gum drop, attached to his rear. Where he got this, there is no telling. He carries it everywhere with him. Perhaps it serves as a sort of cuddly toy like a child's doll. This is fascinating. I must search for more spiders.

August 13.— My renewed search for spiders led me to the basement of the west wing. This area was disappointing in that, much used, it was swept clean. Here the laundry for the entire hospital is done. Two large tubs, churned by immense mechanical arms, whirl the linens ceaselessly. A steam engine heats the water and turns the washing arms. The movement of gears and the release of steam fill the room with clanking and clattering and hissing. Here is the origin of Robbie's endless "shrr, shrr, clunk clunk."

I heard someone coming. To avoid being seen I hid behind one of the large tubs. Matron scurried in quickly with a young woman shuffling in tow tied by a long strip on linen attached to her apron strings. Matron did not see me, but the young girl stopped and stared at me as I inched further behind the tub. It was there the opening to a new world was to be found. It beckoned to me. A black hole. Freedom.

The opening, though small, was large enough for me to enter without difficulty. The bolts that fastened the grate had long since rusted away. The chimney led straight up. No spiders here—only black dust which filled my hair—soft, fluffy, and light. A faint, delicious odour lured me upward. In the pitch blackness one must navigate by sense of smell. What was it? The memory of that odour haunts me still. It is a pleasant haunting, a feeling as if shrouded in a warm, thick blanket. I was pulled toward it, not merely attracted, but pulled. I climbed up the narrow shaft pushing my elbows and knees outward. The thin edges of bricks where they meet the mortar were all I needed to boost myself up.

The passage led long way up. I soon realised that there is no outlet on the ground floor where my ward is. Then a shaft of light from above revealed itself to be the fireplace of Dr Seward's suite. Through this tiny gap I could make out the doctor's office, or should I say, laboratory. Every inch was populated with bottles, books, papers and every sort of modern apparatus, each as beautiful as it was miraculous. No horizontal surface was safe.

His dictation machine with its long cylinder dominated the centre of his desk. Many loose cylinders crowded the selves and cubbies behind it. None were labelled and some were covered in dust. An antique, electric generator with its glass disk and hand crank was displayed prominently in a glass cabinet. All manner of scales, meters and metal physician's tools littered a table punctuated with half-drunk cups of tea or coffee.

Yet, the scent descended from above so I continued my climb. Two stories up, I found myself behind the flue of a wide hearth. The passage widened and formed a shelf. I lingered there unable to see, but I could hear and smell and taste the room beyond. The scent was strong. A crowd of people was on the other side. I made out women's voices.

I felt uneasy knowing that I should not be eaves-dropping in such a manner, yet remained there for quite some time. Finally, overcome with the desire to see, I gently forced open the flue, which did not fit tightly and was slightly ajar. Figuring out how took some time, but I realised that I could drop my head down through the flue if I scrunched up and then inserted my legs up the chimney above me. Though upside-down, I was quite comfortable and could see the entire room.

What befell my eyes as I slowly lowered my head into the light I can scarce describe. It may sound odd, but they were like dolls. Those that moved at all did so in simple repeated motions. Their eyes looked blank and expressions were as painted on. The high ceiling played sounding board to the ardent chords of their voices. Some jabbered, some sang, some cried out in horror, yet, there was a calm—no overt movement was tolerated.

This must be the main women's ward. The poorer classes are separated by sex in enormous wards. I gather the men's ward is in the other wing above the private rooms where Robbie sleeps.

During the entire time I was watching, only one watched me. She was a young thing, pale and thin. She must have been a new patient for her hair was still cropped short above the ears. She looked at me without blinking and no one made notice of her; they were occupied preparing the linens for wash. At first, she was unconscious of her appearance, but then began to tug at her roughly-cut tresses pulling them as if she hoped to make them longer by doing so. I smiled to show her that it was no matter. She smiled too and began to sing. It was a happy, silly tune of a child's game. She closed her eyes and turned in slow circles to the time, her face uplifted as if warmed by the sun. The length of linen that hung from her waist showed me it was she I had just seen in the basement some ten minutes earlier.

"Daisy! be about your work," Matron scolded.

Before Matron saw me, I lifted my head over the flue and in my haste, returned to the basement facedown all the way, with less trouble than it took to get up.

14 August.—Each night I can sleep less and when I do sleep, I dream of dreadful things. Perhaps to-night's dream was inspired by my strange encounter with Patient S. to-day. Yes, for the first time I found the courage to view him through the trap. Much as George had pictured him, he was skin and bones—without the dignity of one

stitch of clothing. He did not appear surprised, but was looking up at the trap when I peeked in.

His large, oddly round, moist eyes, though sad and hollow, surprised me with a hint of mischief. What those eyes have witnessed his tongue was reluctant to tell. At first he did not speak but only looked at me. Then, after a while, he tentatively began. He talked of his lover and as he talked, a glimpse of a smile passed his lips. Yet, then he grew sad and confided in me.

"My love was taken from me, they wouldn't let us be together. Taken so young. He was only twenty-three. He was a sweet man—gentle as you are, Mr Renfield. We lived together at university for two years. We had a cat and held many gatherings of the elite. We liked cats."

I am not sure if he meant his lover and himself or just himself. Sometimes he referred to himself as the queen and spoke using the "royal we." Somehow he knows about my asking for a cat. Can asylum gossip reach even to his seclusion?

He began his weak singing. The Gilbert and Sullivan tunes he always sings bring me back to Whitby and the pleasant times with the ladies of the Philosophical and Dramatic Society. Their meetings were held at the home of Rebecca's aunt, a Mrs Wills. This gentle pleasure lasts only a moment, for when I think of Whitby, I cannot help but remember my vision. My people's faces stare at me in my mind, wide-eyed and blank, frozen at the moment of recognition of imminent death.

In my dream, Rebecca appeared to me again. She called out to me for help. God rest her soul. It was she who first appeared on the doorstep with a hot steak and kidney pie my first lonely week at Hollow's Den. I should have liked to invite her in, but even the curate must have a chaperon. A comely woman, she still bore much of her youth. It must have been she who came knocking on my door that Easter morning. I had not the courage to face her then. She should be angry with me and yet in my dream she looked so forgiving.

It was at the house of her aunt, a fine building by the west cliff just inside the crescent, that I was given a small reception on my installation as curate. Everyone was most kind. I felt awkward, for even though in my native land, I was more accustomed to the rough life of the bush than to polite company. And this house in Whitby, distanced as it is from the city, lacked none of the modern conveniences and fine appointments of the London houses. We sat indoors. We should have sat outdoors on such a fine day in Zambezia. Yes, I remember now that I felt somewhat closed in and yet grateful to be back in civilised England all the same, for the neat doilies and fresh cut flowers reminded me of my mother's home.

I was introduced to several members of the society. Mrs Stoughton was president and was in charge of all their activities including, sponsoring the local players and arranging a theatre outing each year—"for the enlightenment and edification of Whitby women."

Mrs Stoughton resembled a vase, her waist cinched in so tight, a spray of pink rosettes tacked to a delicate matrix of sheer net from her bodice to her high neckline. All the women were well dressed and refined, but Mrs Stoughton drew your eye and your attention. She really knew her worth. I would later find that it was she who did the books for St Ann—constantly reminding me of how many cubic yards of gas were used for our Thursday evening services.

The Widow Johnston always wore black, which was her duty to her late husband. The jet beading of her bodice shimmered with the light from the candelabra. She was an unwitting, living advertisement for the local jet trade. And also, a tribute to our most gracious sovereign, the queen, who still wears mourning covered in Whitby jet though her husband, the Prince Consort, has been dead for over 30 years.

Another member, besides Widow Johnston and her mother, was also in attendance. Mrs Weakes, a bit younger than her companions, giggled and snorted at every comment. She was, on the whole, rather giddy. She had in tow a young charge about seven or eight and a bit pudgy. He hid behind her and eyed me suspiciously over the bow of her bustle. As she bent forward to reveal him in his tidy sailor suit, I could not help thinking she resembled a ship's figurehead. Try though she might, she was unable to manoeuvre out of the way. Her entreaty of, "Come out, Billy, he won't eat you," did not help matters.

Mrs Stoughton announced it was time for the entertainment and invited all the guests to sing at the piano. Splendid entertainment too, for there were several accomplished singers. Widow Johnston, Rebecca—only her aunt called her Rebecca—so shy as she was, did not announce her song, but only stood and nodded politely when asked to sing. It was the first time I ever heard her voice. Mrs Barstock, her aunt, accompanied her at the piano. Rebecca sang, "Come Home, Father," which was her song. She sang so high and clear that my eyes became moist. She was like an angel, an angel in black.

I retreated to the hall trying to dislodge myself from the company for a moment, not feeling quite myself. I stood in the gloom of the dimly lit space and watched motes of dust float in a shaft of light from the window.

From behind me Billy grunted. I turned to find him with his chest puffed and his squinting eyes glowering at me menacingly. That pugnacious face! He was the most frightening child I've ever come across. Soon, Mrs Wills, having noticed my absence, sought me out. Far from relief that she might protect me from the little menace, I felt cornered by her presence.

"Africa," she began, "you must be very proud of your accomplishments." And after only a brief survey of my missionary work she abruptly changed the subject. "You know, Mr Renfield, the custom of curates not marrying has long gone out of fashion. Your being in the bush so long, you probably have not kept up on such matters."

I assured her that I had heard the news and inching myself away, found myself once again in the drawing room surrounded by bewitching music and strange women who seemed to find me utterly fascinating.

After the singing, Mrs Stoughton invited me to join the Dramatic Society on their yearly trip to London. They travelled by train and there they would "experience" theatre. There was theatre in York and in Whitby itself, but London had a special lure: Gilbert and Sullivan at The Savoy and Shakespeare at The Lyceum. These were the choice of the Whitby theatre elite.

"You must come with us on our excursion, Mr Renfield," said Mrs Stoughton.

"Adventure," Mrs Weakes suggested as if to say that that term fit better than "excursion" for the subject at hand.

"I fear I have not seen a play for quite some time," I said.

"The theatre, Mr Renfield, is a reflection of life. We can really see ourselves..." said Mrs Stoughton.

"Unlike when looking in a mirror," completed Mrs Weakes.

" 'All the world's a stage...' "

"That's Shakespeare," said Mrs Barstock.

" '...full of sound and fury...' "

"That's Irving!" interjected Mrs Weakes, her chin slightly raised to one side and her eyes fixed on some distant object. Mrs Stoughton suffered her young companion's gushing with grace and dignity. She forgave her, indicating the interruption by simply closing her eyes for only a moment.

"Did you say *Irving*?" I said, recognising the name, but at first not knowing from where.

"Of course, everyone knows Henry Irving, the actor," Mrs Weakes gushed, now fully with us again.

"I met him." They caught their breath in unison.

"You met Him?"

"Yes, on the docks at Portsmouth. There's not much to tell, really. You see, he stepped on my foot and I said, 'I beg your pardon,' and he said, 'Sorry, old chap.' "

"Oh, how wonderful!" said Mrs Stoughton.

"He nearly knocked me down."

"He actually spoke to you?" Mrs Weakes sighed.

"Yes."

At this she swooned and while Mrs Barstock ran for some water, Mrs Stoughton and Mrs Wills held her up and fanned her brow lest she fall.

It is simple memories like these that keep me sane. God help them, their gentle souls are here with me.

PATIENT LOG

(Entries kept by warder, George Simmons.)

Patient: R. M. Renfield

11 August. 9:00 a.m.— Patient quiet. homesick.

12 August. 10:00 a.m.— Patient not sleeping good was up all night. Complains of bad dreams.

13 August. 10:00 a.m.— up all night again.

5:12 p.m.— Patient found covered with black powder when I brought him dinner.

14 August. 10:15 a.m.— Patient quiet to-day, talked of his home in Witbe.

15 August. 9:45 a.m.— Restricted to room. Patient up all night riting.

16 August. 9:30 a.m.— Restricted—patient writing alot again. Agitated. Still not sleeping much.

REPORT OF DR PATRICK HENNESSEY

10 August.— Patient Renfield is very sensitive to his surroundings and thus the storm made him agitated for when the other patients are upset, he becomes upset as well.

Renfield is also suggestible to a high degree to the will of others. The patient has become so dependent on Dr Seward that their relationship is now not unlike that of parent and child. Renfield, child, is servile and defers to the doctor, parent, for advice and approval for most of his activities. While Dr Seward is away, Renfield is nervous and indecisive.

RENFIELD'S JOURNAL

17 August.— Dr Seward has returned and his head is full of thoughts from Whitby. I search these thoughts for news of my friends, my congregation, but none are forthcoming. His mind is excited. Lucy has been ill, and the doctor must visit her in a much different role than before. Yet this is not the cause of his excitement.

Lucy, though ill, has found the strength to play matchmaker, and recommended her dearest friend as the perfect match for the doctor. Mina, Lucy explained, is intelligent as well as beautiful. She is educated and is also schooled in the art of typing. Her interest in modern machinery fascinated our dear doctor. And, Lucy confided, the doctor "simply must protect her from pining away for a simple clerk who left to make his fortune on the continent and never returned." She summed up by adding that it was his "duty as a gentleman" to pay her call.

Their first meeting would happen that afternoon as Mina came in to check on Lucy. Mina had some little task in Scarborough and Lucy insisted that the doctor escort her for mad cows were known to menace those young ladies who dared cross their path. This pleasant journey, and the fact that Lucy will marry next month on the 28th, were enough to germinate an interest in this young woman.

So the doctor has turned his attention to Lucy's young friend, Mina. He hesitates for she is a school mistress, but he can refuse Lucy nothing. How his wants have changed. First he wants the fair and delicate, witty ingénue; now suddenly he has fixed his fancy on the dark and independent new woman. She is constantly in his thoughts.

Later.— God is calling to me. He is close. He asks me to prepare for his coming. I said, "Yes, Lord, I will do your bidding." He is pleased with me and asked me to call him Master.

18 August.— The voice is clear to-day, clearer than ever before.

God is calling to me.

He is come.

The Master is at hand. He is calling to me from the tower I see from my window.

He says: "Come to me Renfield. Come to me. You must go to the chapel of the great house called Carfax. There you will await your instructions. Take care not to disturb anything in the house or on the grounds for the ancient dust holds many tales of the past. Come to me. Come to me at sundown." God is speaking to me and I will take down his words for they are a new scripture.

"I will give you all you desire: strength, health, respect. All will be your servants and none will be over you. My right hand, you are, Renfield. Lords and kings will kneel at your feet; the birds and the beasts will do your bidding; and you will live for ever. This I promise you. You in return will give me your love and devotion. Worship me. Worship me and all I have promised will be yours."

God has spoken!—and to me, the lowliest of creatures. I will prepare to meet him.

I smell something. Could it be blood? Sweet blood of Christ, it is coming from Carfax and wafting in the wind to me like the scent of cherry blossoms. It is intoxicating and I want more...

George is watching me through the trap. The man has a gift for bad timing. I will pretend not to notice. I will wait for I must leave in secret so I may come and go as I please...

George came in and I dismissed him. Yet, he would not leave. He was pretending to have an interest in my nature studies. This is a sham. He thinks that I would merely tell him of what I know. Ha, I say. No, my stout friend, thick within and thick without, you must wait. You must wait for your reward. The Master is at hand. The stone face of the tower, reflecting the setting sun, glows red. Soon it will be time. I must leave!

George has summoned Dr Seward. Do they know? No, how could they. They merely are carrying out their duties. The sun is down completely and his voice calls me to him—no longer a vague, dull hint of a thought, but a clear voice—as if whispering in my ear—calls to me.

"You are strong," comes the voice.

20 August. Midnight.— God is calling me impatiently, "Come to me, Renfield. Come to me." I must go to him. Go to him now. "Come to the chapel. There I will see you with my own eyes."

I wait patiently for the doctor to leave. He has not shown his face, but I hear his thoughts just outside the door. "Mania" is it. When I am rewarded, so shall he be. And it will not be long for the doctor is tired and must sleep soon. Then I will slip quietly away. No one will even notice I am missing.

If only I could escape out the window the way Samson's companion did. But wait, God has given me the strength and my spider friend has given me the idea. I feel strong—strong as the towering keep that watches me from Carfax.

BOOK II

(Pasted in the front cover of Renfield's prayer book.)

Teach the ignorant

Forgive the offender

Bear with the oppressive and troublesome

Reprove the sinner

Counsel the doubtful

Console the sad

Pray for all

Chapter 1

PRUDENCE

RENFIELD'S JOURNAL

(This passage and the others like it have been faithfully translated from the Rumanian thanks to Arminius Vambéry of BudaPesth University. Note that some of the passages were written in the old Cyrillic alphabet no longer used in Rumania. S.D.)

20 August.— You have been naughty my child, very naughty, or so your Dr Seward would see it. In mine eyes, my servant, you have been dutiful, and for that you shall be rewarded. For all those who serve me shall be rewarded.

You have learned much, my pupil. Though pursued by three angry men, you hesitated to contemplate having Ham for dinner. You are beginning to feel the power, my power that I share with you. You will complete your mission soon enough. For now, my servant, seek you smaller prey. Ham is much too clever to let you catch him.

Ham's brothers were drowned at sea by your fishy friend Capt Colbert, but they were not as clever as he and not as strong.

This does not shock you. You suspected Capt Colbert all along, did you not? Why would you not defend Widow Johnston in her accusations toward him? Why, Renfield? Are you weak? Fear not, it was I who punished him. I am the judge and the executioner. I will deal quickly with those who would stand in my way. I am the Corrector, the remover of human error. It is my birthright.

In time, I will reveal to you my true self.

PATIENT LOG

(Entries kept by warder, George Simmons.)

Patient: R. M. Renfield

18 August. 10:00 a.m.—quiet—Patient crawling about, counting spiders.

8:00 p.m.—Patient sniffing at window was a mite snippy with me. Not surprising he's getting a bit uppity yet with all that writing and all. He made like I was not good enough to speak to him. All he would say was the master is at hand. Called Dr S. so as he might see what I mean. Seen this sort of thing before and there's no worst thing than a patient what gets religion.

19 August. 2:43 a.m.— Patient escaped through the window breaking the frame. He's so strong he pulled the window right out of the frame. I come right away but the skinny devil slid hisself out headfirst. Thought it best to wait and watch where he went and told Elwood to fetch Dr S. When

we caught him on the grounds just over the wall he started in on hitting me and the others. We got him back all right.

9:45 A.M.— Solitary. Patient raving—says he must see the master. Straight-waistcoat.

20 August. 10:15 a.m.—Solitary. raving. Careful watch.

21 August. 9:45 a.m.—Solitary. Another fit but was quiet last night. Careful watch.

22 August. 9:30 a.m.—Solitary. Careful watch.

8:30 p.m. Calm before dawn and at night but raving during the day. Dr S. told me to take off the straight-waistcoat and allow the patient to air out like. The doctor thinks maybe he'll show us something if we let him run free like. We watched and waited but he wouldn't go.

REPORT OF DR PATRICK HENNESSEY

(*Cyclothymia, now called manic-depression or bi-polar disorder, is characterised by mood swings from very sad to very excited. The reader should be made aware that though this diagnosis may be consistent with Renfield's symptoms, it was noted by his colleagues and subordinates alike, that, in his tenure at this asylum, nearly all of Dr Hennessey's patients received this same diagnosis. G.D.*)

22 August.— The patient has been violent for the last three days. Following an escape attempt, Renfield was removed to isolation in Ward B and restrained. This treatment did not have the usual calming effect on the patient, but on the contrary, resulted in the patient becoming even more violent.

The attempt came in the small hours of the night when we are short staffed. It is not clear how the patient was able to break though the window of his room to make his escape; perhaps this strength derived from a fit of pique. Once outside, the patient immediately ran to the empty house next door, there proceeding to pound on the door, ranting and raving all the while, until we came for him. He struck out at us and was hard pressed to regain his composure.

The patient shows distinct signs of cyclothymia, the extreme shifts from melancholia to mania differ from the classic case only in their unusually short cycle. Many patients take months or even years between the manic and melancholic stages of this illness; Renfield, however, is a most fascinating case for his mood swings to both extremes each day. Each morning the patient wakes and immediately becomes agitated. He will not touch his food yet is filled with enormous energy. By noon his state has developed into a paroxysm where he screams and kicks, his whole body shaking. This fit abates somewhat until sundown, at which time he becomes calm, so calm in fact, it is not unlike the serenity one receives after a good long rest.

Dr Seward has ordered the patient returned to his room finding that the patient's night behaviour merits release from isolation. The doctor has specified, however, a straight-waistcoat must be worn by the patient to restrain him during the daylight hours for his fits occur only at this time.

RENFIELD'S JOURNAL

22 August. Sundown.— Someone has been writing in my journal during my stay in the quiet room. The hand is large and ornate, not like mine at all. And though it seems fantastic, the text is not in English. I am skilled in languages, and yet I do not recognise this one. The alphabet, though similar, is not quite the same as my own. *Ecce signum*! This can be no joke—God has sent me a message—I just cannot decipher it yet.

God calls to me. I hear his voice in the whispers of the breeze and in the whispers in the corridor.

I will be with you soon, oh Lord.

So close, so close, I nearly saw you but for Dr Seward and the warders, the heartless ruffians, would not let me. I fought them and got in a few good licks to be sure. My reward was three days in the quiet room chained to the wall. For now I will be calm. I hide my true feelings from them all for they will never understand. Soon I will see you, my Lord, only I must be patient.

My escape did bring me one thing. I met an old friend on the grounds of Carfax. A small black shadow darted in front of me as I crossed from the wall to the chapel. Soon after, my foot caught in what I thought to be a croquet wicket, tripping me forward onto my face. A large black cat scooted out from under me, and though devoted to the task at hand, I could not help but notice there was something terribly familiar about him. He stayed just out of reach, the rascal. If only there was time I could have had him. He teased and taunted me relentlessly. Still, first I must have more sparrows. Yes, I will ask for more sugar, they would not refuse me that. But, where will I find more spiders? The Lord will provide, I need not fear.

When I got to the chapel where my Master dwells, I found the door locked. The Master spoke to me through the door and said, "Renfield, you will be rewarded. Prepare, for I will instruct you…"

Just then we were interrupted by Dr Seward and his men. They had come to bring me back to the asylum. I needed more time. I resisted them with all my might. And, for this, I was placed in the quiet room for three days and three nights. As they dragged me back to the asylum, I noticed how grand the building is. Fine grey stone walls sport a neo-classical triangular awning held aloft by four immense columns. And, like a crown, a white columned cupola perches on the centre of the roof.

All in all, it was quite a peaceful stay in the quiet room. The master, each day, sent forth spiders—big juicy ones—so that I would not hunger.

Spiders are rather tough yet it is no trouble to get some nourishment from them. Spiders have big strong hearts in the middle which pulse the blood down two opposite legs, then the next two, and so on, just like the pistons of an engine. The legs are hollow. A long channel runs the length and carries the blood to the ends—not unlike a sipping straw. If one nips the end off of one leg, the heart continues to pump blood and thus gives a tiny squirt every fourth beat. Once the blood is drained, I simply discard the hollow carcass.

Each night the Lord shared his view of his earthly creatures with me. The days I slept so deeply that I awoke refreshed and invigorated. I do not know why my days reversed themselves in this manner, just that the Lord shared with me only visions of night...

What is this? Samson is acting very strange. He has unhooked the paper ball from his abdomen and is turning it over and over with his front legs. Now he is biting it. Perhaps it is some morsel saved for leaner times or for a special occasion. But wait, the opening in the ball is exuding dozens of tiny, eight-legged creatures. They swam around Samson. Now they are climbing onto his broad abdomen. Layer upon layer they climb on his back. Oh! The weight of them has reached its limit and they topple to the desk. Yet, no sooner do they fall, than they collect themselves and begin climbing the long hairs on Samson's legs. Samson waits patiently for them to regain their places on his broad abdomen. One cannot see Samson's lower body through the crowd of tiny, clinging beasties.

This is a most embarrassing development. These little creatures must be spiderlings and the paper ball must have been an egg. Samson, therefore, must be a female!

Samson has discarded the paper ball and has climbed upon my fly-box which is his—I mean her—usual way of saying she is hungry. From now on, in view of this new development, I will call Samson: "Delilah."

Later.— Matron stands outside my door. This is unusual for her. She attends to Angie and Mary in the early morning and then is off elsewhere for the day. That is except laundry day when long hours leave her neat, rounded folds of hair at many loose ends. Today she has arranged her hair so it is now parted in the middle, though just slightly, like a new woman. She knows it is quite becoming. She smoothes her long white apron over and over. Oh! It is the first time I've seen her smile.

Her thoughts? The few I get are clear. At Conley Hatch they have a husband and wife team. He as patron. She as matron. This is the usual form in private asylums. And Matron has a strong liking for tradition—she has pinned her hat on our Dr Seward.

Speak of the devil. The doctor has just hurried by flushing out all personnel—the workers as well as the slackers. They quickly make themselves scarce or busy in his path. Sadly, Matron has flown the coop thinking it best to leave her approach for another day.

It is curious that everyone in the dayroom, excepting Robbie, of course, noticed her budding romance long before his dalliance with that wealthy, Westenra woman, Lucy. Yet, the dear doctor is as oblivious to her acute awareness of him as he is to her bachelor status. Why does he not notice her? If not for her stern countenance and curt manner she should prove a most attractive woman.

The poor doctor's heart is broken once again. Mina, his new object of desire, has left for the continent having heard from her young man. And so his attentions are turned once more to me. He has thrown himself into his work and I, it seems, am now his favourite case.

Dr Seward has taken an interest in Carfax and hopes to use me as a means to gain entry. He does not know who or what is at Carfax, but is very interested to find out. So much, in fact, that he was willing to let me run free. Tom informed me the gate at the stairs was left unlocked, as well as my door. George casually left them that way, feigning distraction by some pressing work (an extremely poor choice of ruse for such as George). He then occupied himself elsewhere, but his thoughts were on me.

I think it better to wait. I must find a safer time to slip out. Now all eyes are upon me.

23 August.— Tom is ill, a cough has settled in his chest and he fears he will succumb to the influenza. While visiting in his room, I tried to comfort him and feed him some broth. I told him he would be well with a little rest and a little prayer. He said he could not pray for health when it was God who had "smote" him with the illness in the first place. I was flabbergasted at Tom's belief that illness is caused by God's anger with us, that God afflicts us with pains and troubles for our transgressions.

"How do you come to believe such things?" I asked.

"Father...," he winced and then apologised with his eyes. "Reverend Sir, I have a terrible sin on my soul. It weighs upon me. That's why they put me here. The sin, the shame... it affects the way I act, everything I do. I can't hide it, it shows. At the job or with my family, even just walking down the street, people would look at me as if they knew, as if they could see what I have done. I have no peace. God is punishing me because I've done the unthinkable and not confessed."

"And were you never ill before this sin?"

"No, it started only after my first time."

"First time? You mean you continued after you knew what you were doing was sinful?"

"Yes, but I can't help it. I love her. Her memory will not go away. I heard her voice in my head. I tried to push her memory out by concentrating on my work. When I was not at my work, I went to the pubs and sang along good and loud, but the voice was still there. I drank and drank to drown out her voice, but when I sobered up, the voice came back calling me to her."

"Her voice? Who is it that is calling you?" I asked, and in his mind he pictured the woman and her basket. It is only now while transcribing this discourse that I remember where I have seen this before. He often pictures a woman in his mind, a woman sitting on a stone bench with a basket on her lap. Yes, I have seen this before.

"My wife. My wife is calling me," he said as he collapsed, burying his face in his hands to console himself. He rubbed his forehead with the tips of his fingers and sobbed quietly to himself. "You can't possibly understand what it's like to hear a voice calling to you in your mind—calling you from the grave."

I dared not enquire, but wondered why he asks so often to see his wife though he thinks she is dead. Does he even know?

"God will forgive you, only you must ask to be forgiven and you must repent."

He turned his face from me and rested his head on the wall. I thought it best to leave him alone for a bit.

Later.— The Master is calling to me. He is in the chapel at Carfax. I watch with my mind and can see as if through a bird's eyes (only birds do not fly at night).

A mouse, with whiskers wiggling, sniffs along the base of the chapel doors. There, between the doors and the doorjamb, a narrow opening beckons. He is going to enter. Reaching with my thoughts, I take hold of his mind just before he flattens his bones and squeezes himself into the chapel. There I see as he sees, hear as he hears.

The last rays of the sun stream in through the blues and golds of stained glass. In the dim silence I see the pews have been removed—the open space seems enormous. I flex my (or his) tiny paws, so like hands with long fingers, their bone and sinew visible through tight, translucent pink skin. The view changes constantly as his eyes dart about. The ceiling is a long way up. There the moths' dance distracts me as they flutter amongst the cobwebs. Oh no! A piercing shriek sends me darting toward the nearest corner for cover...

That gave me a start! Yet, it is only my cousin the bat, hanging from an Italian ceiling sconce, stretching and waking for the night.

Exploring the hall's perimeter, I find all manner of refuse: shards of wood and plaster and glass all covered in soft powder of a hundred years' dust. There is only so much dust... After turning an object in my paws at every possible angle to sniff, peer at, and taste, I toss it aside and clean the dust from my paws and face. The cobwebs stick to my whiskers which I comb with my paws, rolling it with dust into clumps until they lose their clinginess and can be tossed aside.

Food, I need food. I am ravenous. I taste the dry dust on my paws as I clean them and it makes me thirsty. I sniff the air. Nothing. Wait, perhaps there is something. I lift myself onto my hind legs steadying myself with my tail, to sniff a higher layer of air. All is still. The air moves more quickly along the floor than way up here, four inches up.

I must clean my fur again.

All is quiet and yet I am nervous. My heart beats so that I can feel the blood course through the veins of my starched ears. I am all atremble, ready to spring, to turn, to run, at any sound or any cause or origin. Run—that is what I will do. That is what I do.

I hear the Master calling me, "Come to me Renfield, it is time!" I feel his presence and begin to quake. My body—the mouse's body is pulled by an invisible force. We run in circles faster and faster... The bond is broken. I understand now. It is time. I must run to the Master.

Chapter 2

TEMPERANCE

(Renfield's poetry pencilled inside the back cover of his prayer book. Dated September 5. S.D.)

Sadness — gladness — madness, those

two at angles juxtapose

to create the third.

Then where are you oh human kind?

when thy brother hath gone lost

his mind is full and empty both

his tongue and gestures swear

the oath of fearful loss and gain.

His eye doth hear and sight from ear

doth paint the florid scene

which is only an allusion

to that which is really so.

PATIENT LOG
(Entries kept by warder, George Simmons.)

Patient: R. M. Renfield

23 August. 3:00 a.m. Patient got out on his own. I was just checking in on him like I do every night when he shot by me like he was no wider than a board. He ran acrosst to the old house again like there was something there. We went after him. He acted strange. He started in to fight, but then for no reason stopped and wanted to come back with us. Padded cell.

24 August. 8:00 a.m. Padded cell. Patient restless, chewing around fingernails until they bleed.

25 August. 8:30 a.m. Padded cell. Patient restless again. Won't eat nothing all day. Sucking on his fingers. Was calm in the night.

26 August. 9:00 a.m. Padded cell. Patient talks and acts normal enough in the evening but is worst all day. He shouts and upsets the others. Won't talk none to me or the doctors. Wants something hard to write on.

27 August. 8:00 a.m. Padded cell. Patient unchanged. Won't eat nothing during the day or talk to people.

28 August. 8:00 a.m. Padded cell. Patient unchanged. Dr S. instructs me to keep him in padded room myself.

REPORT OF DR PATRICK HENNESSEY

29 August.—The patient Renfield, considering the developments of last week, falls directly in what is called the cyclical phase of the mood shifting disorder, cyclothymia. Attempts to approach the patient in regard to speaking of his ailment have been abandoned, as his manic episodes, which quiet only at night, make discourse virtually impossible.

In regard to the patient's recent escape attempt, it was considered prudent to place him in solitary confinement until his roaming instinct has expired. The patient is conscious of his motives and deliberate in his actions, yet, under cross-examination, he defies any and all attempts to ascertain his reasoning for said event; he cannot, or will not, explain his actions in regard to escaping to the abandoned property on the far side of our west wall.

The patient was heard speaking at the chapel door, the chapel belonging to said property, when Mr Simmons and Mr Elwood arrived to retrieve him. The patient, as before, was reluctant to leave the doorway, continuing his chatter until he was forcibly removed and returned to the asylum. One cannot speculate, at this time, whom the patient believes he is speaking to, yet, it is conceivable to conject that if the patient is speaking to an empty building, yet believes he is speaking to someone, that he is most likely hallucinating.

This being the first instance of promoted pathological behaviour, it must be a significant sign as to the patient's condition. I therefore conclude, that the patient's condition is deteriorating and concur with Dr Seward that solitary confinement is the best prescription for taming the patient's unsettled mind at this time.

RENFIELD'S JOURNAL

4 September.— It is all over now, my experiments are ruined!

To-day is a sad day. During my stay in the quiet room Delilah had no food. When I returned, I found the only fly in her box sucked dry. How dreadful to think she might have survived if I had left her box open. There is no telling how long she has been dead. She was company to me and I will miss her.

Her children, or at least most of them, are still alive, no doubt endowed with some food reserve at birth. How they cling to her lifeless body. They are true spiders now and have developed the long legs and colouring of their mother. Still they are so small that ten of them can fit on the tip of one's little finger. Their tiny, determined faces look toward the sun's last rays reaching in from the window above.

The sun has set and soon the last light will slip over the horizon. And with it will go my hope. The Master promised me. He promised to give me... He! Was he real or am I under delusions as Dr Seward says? It is gone. That feeling that I was being watched over is gone. How can this be? When I pressed myself against the chapel door at Carfax I felt a real presence. I was ever so close to the Master. He spoke to me through the door. The Master touched my mind as he had that first time I lay on the floor of the quiet room. He spoke to me. The voice was commanding, yet soothing. It said, "You are a good servant. All good servants are rewarded." As the voice penetrated, my mind became clear. Thoughts untangled, reason and purpose expressed themselves all around me. Nature, industry, and the human condition became as one simple, elegant equation. Everything made sense.

When the warders caught up with me, my first instinct was to struggle, and struggle I did. Yet, as the warders took hold of me, I heard the Master's voice. The Master bid me to be calm and I became calm. He instructed me to not resist them. And, as my mind relaxed, it was able to escape my body (which the warders took back to the asylum.) He spoke again and said, "Soon, soon you will have your reward." These words lingered in my thoughts, and then his presence left me as suddenly as it had come.

I followed the warders back in good spirits, never knowing what was to befall. To my horror, I was led to the quiet room, but I gave no trouble for I believed the Lord would provide.

I do not know what to do. While weeping for Delilah, I spread out the sugar from my tea as the last rays glowed red in the distance. Dr Seward was kind enough to give me an extra share...

Oh what is this? The spiders! Delilah's children are on the move. They turn one by one as if called by a voice that only they can hear. They leap the gap between the desk and the wall though this is quite a feat for such tiny creatures. Here, each heroically climbs to the windowsill. Up they go. They make slow progress though they run so fiercely. Yet, without faltering, they continue without rest to the very top of the open window and wait there.

Silvery threads stream out from each and wave in the breeze outside the... Oh wonders of nature, they can fly! The wind catches their silk threads and whirls them up into the air. There are others there, too. Thousands of specks, like dandelion seeds, float silently by. They float over Carfax as high as the keep, going higher and higher as though they could make it all the way to London. Such a strange and marvellous sight right here in this great, dirty city. No one takes notice of the spiders as they drift by and land on their carriages and shoulders and hats, not even the horses...

A most curious thing... A thought, like a dream, entered my mind as I looked out over the city rooftops. I saw a tall thin man. I saw him clearly, though this thought lasted only a moment. I could tell he was standing on the asylum roof, his black-clad frame between the white columns of the cupola. He stood there silently looking over the night sky. I made out his features by some curious light—it was Jamison. Then, suddenly, as soon as I was sure my eyes were not deceiving me, he sprang straight forward leaping off the edge of the building directly above the front entrance of the asylum. There the vision ends. These thoughts become more strange each passing day. I really must get more rest.

Later. .— The Master has called out to me. I heard a rush of wind and suddenly I was surrounded with blinding light. The wind roared and whirled around me as I stood in the middle, the eye of the storm. All at once I knew. I knew it was He, and I knew I need not fear. "You must ready yourself for the Master, for I will come to you. Prepare yourself. Gather the strength around you. Concern yourself not with lesser prey. You will be given larger prey, which I will send to you. Yea, like the husbandman, you will tend your cattle so that you might always drink."

Lifting swiftly, the light dissipated, retreating in all directions at once. So too, lifted the sound. When my sight returned, George, Burly, and Dr Seward were standing over me and I was kneeling on the floor. Did they see the Master? No, I am sure they did not. To hide my embarrassment, I stood quickly and busied myself with my fly box by the windowsill.

There he stood! He was still, like a gargoyle perched on the wall of Carfax. The whiff of feline scent wafted into my window. Ham was watching me. Then remembering my Master's words and the doctor's growing concern over the noise and nuisance of keeping flies, I dumped them out the window.

The Master has heard my call. Forgive me, Master, for my doubt. I will have faith.

(*Below is another section written in Romanian with Cyrillic lettering, liberally sprinkled with German and Hungarian. This section was not dated, but appears in*

My land, full of hills and valleys caused by the wrestling of the earth, displays the beauty of life's struggle. Nature pushing up mountains with flaming lava boiling below, valleys gouged out by rushing water churning sand against rock, this is my home. Trees cling precariously to the steep slopes tested repeatedly by wind and rain until they are twisted and gnarled, this is my dwelling place.

Many have coveted my land. They would take this from me, from my people. They would lay ownership of my land, my people. Would they also lay ownership of me? They owned my brother.

My brother, if you would call him my brother, handsome and debonair, loved by the boyars and peasants alike, disgraced me. Charm and grace, that would be enviable in any woman, bore him through life as on a cushion. I would face my enemies in battle, he debased himself in their beds, and yet, the people would have him prince in my stead.

I grew to loathe him and all that is soft and giving. He cannot rule who is ruled by his passions. A ruler must show strength and courage. A leader is an example to his people. My brother, like his mother before him, was soft.

When I came to power, I soon found myself surrounded by enemies, even from within my own court.

Where was loyalty but on the tongues of liars. Traitorous boyars, whose allegiance changed as frequently as the wind, schemed endlessly to depose me.

The Turks, as well, in their own way, dressed and educated with such refinement, yet, they were base in their ways and hypocritical. How can you dine with an enemy who would convert you or kill you? I was forced to do this every day for seven years.

I have no respect for the respectabilities of modern man. Were not the Saxon merchants the very picture of respectability? I needed their support to man the border from the ceaseless claims from without. Soon I found that even they could not be trusted, for they sold to both sides.

My country was full of brigands and highwaymen. It was not safe to travel even by daylight.

I devised a way to discourage crimes in the state. It may seem unique to you, but my method is not so dissimilar to the methods used by others in the past. The English Tudors displayed the heads of executed criminals on spikes in a public place, a bridge or city gate, for instance. The Romans of biblical times left people to die, starving, tied to a wooden cross, as you well know. I found a way to combine the two with beautiful results. Impalement is a slow death; it can take days to die.

Some would come who would take their kin from the spikes. I would not have this. I could not trust the ragtag remains of my honour guard, so I sent them away to rest. Alone, I sat and watched over my dying enemies, myself. There, amid the squalor of death, I made my ablutions. There, while the screams of those who would oppose me rocked the mountains, I took my rest. There, surrounded by the rotting corpses of a thousand, I took my meals. I saw to it that not one of the enemy was robbed from the grave.

5 September.— The quiet room has become my second home and I do wish that the name "quiet" was just that and not a sarcastic witticism. This was by far my longest stay there. Patient S. regaled me with songs and stories from his past as we passed the long hours in our separate adjoining cells. When he kept his train of thought, these could be pleasant and amusing. Though his singing voice has faded with his strength, he made up for it by putting his heart into the lyrics.

His poetry, however, is frightful or should I say, frightening. Such a waste of talent. His clean meter and clever inner rhymes are wasted on the most vulgar and vile subjects: sport mixed with buggery and murder mixed with scatology. One could only pray for thicker padding on the walls.

Angie says Patient S. gives her an eerie feeling. And, I must say, there radiates something (how can I say it?) disquieting in his manner. What is more, and Angie is spared this, is his memories are frequently of blood and death. My only hope was to distance him from these thoughts lest I be horrified and upset by them.

I asked him of his family and he had many warm thoughts. He told of a time he had danced with his grandmother. She loved to entertain, and always asked the children to sing or recite with her or create a tableau.

Sometimes, during longer visits, they would perform a play. She loved music, and as soon as he was tall enough, he was made to dance with her. He, then, dreaded these visits. Now he reminisced fondly about them. She, his grandmother, has been told that he is dead. He will never again be asked to recite for her. Would he suffer his grandmother to hear his shocking verse?

Patient S. is not the only other patient who writes poetry. Robbie's mind, which once spun with random thoughts, now produces what one might construe as poetry.

For instance, Robbie recites verses in his head such as:

> "bats cats shiny things, bats gnats, walloo cats
> spinning, spinning, spinning wildly, spinning
> orange big cats, orange big walloo cats..."

I am not sure what "walloo" cats are, but Robbie often includes them in his verse (if I may call it that).

Robbie likes things that repeat. Repetitive sounds, oscillating movements, spinning objects, all these appeal to a mind that spins and repeats in its thinking patterns. If one could describe Robbie's thoughts, it must be as a whirl of colours mixing round and round like the steam powered clothes washers that he enjoys so much to watch. They mirror his mind.

Poetry, once my dearest companion, is distant from me now. Perhaps I should invite poetry back for a spell.

Later. — The doctor is in tonight. He goes out more and more as of late. He has ordered those new electric lights. They have not yet arrived and he so wants to be here for their installation. But, he must away. His Lucy is ill yet again and he must attend to her. We must not judge him too harshly for his is a difficult road. Attending to his would-be wife is a drain on his otherwise vigorous constitution. It is no wonder that he must drown his sorrow with his new-fashioned elixir.

When surrendered to his "little vice," the doctor's mind seems to float about. The clear logical flow of words gives the stage to visual scenes that seem to fill the space around him with sights and sounds and textures and scents of a world that exists only in the space between his ears. His inner voice has stopped, and in this quiet, the world speaks to him. The details of his musing are so complete, that while I read his thoughts, it is as if *I* were having the fantasy.

Again he pictures himself at the ball. A servant proffers champagne on a tray, but he waves it away. He stands at the head of a receiving line where the ladies approach and curtsy before him one by one, their fine satin flounces gracing the floor. He bows and kisses each hand as it is presented and peers back at each hopeful pair of eyes. It is clear why they strive to flatter him so, for in his fancy, he is "Sir" John—knighted for his brilliant treatise on the new philosophy of psychology. (He should be working on his manuscript instead of daydreaming if he hopes to ever achieve this end.) The perfume of each mingles in the evening air as a waltz whirls around in Viennese style.

Lucy is there, full of giggles and teasing winks. She breaks protocol and drags him from the line. With a bashful smile, he shrugs at the other men as if to say, "What can I do? I am helpless." Somehow the two merge into the circle of dancers and he presses against her as they turn and turn. As they spin, the room is a blur; the flames of the candelabras are ribbons of light.

Chapter 3

FORTITUDE

RENFIELD'S JOURNAL

(*Continued*)

6 September.— Though I had been absent for over a week I noticed little had changed when I entered the common room to-day. Jamison looked up, and looking me over from head to toe, decided I looked entirely too well to have been in seclusion for so long. I assumed my usual seat at the table and assured him that diet and exercise are all that is needed to keep one fit, even under stressful circumstances.

When I sat down with Jamison, or Reed, as I now call him for there is no need for formality here, I noticed Robbie standing more closely to us than usual. Reed, beaming like a proud parent, said that Robbie and he had spent some time together in my absence. (Tom, seeing that these two have become quite a twosome, now calls them "the idiot and the oddity.") Robbie, his head thrust to one side as if avoiding some loathsome sight or smell, was indeed attentive to us, though this would hardly be noticeable to any but the keenest observer.

Robbie's mind spun a new poem.

"The day the night the wrong the right, Wah-loo
the black the white the dull the bright, Wah-loo
the fat the slight the loose the tight, Wah-loo..."

This, of course, continued and repeated itself without end. Reed has exposed him to the wonders of iambic pentameter. I dared not give away to Reed that I could hear other's thoughts, yet he was not surprised that I noticed the change in Robbie.

"He's really quite bright," Reed said.

I had to agree. Robbie, now a member of our reading circle, shows his pleasure for a recitation by rocking side to side and his disapproval by rocking forward and back. He does not like Trollope for the point of a scene takes too long to come around. The Brönte sisters, however, captured him completely, keeping him, which seems impossible, almost attentive.

Angie and Tom prefer the "readings" that George gives from Burly's illustrated papers, The *Penny Illustrated Press* and *The Police Gazette* being their favourites. Debates ensue over the guilt of suspects and the quality of the police procedure. Most important of all is the circulating of the pages for the close inspection of the artists' renderings of the crime scenes, the suspects, and the victims. Angie holds a fascination with crime scenes; her head is awash with gruesome pictures of snatchings, muggings, and slashings.

To-day, however, there will be no reading. George has been given extra duty for Dr Seward is expected to be out on call every night this week. While George is in charge, his usual duties are to be given over to Burly.

The lout, however, does not move from his chair in the corner unless... He rarely shows himself at all. And how could George expect him to read to us? Burly, though he spends his day staring at newsprint, cannot read. He pictures the letters in his mind not as symbols representing sounds, but as icons. Double-o's are eyes starting back at him. The t's are tiny crosses—a residue, no doubt, from early religious education. The letters move as well. They scamper to and fro like ants across the page. The blank spaces between the words and lines of text capture the focus of his attention. They form pictures as clear to him as the engravings on the page. And those engravings— move. Gruesome acts unfold in mechanically etched swirls of ink.

Despite Burly's lacking alacrity, George is bolstered by his superior position. And so, George has been strutting around all day: the cock of the walk. We all must take care not to ruffle his feathers.

George inspected our rooms twice this morning. Dr Seward would never have allowed this. Yet, George, fully aware of Dr Seward's confidence in him, knows that no complaint can sully his position.

George, pleased that there are no longer flies in my room, congratulated himself on a job well done. He made me remake my bed three times. Then he made me straighten the papers and drawings I was in the midst of working on into two neat piles. This I did without protest. What is the use of complaining, it only spurs more commands from such as George.

Angie and Robbie, of course, brook none of George's condescension. Angie, quick and clever as she is, pleads incompetence to any task that does not please her. Few do. And as for Robbie, what is there to say. An order, even with the best intentions, ignites his ire and such wretched wailing none of us can stand it; George knows better than to bother trying. Tom, however, is his helpless victim.

George rousted poor Tom from his sickbed and had him make the bed again and again.

"But George," Tom protested, "I did pull the sheets tight."

George tested them again, and not satisfied, ordered Tom to make his bed for the third time. When finally, he was satisfied, George found fault with Tom's shirt. "Button your top button," he ordered. Tom hurriedly tried to comply, but found his neck suddenly larger around than it was before. "Don't ye care 'ow ye look? Is that the way of a man what wants so much to visit 'ome, cares for 'isself?"

Tom, red-faced and barely able to breath, was finally able to secure the button. But he was also, unfortunately, able to speak. I could not make out what was said, but saying anything except "Yes, Sir" to George when he is "in charge," is perceived as an act of defiance. George, "in defence," threw Tom to the floor. Tom has long lost his ability to ignore this bullying.

Angie piped up her "Georgie Porgie" tune. She did not sing the words, only the silly, little rhythm. "Dah-te, dah-te, ta ta ta." Without prompting, we each, one by

205

one, joined in, punctuating the meter by clapping our hands on our doors.

Dah-te, dah-te, ta ta ta. Dah-te ta, dah ta ta ta.

George fled the ward without a word. We are all grateful that George did not fetch his stick.

Later.— The Master has many powers, and through him, and through the beasts he commands, I am shown the world outside these wretched walls.

Each night we fly about London. Tall buildings stand silhouetted by moonlight like dark stems in a lifeless garden. The "teeming numerosity" of Henry James has retreated indoors. The night's quiet calm shows the city in all its glory and hides its shame. All around us are the songs of a thousand tiny "fairies" dashing by in all directions faster than the eye can see. They call to us with tiny hums, whirs and chirps. The Lord pays no attention, but I am curiously drawn to them. I feel the air in my eyebrows as we descend, yet I am here in this prison. I reach up, touching my brow, and here there is no wind.

He took me to a stately mansion. Rather, He went to a mansion, and through Him, I peered into the bedroom of a young woman from the glass doors of her balcony. She was much like the Lucy of Dr Seward's reverie; only the Lord shares His thoughts so fully that I feel I am there. I *am* there! She is beautiful, so thin and delicate—the blue web of veins shows through her white skin.

She opens the double glass doors for us as if in a trance, then she reclines on her bed, her breast heaving as if each breath could be her last. Her burnished-gold hair is down, braided for the night. I have never seen this simple sight before. The long braid that will be twisted, curled, and piled on top of her head in the morning, now hangs to one side with simple grace. I never expected it to be so long and so big around. Her dainty fingers grasp the braid and toss it over her pillow revealing the firm, soft, delicate curve of her neck. It is perfection adorned with two red beauty marks. We are so close I can smell the perfume that she wears behind her perfectly shaped ears.

Oh, but I am rambling. Solitary has ruined me. I am rested but disoriented. Dr Seward has forgiven me enough for my little "excursion" that he has returned me to my room, yet I must sleep all day in a straight-waistcoat. I do not mind for I sleep so peacefully—the Lord sees to that—I only realise that I have been restrained when George comes at tea to release me. I have been the good little patient that is expected of me and soon I will answer to the Lord face to face. I, Renfield, the chosen of God, will be granted audience and receive my gift directly from the Almighty.

(*Here we find another Rumanian passage. S.D.*)

I like this custom of *décolletage* after sundown. English women in their evening dress appear so appetising. The ladies' gowns, cut low, reveal the neck and shoulders. There, blue veins flirt under subtle elastic skin to delight the eyes. It is as if they knew I were coming and dressed accordingly. For this generous gift I will forgive them for the bustles they wear to make their hips appear more substantial. They would have men believe they are full figured or "*zaftig*" as we say in my country. Yet, it is a sham, a false lure like the silk fly at the end of the fisherman's line. I will not be deceived again.

7 September.— The Master has written in my journal again during the night. If only I could read it. It must be very important.

8 September.— Jamison has embarked on a writing project of his own. He shall gather his poetry into a book—a book he hopes to publish. I had known his plan long before he revealed it, of course. His thoughts mused on the idea frequently. Still, it was not bits of fact that led me to this conclusion, but rather his manner of thought itself. He pictures leaves falling from a tree, one by one, though the leaves are green just outside in plain view. At other times his thoughts turn to water dripping one drop at a time. It took some doing, but I now realise that my friend thinks in metaphor. Sad and lonely motifs cascade within, but he never thinks the words sad, lonely or other words like them.

Quiet talks with Reed have become difficult for Tom insists on joining us. Reed and I were discussing the poetry of Clare when Tom broke in. "Dr Sewer," he said slapping his hand on the table with a loud thud, "is not in to-day." This is Tom's way of conscripting my aid in playing some prank on George. I do occasionally stand guard at the door, my ear to the wall, to tell if someone is coming. If I did not, Tom would only get into real trouble, and his japes are harmless.

"George is busy in the main building," coaxed Tom, "we must explore the tunnels!" His excitement made his wheezing more pronounced. He should be in bed, yet since it was not his intention to escape to-day—only gather information—I decided to join him.

Down the stairs, single file, we crept to the basement. Reed occupied himself in the photographic room, studying the pictures of patients from the past. Each portrait is poised and calm, yet their eyes betray their thoughts: uneasy, unsure, insane. Tom went exploring the tunnels, certain that there must be a means of escape somewhere. He disappeared down into the darkness, unaware that I did not follow. As Tom's cough grew faint in the distance, I found myself drawn to Patient S. His singing was so weak I could not but pity the man.

I peered in through the trap. Though it seems hardly possible, I found his sad, hollow eyes even more pitiable than the first time I had seen his face. He saw me looking at him and wondered what I was thinking. "Is he judging me?" he thought. "Does he believe I deserve this?" These thoughts gave no hint as to his reasoning, yet he firmly believed I was, indeed, judging him.

Why would I judge him?

I wanted to leave his door at once, but I could not. Fixed by his stare, I was drawn into his mind, and there, I was subjected to his fearful memories. It was subtle at first. I felt light-headed—foggy, if you will. Forgive me if I protest my innocence—it was he, though weakened by long illness, who was controlling my thoughts. Strange as it may seem, he had the power to mesmerise me. His thoughts had reached into the past, and with his, my thoughts were drawn as well.

It is night. Hiding in the shadows, thick blackness shrouds over us, protecting us from prying eyes. We pass through a doorway leading into a courtyard careful to avoid the lamplight. Soon we stop outside a door marked "13" and turn to peer into a broken window. The room is shabby, containing only one chair, a bed and small table beside it. By the light of the hearth a young woman sits in the chair looking back at us. Pretty, though dishevelled and a bit tipsy, her face reflects the flames—sometimes hidden in darkness and other times streaked with soft orange light. She is expecting him. He is someone special. Half-dressed, she crosses to the door and bids him enter. She latches the door behind him then caresses him pressing her mouth to his. He is unmoved. "I knew you'd come. You have a name, fella?" she asks, his stiffness not affecting her jovial nature.

He gives no answer, only holds out some sweets in his delicately gloved hand. These delight her. She snatches them and she eats them immediately, not stopping to thank him.

He is still. Can he be using his mesmerising eyes on her?

She opens her dressing gown and lies on the bed inviting him to join her.

The blast of George's whistle shocked me back to the present. Had we stayed too long and been found missing? Reed took the stairs three at a time, his long legs not unlike a spider's. He was already seated calmly at the table reading when I reached it, still reeling from the sound of the alarm. No one in the common room made the slightest indication of our return. Some moments later, Tom, winded and distraught with fear of being caught, rushed in, unable to calm himself. The whistle blew again signalling us to silence. It was from the adjoining corridor. We released our collective breaths and laughed.

Standing at the door, we watched Daisy perform her slow sun dance for the warders. Apparently, she had wilted again. But everything is all right now; George has thrown a bucket of water on her.

A group of workmen gathered downstairs had caused this stir in the usual atmosphere. Daisy does not like too much excitement being a sedentary soul. We were all ushered back to our rooms though it was not yet 7:00 o'clock...

The electricity has arrived! Such a commotion, workmen coming in and out, cable everywhere. It seems the workmen arrived while we were in the basement. George thinks "they should 'ave been done by now," and scowls with displeasure. I am pleased, however. I did so want to meet these men and learn of this amazing technology. Men like Faraday, contemplating immense questions over the substance of sight and sound, are what I expected. The men who came to bring us electricity, however, are not as he. My anticipation of conversing with men of "brilliance" was dashed at the first sight of these rough-cut, dull men in their rubber-coated aprons. This cannot be them I thought, surely someone has died and they are from the morgue.

They set up their ladders in the centre of the hallway. Rolled in on oversized spools, cable is clumsily strung along the ceiling with small porcelain hooks. The cable is covered with tightly woven, white string. And before each room, a clear globe, the size of a fist, is hung so that the light can shine through the trap when it is open.

I watch with much interest as they go about their task; they ignore the others and me completely.

Tom thought perhaps he might steal one of the globes so that he might have light whenever he pleased. Then he laughed to himself, for wanting it let him believe, only for a moment, that that was possible. He soon realised that there would be no light without a cable.

I reached out to the thoughts of one man as he climbed the ladder just outside my room. (He was actually very aware of us watching him, and yet he had not shown us any sign of this at all.) At times his thoughts were focused on the task at hand. At other times his mind wandered as his hands worked away as if independent and self-controlled. He worked quickly, not because he feared us "rummies," but because it was late and he wished to return home in time for dinner, and after, attend to his many projects. "Gardening—the hedge needs trimming, but it will be dark by the time I get home. Did the bitch have her pups? Promised the wife to put a coat of varnish on the new chest of drawers. Wonder what the boy is about today—tore his trousers yesterday. Can't wait to finish all my chores so I can continue carving my newest pipe—this is a fine one—no need to hurry when carving a pipe." The wife does not understand—why should he carve pipes if he does not smoke.

Stripping the cable ends to reveal the copper wire inside, he bends it into a hook, hand fits it with care into the fixture and screws it down tight. Then, carefully, he presses a globe up into the socket. After a short conversation between the other men in rubber aprons confirming that all is in place, they sound off. We hear the clap of metal as a switch is thrown.

A hum—a high sustained ping—sounds from each globe as the arch of orange, glowing wire emits stark, piercing white light. Sharp, angled shadows slant away from the globes, reaching out to each other, forming layers of greenish-grey shadows on the floor and walls. This is observed in silence. No one moves. No one speaks. We just stand staring at the wonder of it.

Chapter 4

JUSTICE

RENFIELD'S JOURNAL
(*Continued*)

10 September.— Angie tells many stories and I must admit I give no more worth to them than the tale of a child concealing a stolen sweet behind its back. Yet, through her thoughts, Angie has told me, unknowingly of course, the story of how she came to be shut up in this dreadful place. This story may be of relevance for it is similar to another tale that I have "heard" only this other story does not come from Angie. *Relata refero*.

"I weren't feelin' quite meself that night on account of this lit'l spat with the barman at the *Queen's 'ead*. 'e took what I 'ad an' gave me a poke to boot. With me money run out, I thought it bes' to find somewheres to flop."

In her agitated state, she pictures a small room; sometimes she shows the journey through a side door into a courtyard to that room. The light and noise of the street are shut out in the short alleyway.

Searching with difficulty in the dark, she makes out the faded mark on the door, 13. Rounding a corner, she peeks in through the window to see if Emma is about.

She notices the window pane is broken. The fire has died down, but is still alive and the candles are not yet snuffed. She reaches in through a broken pane to release the latch of the door calling softly, "It's me, lovey. Can I stay a bit? I'm short with me doss and ain't slept." This scene repeats in poor Angie's mind, relentless, unchanging.

Fumbling in the dark, half drunk and dazed from lack of sleep, she opens the door slowly, confident that there is no man there (Emma and her common-law husband have gone their separate ways) yet wary that she might wake her friend.

"I smiles, for Emma is in bed, asleep. I quietly closes the door behind meself and latches it slowly so as not to wake `er, and tiptoes into the room, `cept that I trips over the leg of the chair and falls thump on the floor." But luckily there is no stirring from the bed. "Must `ave `ad a sip or two, `erself, I thinks as I lays meself in front of the fire for a warm. Good ol' Emma, always willin' to put a body up when she's down."

Gazing at the fire a peculiar thought touches her. "There's a queer sort of smell in the room like." She notices the remains of a bonnet in the grate and finding this a proper enough explanation for the smell, dozes off to sleep.

She cannot have slept long when she half awoke, her head heavy with a hangover. "I wakes up an` couldn't get meself comfy, sos I thought I'd see if Emma was awake too." The smell was growing stronger. She rolled over and looked up at the bed. Emma must still be asleep, she thinks. The sun was coming up and the brightness in the room makes it difficult to go back to sleep, and to go back to sleep is all she wants. She spied what looked like a pork roast on the bedside table. "Curious to leave meat unwrapped like that, I thinks to meself. It must be goin' off—that must be the bl—ing smell." She dozed off yet again.

Then, waking with a start, it is full daylight. Emma must "certainly `ave `ad a drop in," for she did not make a sound, she was "dead drunk."

"Emma," I calls, "but me bones are givin' me some trouble."

There was no response.

"Emma, it's me, Angie." Slowly she pulls her drained, dehydrated body up on her knees. Her head aches above the left eye and her limbs are heavy and sluggish.

"Emma?" she calls louder. "Mary Kelly!" she tries, using one of Emma's other names.

There is still no response and with some irritation, she pulls herself to her feet and approaches the bed.

There the view of Emma "Mary" fills my mind. If Angie's thoughts did not identify this as her friend, I would not have known it had been a woman at all. Black smears stained the sheets and walls all around her. She had been dead for some time. Air hissed from Angie's mouth: a silent scream. Emma's internal organs lay at her feet and one breast by her head. The other lay limp on the bedside table. All the flesh was torn away from her body from the neck to the knees. Her face was slashed yet her eyes were intact. Her eyes were open and their gaze seemed fixed on Angie as if silently trying to tell her what had happened.

Angie ran for the door. The lock would not release. Her hands would not function. In a flash she lifted the window and slipped out, having been shocked awake and sober in an instant. Out she went, the window falling shut behind her.

She walked the streets pushing her way through the crowd, muttering and cursing, hoping upon hope that distance would abate the sight of her friend's mutilated corpse. It did not. (It has not even to this day.) She walked for days until she collapsed in the street.

Days or weeks later, she cannot remember which, her friends, fearing the worst, searched for her and found her in a convent that provides beds for vagrants. She would not speak, only try to scream, which she could not. Her friends brought her here. This, to me, proves that she must indeed have a benefactor, for how else is a common harlot provided for in the paid ward.

11 September.—My God! How much of this must I endure? This evening everything changed. He has crossed the line! It is bad enough that he bullies Tom and me, but to torment the helpless is unconscionable. George, the black-hearted villain, had cornered Robbie in the common room for throwing his food. And, with his stick, George struck Robbie, again and again. How could anyone do such a thing? I stood in the doorway, wondering what to do, when Reed leaped forward, and circling George with his long arms, pulled him away.

Had Reed not stopped him, George might have killed the lad.

"An` what do you think you're doin'?" George said turning on Reed, sizing him up. Reed is thin but very tall, leaving George to wonder his prospect of winning if it should come to fisticuffs.

"I had to put a stop to it," said Reed, still breathing heavily from the altercation. George, spent from his rage and his work on Robbie, decided to forgo any further action.

"Your turn 'ill come," said George maliciously eyeing us as he stepped from the room.

Trying to comfort Robbie, I lifted him and walked him to the table, the table Reed and I share, thinking this would give him a sense that we included him and wanted him to be our friend. To our distress, he just sat there lost in his own world. He had no thoughts about what had just happened and no thoughts of us.

In Robbie there is no love or human closeness of any kind. I lack the same only I long for it, where he cannot even know what it is. In him there is something lacking: that drive, that electricity, which delights in the sight, the smell, the touch of another. If he were not forced to be here, surely he would wander off, alone, perhaps into the woods. Soon he would hunger and thirst and soon after he would die. His will to live is not strong enough, not strong enough to hold onto life.

Letter to Rev Renfield from Mrs R. Johnston
(*Unopened*)

"15 September.

"Dear Rev. Renfield,

"Bishop Fairfax informs us that you have extended your sabbatical to quietly reflect and deepen your spiritual awareness. I do wish you would reconsider extending your stay, as the ladies of the Temperance Union await your immediate return. We need your help. We need your leadership and guidance. The bishop has closed the chapel of St Ann. He refuses to listen. Though the work we have done has raised almost enough money to pay for the repairs it needs, the chapel has been boarded up so we cannot mop up after the rain or high tides. Rev Jenner was, regrettably, of little help. He has resigned and taken up a ministry in Brighton.

"Oh, Rev. Renfield, what are we to do? There are rumours that the chapel is to be sold to a publican and converted into a tavern. The consequences of this conversion could be catastrophic! A saloon directly across the bridge from the Temperance Hall may prove too much a temptation. All of our hard work will be undone! Please help us Reverend. Your strong persuasive way is our only hope of saving St Ann.

"Yours with hope and strength,
"R. Johnston, Mrs."

13 September.—Down here near the earth, the smell of the grass, the texture of the soil, and the sound of the insects and birds, fills my senses, tickling and pinching. I take pleasure in the many smells, but the noises are too loud, too sharp; they irk me. My heart beats so quickly and yet I am calm. Strength surges through my body. With each intake of breath I advance. Comfortable in my skin, each step is light yet with coiled tension. This enables me to spring—instantly—in any direction. Brushing the air with my tail, I test the wind which tingles the scattered, thick sensitive hairs on my back.

Smells, strange and familiar, drift past from every direction. I breathe deep, mouth open, to wallow in each new and tantalising scent. From the sickly sweet odour of blossoms competing for bees, I lower my head to whiff the earthy floor below criss-crossed with the paths marked by a dozen citizens of the grounds. There! A scent more attracting than the rest. Calling, taunting—it beckons. It is a mouse that has unwittingly crossed my path. I smell it, but where is it? Its smell, a mixture of blood and ammonia-rich urine, winding a trail through the tall grass, attracts my attention. I could track it, but why bother.

I continue on my way. The scent is strong but ... there! It shivers with fright just before me, front paws together as if praying. It does not move. I strike it to make sure I am not mistaken. Move damn it! Or is it already dead? I sniff its whiskers. Trembling, they tickle my nose. A taste perhaps?—I could always spit it out...

Oh! It is gone. The chase is on over the wet grass. I leap front legs together, hind legs thrusting me forward. As each jump arches forward, balance remains in perfection until I gracefully touch down, the spikes of grass impaling my fur as I descend. Sensing his movement by watching for twitching at the top of the long blades of grass, I bound helter-skelter through the field, each pounce just short of my prey.

Dash it all! It hides under a log, just out of reach. Stretching out one long front leg, claws extended, I feel for the soft, warm give of live flesh. Close so close. Waiting for the faint outline of movement, my eyes adjust to the moist dark under the log.

Its eyes, shiny black dollops of treacle, stare back at me. I settle down on my haunches—this could be a long wait. As it shivers in the dark, I swish my tail back and forth, beating time.

It is on the move again. Another circle around the yard, but he will not make it to the log again. Got him! He is knocked senseless by my weight. With both paws I push him, struggling with all his strength, into my mouth. He is rather small, no doubt not yet fully grown. I hold him between my jaws, his face jutting out of my mouth. He waits precariously pegged between my four long fangs, trembling, silently hoping for a chance to escape.

What do I do now? I am not hungry.

14 September.—The Master's thoughts are more distant. He has not taken me tonight to Hillingham to see our Lady, yet I feel his presence.

There is another now in our little family of thoughts. She, a friend of Lucy's, will soon return to London. Our collective mind anticipates her arrival. Her presence is strong. I sense the concerns and the trivialities, the memories and the plans of her mind. She thinks of her husband who is ill, stricken with brain fever. Lucy has recommended our own Dr Seward.

Master, can this be? He calls her Mina. It is the Mina of the doctor's daydreams. She also thinks of Dr Seward and remembers their walk on the cliffs in Whitby. She is thinking wicked thoughts. Miss Harth's indiscretions back in Whitby I could sweep aside, but this I cannot. Dr Seward is somehow a connection for his thoughts and the Master's now concern the same woman: Mina.

17 September.— The doctor is in to-day for the first time in weeks. I hear his furtive thoughts as he scribbles away up above me. His thoughts are loud and I hear them ring in my head like church bells. Work-a-day, work-a-day. His much neglected ledger, barely tamed by the endless scratch of his pen, threatens rebellion at any moment. I feel the blood rush through his head in spurts and with each, the pain of his overworked, sleep-deprived mind. The blood, the blood calls to me.

He has given his blood to Lucy! How curious. Yes, he has shared his blood with her and is now confident that she will be well. How lucky he feels that his new transfusion apparatus has been put to good use.

Share your blood with me, doctor. The Master tells me that you will supply the strength I need: you, the cow from whom I will milk, and you, the bull from whom I will gain strength.

But how will I share his blood, oh Lord?

The Master has shown me the way.

Later.— We are on our way. Each night I look forward to this more, for each night, I am more a part of it. To-night, however, is special. To-night our lady, Lucy, will become a bride.

The stars seem brighter to-night. The wind, too, seems stronger or is the Master flying faster to-night? Brisk air rushes past us in a whoosh and insects dash all around making gentle whirling and buzzing sounds. How I delight in these little tunes. And now a new addition! A grey wolf follows us on our journey. He trots below, howling his baleful tones all the way. Occasionally lifting his eyes to make sure he keeps us in sight, he proceeds just before us as if he knows where we are going. Can he feel our Lord's thoughts as well? As we gently tap on the French doors with our wings, the wolf struggles through the hedges that surround our lady's little balcony.

Oh, what is this? Another woman has entered our lady's chamber. She is frail and has sat down on the bed next to Lucy. Lucy holds her warmly in her arms. She must be an angel for she is bathed in a resplendent light.

The wolf has managed to jump from a stone bench by the bushes to the roof of the bay window below and then leap onto the rail. Now, in his impatience, he has broken right through the glass panes of the door. Why does he howl at these women? Why has he followed us here?

Now the angel is pointing—pointing at us. No, it is the wolf she is pointing to. "Mother," Lucy cries, "what is it?" Frightened, the older woman clutches her heart and breathes only with much effort. Now she has fainted dead away.

Four servants rush in but suddenly stop. They seem dazed and stare straight ahead. All is quiet for a moment. Why do they not help the angel? Why are they just standing there? Lucy sends them away and insists that they go to the dining room for a sip of sherry.

The wolf is struggling in the hedges again. He was more frightened by this ordeal than any of us; he jumped off the balcony so suddenly that he landed awkwardly in the hedges. There he wrestles to break free of the densely packed branches. And, he got enough scrapes and bruises to last him for a while.

The Master gently lowers us down to the bay window of the dining room just below Lucy's room. We see the maids in the dining room conversing with uncomfortable and excited gestures. The maids are a queer lot. They have suddenly stopped their chatter and are staring straight ahead again. The Master calls to the one nearest the sideboard. I can hear each command and reply clearly in my head. The Master asks her (Penelope is her name) to add some of Mrs Westenra's medicine to the sherry. This she does and they all dutifully drink. I am fascinated by this, but the Master has flown us up to our lady's bedroom again, leaving me to wonder at the maids' odd behaviour.

The angel is deep in a trance, a trance deeper than that of Lucy or the maids. She lies on the bed unmoving. No doubt the power of the Master has overwhelmed her.

Lucy calls to us. "Come to me," she calls, "Come to me, my darling." Her dainty steps cross to the French doors and she opens them both, standing momentarily framed between them, her bare feet blind to the broken shards of glass, her sheer shift pressed against her by a gust of wind.

Chapter 5

FAITH

RENFIELD'S JOURNAL

(*Continued*)

Midnight. — The doctor was most gracious and generous. It was, however, difficult to retrieve the blood that spilled on the carpet—I did not want to waste a drop.

REPORT OF DR PATRICK HENNESSEY

18 September.— The patient Renfield, though seemingly of affable disposition and sedentary ways, displayed such violent behaviour last night that his permission to remain in the private ward must be reconsidered. The patient found his way upstairs into Dr Seward's study, and there, charged at him with a kitchen knife. The doctor, in self defence, struck the patient in the head with his fist. The patient took no notice of the blow, but became quiet is if his mind were occupied elsewhere.

The attack on Dr Seward's person, or any other doctor or asylum attendant, requires swift action, with punishment severe enough to discourage this behaviour in the patient and in other patients who might benefit from example. In order to maintain discipline in an open ward, the exercise of authority must be maintained with constant, even-handed vigilance. Dr Seward, believing that this attack was an aberration in Mr Renfield's behaviour, has not seen fit to punish or isolate him. In its stead, Mr Elwood has been ordered to place the patient under careful watch.

Dr Seward has ordered the patient to wear a straight-waistcoat during the daylight hours, but has ordered the patient released every day before the evening meal. During the interval between sundown and lockup, the patient is allowed free range of the ward and to dine with his ward-mates in the dining hall. It was at this time that the patient must have procured the kitchen knife. Opportunity makes a thief.

One must not underestimate the cunning of this patient. It is my belief that the escape attempt of Mr Tooley that occurred while Mr Simmons and Mr Elwood were restraining Mr Renfield may have been planned; Mr Renfield, brandishing his knife, was merely trying to create a diversion to allow Mr Tooley to sneak away unnoticed. This would explain why Renfield's attack was only half-hearted, merely cutting Dr Seward's wrist. The patient had ample time to strike out at Dr Seward again and again, yet he did not. Rather he stood cleaning his knife as if waiting for the warders to come for him.

I have not placed the patient in the padded room as of Dr Seward's wishes, yet, should any further violent act occur, I will be forced to handle this matter to the dictates of my conscience as guided by the medical doctrine that I hold dear.

(Dr Hennessey studied in Paris under Charcot who was the most influential neurologist of his day. It is not inconceivable that, being a contemporary student with Freud, he knew him and was influenced by Freud's budding theories. There is, however, no further evidence of their contact or any existing correspondence between the two. G.D.)

18 September.— George and Burly have been acting very strange to-day. They stayed their distance from me and their thoughts betrayed a fear of me. Me, hurt the doctor? How could one think of such a thing? My only thought is to help the man.

Dr Seward has left Mother Hen in charge while he is away. There is an uneasy atmosphere between the two. (Dr Hennessey thinks Dr Seward is too brash and changeable which he attributes to Dr Seward's youth and inexperience.) Each holds different theories on the causes and cures of insanity. And each practises much different methods of diagnosing patients, with different criteria, resulting in markedly different opinions. Dr Scward believes I suffer from religious mania, which I take great exception to. Dr Hennessey believes I suffer from cyclothymia. I do not know what cyclothymia is. Yet, it cannot be anything too serious for he believes Dr Seward has cyclothymia as well.

Dr Hennessey and Dr Seward are at odds over more than just my diagnosis. It seems Dr Hennessey studied in France where a close friend and fellow student, Sigmund, is inventing a whole new set of theories in psychology. Mental illness, he believes, originates deep in the mind. People have a lower consciousness, like the instinct of animals, called the "subconscious." In this lower place lie our unconscious desires. There seems, however, to be only one desire and that is for sex. And there, he believes, lies the whole of our makeup. Dr Seward believes in a whole pantheon of different diseases of the mind, each with its own distinct physical cause, and is only too happy to add to the list. Though Dr Seward believes important clues can be found in a patient's words, he is becoming increasingly interested in the chemistry of the brain.

Dr Hennessey still adheres to his theories though they disagree with Dr Seward's directives. (Sigmund has been publicly ridiculed for them.) And, of course, he has not revealed his interest in the subconscious to Dr Seward. His thoughts reveal much different beliefs then those he shares with the doctor. Secretly, his faith in the importance of childhood sex drives, drives his practice of medicine. He will, however, not jeopardise his position though he believes Dr Seward brings us "back to the dark ages" of medicine.

Frankly, I do not much care for this theory. It is not surprising that young Dr Hennessey and his friend Sigmund would come to such notions. Two lonely youths, far away from home, living like church mice in the student quarter of Paris, look deep into themselves to find the universal truth that drives us to toil for existence on this cruel earth—and what did they find? What did they find but their own budding manhood with its lustful thirst for carnal knowledge—spurred on by the local French "coquettes," no doubt. As for Sigmund, thank goodness his superiors put a stop to this misguided youth before he made a fool of himself.

19 September.—I do not know why exactly I was compelled to visit Reed to-day and yet I am glad, for I was able to cheer him a bit. Reed has descended into melancholy and sits dejectedly in the common room. Distracted, he fingers his packet of poems—completed save for a few final touches that will not avail themselves to him. Even reading has lost its ability to console him. In fact, the difficulties that prevent him from focusing and concentrating on the page have made him even more dispirited. Though I fear that I too may succumb to melancholy, it is my duty to comfort him.

"This too shall pass," I said trying to cheer him.
He nodded, knowing he has come through such as this before.

"There was a time I played at this," he said sitting across from me at our usual table. He did not look at me, but gazed at the trees just outside as they dropped their leaves one by one. "To be jaded and affected was what distinguished one from the lower classes. I studied my face in the mirror to perfect a look of indifference with just an air of feigned *ennui*. The women liked this and so I posed all the more. The more they clamoured, the more I served them cold disdain. Why don't they prefer some robust farmer and not a dandy like myself who spends their money?"

Unable to answer this question, I looked at my hands and wondered if they (his women friends) would have liked *my* poetry.

"You must have courage to live, man. God will help you."

"God, I don't believe in God. Does anyone anymore?" It is not surprising—this lack of faith—for Reed once ran with the Aesthetics.

"God is alive. He talks to me. He has given me a purpose." When I said this I remembered my recent lapse in faith and was ashamed. "God is near," I confided, having been reluctant to share my private thoughts on this matter. But soon I will have to. I pray God will reveal to me my purpose soon—meanwhile I will pray for guidance.

Midnight.—Oh merciful heaven! What should I tell the doctor? Can I tell him? Would he even listen? He would never believe in my abilities, my visions. How can I make him believe me?

Oh doctor, all your effort is for nothing. You do not know that I have seen you—you and Dr Van Helsing at Hillingham. You see, the Master takes me to see your Lucy. She is much the way you describe her in your mind, only not so demure. How can I tell him!

I can see through the eyes of the Master and I have seen Lucy to-night, her slight frame more frail than ever. I thought I saw the moon shine on her face, but there is no moon to-night. Oh doctor, all your procedures and fuss are for naught. You even gave her of your blood!—but for naught.

The Master has said his farewells, "You are one with me now, Lucy," he told her without words. "Now you will pass through to the other side. A new plateau awaits you here. Come, come unto me, and I will give you new life."

This Lucy accepted with silent, humble gentility and smiled showing her many teeth.

The Master instructs me...

REPORT OF DR PATRICK HENNESSEY
(*Supplement*)

20 September.—This evening, just after 6 o'clock, the patient Renfield became incensed by a group of workmen in the street delivering large crates to the property just outside the west asylum wall. He broke through the window of his room, escaping to the street, and there assaulted the workmen, claiming they were trying to kill him. Simmons informed me, that during the attack, the patient cursed like a sailor. I have forwarded a full report of the incident to Dr Seward who is on call this week.

I am surprised and alarmed that the patient, now known to be violent, was not secured in some way. This second act of violence prompts me to recommend immediate transfer of this patient to the violent ward where careful watch is more vigilant. Dr Seward, however, reluctant to restrain paying patients, insists the patient calms himself every evening, becoming docile and tractable. Caution dictates otherwise for predictability is rarely, dare I say never, found in an insane person. I must stress that the assured unpredictability of insane patients is what necessitates incarceration of said persons in the first place.

Mr Renfield's effect on the other patients must be taken into account as his influence permeates every corner of Ward D. Warder Simmons reports that Patient Renfield instigates levity and he has, more than once, caught patients laughing together in the dayroom. Mr Renfield has convinced one imbecile patient that he can read and encourages him to do so, out loud, in the dayroom, this charade making a mockery of the feebleminded. Renfield has convinced a melancholy patient to give up banking, his livelihood, and take up the frivolous and financially unsound occupation of poet, for no better reason than it seems to cheer him a bit. Renfield has "forgiven" a patient who has dipsomania, instilling in him a rebellious streak manifesting itself in such acts as, defying warder's orders and insisting on his right to correspondence with, and receiving visits from, his family. This patient had escaped earlier and was missing for hours having been restored by the warders from blocks away. Lastly, I must point out, he humours one poor young female patient who thinks she is a flower, encouraging her to "bloom and grow!"

This, highly unsettling influence, must be checked lest it have devastating effects on the peace and serenity so hard won in a lunatic asylum. I strongly recommend the transfer of this disruptive and violent patient to the violent ward where his disturbing tendencies can do no more harm.

The damage to Renfield's window, caused by him during his escape, has been repaired under my supervision. Iron bars, restricting access to the window, have been installed, the cost recovered for the Repair and Replace discretionary fund. I have deemed this necessary as Dr Seward refuses to grant permission to place this patient in the protecting confines of solitary.

A TIME TO REAP

(This sermon, dated 21 September, and believed to be written while an inmate in Dr Seward's private asylum, is the only surviving non-secular writing of R.M. Renfield. It is unfortunate that no other sermon of his survives for comparison. S.D.)

"...and let them have dominion over the fish of the sea, and over the fowl of the air, and over the cattle, and over all the earth, and over every creeping thing that creepeth upon the earth." Gen 1:26

To live as a man—that is good. God has given much to man: the fish of the sea, the fowl of the air, and all that creepeth upon the earth. Imagine the world of Genesis. The beauty. The abundance. Rabbits frolic here and there. Deer wander on pristine meadows. Cattle drink from a stream unattended. All this is ours, so the Bible tells us. Life was good in the time of Genesis. Life was good for man. Yet, what of the hare and the deer? What of the cattle?

In order for man to live, plants and animals must die. To sustain life, man uses the plants and animals around him for food and clothing. He may shape their bones to make tools and melt down their fat to make soap. He fashions their fur into clothing and wears their feathers as decoration. He trains dogs to help him hunt and oxen to pull his load. All this is given man.

Life's struggle is to man as it is to animals. Man kills in order to live just as the lioness. For the lioness, who must kill to live, shares her catch with her pride. There is an hierarchy of species—a chain, a pattern. Each fish is swallowed by a bigger fish, which is swallowed by yet a bigger fish, and so on. The Lion, who might eat the jackal, who might eat the hawk, who might eat the frog, who might eat the fly, is part of the cycle of life, and, when it dies, its decaying body food for flies.

In Aesop's fables, man is portrayed by different animals. For instance: the wolf and the crane, the ant and the grasshopper, or the hare and the tortoise. Through the likes of the hare and the tortoise, we learn a lesson. We see ourselves as the hare or maybe the tortoise, and thus, their lesson becomes our lesson. Yet, we are more like our animal friends than we know.

As man spreads into the wilderness he, one by one, eliminates other animals. The animals are killed, lest they become a menace or a nuisance, narrowing the world to fewer and fewer kinds of animals. When will it stop?— when there is only man? The once varied hierarchy of life is reduced to only a few strata. Or is it? Man, as in Aesop's fables, impersonates the animals of every level.

Man is the ant and the grasshopper. Man is the hare and the tortoise. Man is the wolf and the lamb.

Man then adopts the ways of the different species he has eliminated. One man is a wolf, one man is a sheep—all the roles and castes of nature are played by man. One man may keep another as a pet, another serves as his prey. So men who see themselves as lions see other men as sheep, fit only to be led to grazing, led to water, led to slaughter. The lion has no remorse; of course, to become a meal is the sheep's lot. You see, in this new order, man preys upon man.

As man spreads across the face of the earth he finds more than the fish and the fowl he was promised. He finds other men. Now it is not the beasts that threaten him, but man, himself. Man's dominion is now in question. Which man has dominion over which beasts? Now man seeks dominion over man. The struggle for existence is with one's own kind—and, to the victor, dominion over man.

All men are not of the same herd. What is good for "us" is more important than what is good for "them"—we must survive. All that is who we are must be protected or we, as we are, will perish. Thus, we create among ourselves the soldier, the defender, the protector against the enemy. A soldier fights for freedom—freedom of his country, his people, his family. Yet, is a soldier then not a "killer of man."

How do we justify soldiers, whose only reason to live, is to be killers of men? It is a long journey to the answer, a journey we know well. "They would kill us!" we say. "They would take the grain from our fields and leave us to starve. They would use all the water and let us thirst. They would take our lands and leave us homeless."

Those who have dominion, see others as a lesser creation. They believe they may do as they like with those that "creepeth." They may inflict any injury, justify any cruelty, and boldly proclaim the power over life and death of the conquered.

That is evil to separate one's fellow man into strata of predator and prey. The strong prey on the weak not to devour them—no! that is the kindness of nature. The human predator sucks the weaker man dry a drop at a time and keeps him alive as a larder with total disregard for his misery. Yet, in one way the human and animal are alike—they show no remorse. They are as the beasts; they have no soul.

For the soulless, the only power is to kill. The only way is to kill. Their only existence is to kill.

Those who could do such vicious acts are as one dead in the eyes of God. The body lives and breathes on, but the soul has fled. "Do unto others ..." Would you suffer your eyes maimed? Your ankles lamed? Your throat cut? The thought of these acts makes the strongest of us wince. Only one dead—divorced from the collective soul of ourselves—entertains the thought, let alone carries out the deed of harming his fellow man or killing his fellow creature without using his flesh for food.

You may ask, "How does the soul die?" That I cannot tell you, only let me warn you of the consequences of a life without a soul. It is a parched existence, devoid of love, anticipation, and hope. Love, that which bonds us to another with affection, is now only a dream, so seeking pleasure takes its place. Pleasure, however, cannot find a foothold, yet the seeking of it becomes more and more imperative. The drive for that which cannot be, fills every vein, until that drive, mistaken for will, attempts to take what cannot be taken. Can you steal love? Can you steal pleasure? No! You can take love, pleasure, away, but you cannot keep them for yourself; once taken they are gone. Thus, like rot, growing yet dying, death begets death.

The simple gift of anticipation, unshepherded, silently flocks away leaving no trace. Now, events happen in succession—no waiting, no wanting, no dreading. No emotion, uplifting or downheartening, pleasing or repulsing, liking or loathing, connects with the act of doing. Life becomes a mere sequence of events until it is no life at all—only existing. Existing, not being, for in being there is hope,—hope of love, hope of comfort, hope of peace, hope of eternal life!

RENFIELD'S JOURNAL

23 September. — I do not remember writing this sermon yet it is in my handwriting. This most unexpected pleasure has softened the blow of my dreadful experiences of the last three days. It seems George believes I have breached some rule of the asylum and needed to be punished. The ordeal has not faded from my memory.

As if in a dream I tried to focus on my surroundings. I had a feeling of tremendous loss. Time ran away and I saw everything as in a tunnel, and I was being pulled farther and farther into the tunnel. I awoke in the bright light of day outside the asylum on the street. George and Burly were pulling me back into the asylum and as my consciousness faded in and out, I heard them curse me.

I found myself facing the asylum. To my left was Carfax. Workmen were loading large boxes onto a dray. I felt the Master's presence in one of them. The boxes! To my right, men in rubber aprons were loading what looked like sacks of potatoes into the back of a donkey cart. The outline of limbs bound under the linen was unmistakable. They were bodies. Mother Hen stood by checking his watch. When their cursed deed was done, I heard the clink of metal as he closed his watch. I heard another clink as he took possession, inspected and closed a small purse. It became my time to curse.

That evening when I awoke, I found myself in the quiet room. The Master's presence did not come for me. I was totally alone except for the whirl of memories from Patient S.

Patient S was only too glad to inform me — to explain the dealings of Mother Hen. Dear Dr Hen had become a disciple of the late Dr Gull. Dr Gull headed the dissection (dare I say vivisection) classes at Guy's Hospital. And Guy's, it seems, pays handsomely for fresh corpses. Pauper corpses. Now Dr Hen presides over Dr Gull's classes every Thursday. His study, they say, is lined, row upon row, with bell jars each containing a single human brain preserved in alcohol.

I once believed it was the paying patients, like myself, who keep this small asylum in the black. I know now it is the charity wards that provide the finances for this solemn institution—not the meagre stipends from the parochial authorities—but the liberal sums paid for the deceased bodies of the poor. They are not afforded a proper Christian burial. It seems that the sanctified churchyard or even these new-fashioned burial grounds prove too dear for even the working poor. And if one can't pay for a burial…

Later.— George reluctantly returned me to my room last night, eyeing me with suspicion all the while. His anger toward me has grown. I, however, am surprisingly light of spirit. How wondrous the world is! What a surprise and delight it is to discover this sermon on my table. I must have written it during the night. It just appeared this morning as if the shoemaker's little elves had been hard at work while I slept. It surprised me in its content as well as its format. When settling down for bed last night a thought about Ham had stirred. Perhaps his catching mice and birds had inspired my dreams and, during deep sleep, like sleepwalking, I rose and wrote this. This is entirely possible, only, this is a first draft and yet it is a complete sermon without a sign of editing. Best thing I ever wrote, it has real fire in it.

The passage on cattle must have been inspired by memories of my days in Zambezia. There, youths would slit an artery of a live calf and drink the blood like a fountain, then smear dung on the wound aiding it to heal. Cattle, as quoted in the Bible verse, are, and have been, an important part of Shona and Matabele life from their earliest history. Could there be a link? The Hebrew Bible was set down at a time and place where cattle raising was an important part of the culture. This way of life was sustained for thousands of years and was shared by the Arabs who also raised cattle. Arab trade routes reach even farther into the interior of South Central Africa than Livingstone's mission. Could the Ndebele have been influenced by the Bible? Had the seeds of its influence already been planted?

25 September. — My first day allowed back in the common room was strange indeed. As I entered I found the others gathered around George who was reading to them. They were arguing some point and hardly made notice of my return. I sat down to listen.

George, reading from *The Star*, enthralled us with a story of young children being snatched in the Hampstead Heath area. Each would mysteriously turn up the next day near the graveyard at Kingstead. In some cases the child was found listless and pallid. But what is most curious is that they all had what looked like the bite marks of animals on their necks.

This sounds much like the condition that afflicted Lucy. This struck me for Dr Seward believes, or at least in his mind treats Lucy is if she was already dead. He no longer goes to Hillingham, and, for that matter, neither does the Master. We have not visited her in a week, yet the Master has told me to hold Lucy as an example, that I must be like her.

I am listening closely to George's reading. I will record as much of the information as I can and later find some way to deliver it to the doctor.

"One child, who was old enough to relate some information on 'is kidnapper described the willain as a 'bloofer lady.'"

"Blue-fur Lady?" asked Angie, with incredulity.

"Yes, that's what I says, 'bloo-fer lai-dy,'" pronounced George. He then spelled aloud, "B L O O F E R L A D Y."

"Perhaps the child had a lisp and he really said 'bloomer lady' because she was not altogether dressed," suggested Tom winking at me.

"Yes, a child would respond to that—underclothing, I mean," Angie said, trying to be genteel in mixed company.

"And it's a good thing it was, she was wearing her bloomers, or the children would be calling her 'St Knickerless!'" joked Tom.

We all laughed, that is all except George, who did not appreciate the joke. George never laughed with us for he feels that if he did, it would foster an unwelcome camaraderie between warder and patient. The warder's dignity must be upheld. Robbie laughed just to fit in which I found rather surprising. He is not usually that socially conscious.

"No, no, no, Bloofer Lady is 'beautiful lady.' A child so young cannot yet articulate and tends to slur his words," said Reed, but they all ignored him. They were convinced "Bloomer Lady" had to be correct.

26 September. — Tom is gone. Tom, coming out of the common room, noticed the gate was unlocked. (He has an uncanny sense for these things.) Checking to see that

George was otherwise occupied, he tested the gate, holding the latch so that it would make no sound. I, thinking he would hold this knowledge for later use, was surprised when he closed the gate silently behind him and set out down the stairs immediately without a single thought on a plan for his escape. I reached out for his thoughts. They dwelt solely on his wife and he was certain he knew where she was. Oddly, he pictured in his mind a huge pile of coal. Soon his thoughts faded, for Tom, in his haste and determination, quickly put distance between us.

I did not expect this though I knew he was up to something the moment he entered the common room, earlier today. He was changed somehow, his posture, his expression, his manner. Pushing the sweaty hairs that shielded his eyes back revealing his forehead, he seated himself in Reed's chair. His face so changed... so sane, so calm.

"You're like me," he said, but did not explain himself.

This was not the first time I glimpsed the real Tom, but it was the first time he revealed himself so completely.

George came in and Tom immediately donned his jovial face. "Top o' the mornin' to ye," he called.

"Why? Why do you carry on with this charade?" I asked. (But I knew why.) I watched his expression knowing he wanted to tell his story. He wanted me to know the story of his life and yet he didn't.

"You wouldn't understand," repeated his thoughts.

Yet, I did understand. I had long known this story for his thoughts told it in pieces each time he looked at me. I understand not fitting in in a new place, among new people. I understand not being viewed as an equal.

Tom's family trades in textiles the world over. When he came of age, he crossed the water to represent his father's holdings. Marrying a young, fresh, Welsh heiress secured him a place in society—the society of like individuals. But his happiness failed to last. He wanted to be accepted in London society.

"The subtle but relentless machinations of… 'them.'" What started out so promising seemed to unravel in his fingers. He could not hold on. Those who appeared so enthralled with the Irishman and his charming stories became bored. They whispered about him and his provincial ways while eyeing him surreptitiously just beyond his hearing. He was useful. They wanted his trade, his connections, but they did not want… "him."

"Tell us another one, O'Tooly," they cried. And so he did. He smiled and played the part. "Dance us a jig," they begged. And so he did. "Another toast to the Queen!" they demanded—and so he did. He'd win by any means. He needed to stay in the game. He could not return unsuccessful.

What he did not tell, what he dared not confide lingered in his mind. In his youth, back in Tipperary, he murdered a stranger. "…an innocent glance at a convent girl. Well, not so innocent." Her brothers fell on him as he made his way home. "Your family fought for the wrong side," one taunted from behind. He reeled on the man, landing blow after blow until his attacker fell silent and then fell to the ground.

Days later he was brought before the Rural Magistrate. (The R M prompting his former ranting toward me.) Being rich and connected kept him from confinement, yet he was not free. Being rich kept him from belonging in his country of birth. He was not accepted in his home, so he came to London. He was too British for the Irish, and now he found, too Irish for the British.

He persevered. Yet, the past found its way forward. When he heard the young man had died, the warp and the woof of his mind unravelled. He was sure they were coming for him. He thought here in the asylum he'd be safe.

When his wife became ill he dropped his foolish façade and pleaded to be released. But it was too late. The warders and doctors were convinced it was the inebriate that was real, the educated dandy, the act. His wife died shortly before I came here. Thus, I witnessed his predicament at its most dire.

Now he has run off. He has no money, no change of clothes, not even a crust of bread to sustain him. What troubles me most is that he is ill. He has not felt right for weeks and lately there is a wheezing in his chest. Now he is out of doors, ill, with no coat and with no one to care for him. I do hope he does not fall to the influenza.

Chapter 6

HOPE

RENFIELD'S JOURNAL

(*Continued*)

28 September.— We trot north, determined, steadfast, knowing clearly our purpose. The Master is sending us (the wolf and I) on a mission: "protect Lucy" and, yet we do not know exactly where she is or what to do when we reach her. We navigate by a sixth sense, a silent signal that grows stronger as we draw nearer.

I enjoy the night air. If people only knew how cool and inviting the autumn evenings can be, they would not hide themselves indoors. Though we travel on several miles, we see nary a soul. A cat perched high on a porch rail eyes us suspiciously, watching for any movement that might be threatening. We push forward resisting temptation.

Many streets are lighted with gas lamps, but we avoid those. Many streets are dark, but we have no trouble. Low to the ground, we see the pavement clearly before us, our eyes adjusted to the dark. Unhesitating, and with clear purpose, we head north, our destination only a short distance away.

How now, this is familiar! It is Kingstead Cemetery. Monk is buried here—perhaps I could...

We turn west, though I pull east with all my will, and I realise that I am here for the ride; I have no control over this beast. It is the Master who has sent us. Avoiding the east side altogether, we trot past the chapel and under the west gate. The west side is much different than the east side, which I saw years ago. Crescent-shaped rows of grey-stone mausoleums line well-groomed paths and ornate gates guard the doors of wealthy family crypts.

We press on. Grateful to be relieved of finding our destination myself, I watch, silently listening and waiting for the Master to show us, to dictate to us, his bidding.

We stop. Silence. As we wait our ears adjust and the sounds around us become louder and clearer. Waiting, I listen to the sounds of the night: chirping crickets, rustling leaves, and unknown creatures scampering underneath beds of ivy. The wolf is patient, but anticipation has defeated me and now I am chomping at the bit.

What is happening? We prick up our ears.

We are not alone. A woman in white steps slowly toward the crypt directly across from us. The dainty tails of her dress dance in the breeze as her bare feet tread toward us. She holds the hand of a little boy, who smiling, totters with quick little steps striving to keep up with her. Looking down on him, she smiles gently coaxing him to keep up. Oops, he falls. Startled, he is about to cry. The woman lifts him into her arms before he can realise what has happened. His frown is snatched quickly away and kissed and cooed into a giggle of delight. But wait. Can it be? It is! It is our lady. It is our lady, Lucy.

Odd, somehow she seems changed to me, yet the wolf knew her clearly even before she came into sight. Her scent was everywhere, and for a wolf, that is all that is needed. The wolf pants mouth ajar and tongue hanging to one side. He is drinking in her scent.

Calmly, quietly, we wait for orders.

We lift our ears. A stranger. A man finds his way in the dark toward us. We carefully slip around a tomb for cover, catching sight of him at the door of a family mausoleum. He has an awl and is wiggling the tumblers of the lock one by one. With each successful tumble, he looks east, then west, as if to say, "Did anyone hear that besides me?"

We step closer. I try to will the wolf to stop, but his ear is not tuned to me, he listens to the Master, only.

The door creaks long and low as the man pulls it, its weight resisting as if stubbornly trying to remain closed. When the opening is just wide enough, the figure slips in with one final glance around the graveyard. He did not see us.

No, no, no, the wolf is following him. No! We will be found out. The wolf will not heed me. Lucy has disappeared down the path and I want to follow her. "The Master wishes us to protect Lucy," I scold, but the wolf is distracted. The man in the tomb, or should I say his scent, has captured the wolf's attention.

Leaning our head over to the side, and inching our long nose around the half-opened door toward the scent of man, we peek inside. Light suddenly flashes in our eyes as the man has lit a torch. Good God! Can it be? To my astonishment, I see Tom Tooley, his face, hands and clothes smeared black with soot. He is sliding the lid off the most recently placed casket. Thud! It slips to the side, perched on end. He pauses only a moment from the sound. Then, confident (though mistaken) that he is alone, he lifts himself onto the corpse lying face down on top of it.

"Sarah," he calls gently, "Sarah, I'm here."

Can this be? Can this be his wife?

"Sarah, I have come back to you. I promise you that I will be a better husband to you. Take me back just this one more time. I've changed," he says as he unhitches his trousers and tosses them off to the side.

The wolf is as puzzled by this as I, and just as mesmerised.

"Ooo-oo-oo-oo," he whines, sniffing and snorting at this enigma.

Tom hears him and looks up with a start. He is afraid. I can smell it. The whole chemical makeup of his blood changes as quickly as the expression on his face. His body betrays him by starting to sweat, thus pumping the telltale signs of fear into the air for all to detect. It is a charged smell—full of energy. To drink the blood of prey in an agitated state is to receive this bonus. I now know why the cat waits to eat the mouse: it is to gain the full effect of the liver!

Rising from the coffin Tom tries to collect himself.

"Ah-oooooo!" the wolf howls, and, echoing as it does in the tomb, the sound hurts my ears—and, even more so, the wolf's.

But wait, someone is coming. Our flexible spine bends and straightens and in an instant we have turned around and slipped outside. Standing perfectly still in a hollow between the tomb and a yew tree, we study the direction of the sounds and sniff the air for a scent, watching for movement. We know his voice. We recognise the odour of his blood! And now his silhouette appears against the foggy dark. His slim, smartly cut figure, shown by moonlight from behind, steps onto the path. It is Dr Seward! A group of men carrying torches follows him down the path searching for something. They must have followed Tom. The wolf is startled. We dash into the nearest hedge...

The bond is broken. The wolf has gone on without me.

29 September.— To-day, during the quiet of the afternoon, the sound of tapping caught my attention. Mina, the one Lucy wanted the doctor to marry, arrived a few hours ago and brought with her a typing machine. She is writing a ghost story and has been hard at it for hours. And, as if to immortalise her friend Lucy, she has cast her as the heroine. The character Lucy, however, dies in the story. What Dr Hennessey would make of that!

In the common room, there was an uneasy atmosphere. Tom has not returned. And now, Reed is missing. I looked at Robbie and Daisy, they are of no use, Daisy's thoughts are only of light and water and Robbie's thoughts, of course, were no help. Mary communicated that she did not know where Reed was. And as our thoughts touched, she rose, and with silent, careful steps, approached the table and sat in Reed's chair.

Mary's thoughts were sad, the eternal sadness of loss, of grieving. We sat in silence. Then reading the same thought at the same moment from each other, we reached our hands across the table, and, with our communion, we shared our thoughts as if we were one.

"Where is the child now?" I asked, consoling her.

Her thoughts came forward and she "showed" me them as she relived them. She pictures a revolving door. "Dead," she says in her mind, but she does not believe it. Secretly she hopes that the child is alive and being cared for. We know better. The revolving metal door I have seen before, but where? She had fixed that door in her mind. It did not meet the ground but opened in the wall at waist height. The minute scraping and squeaking of the door as it slowly turns, she remembers as well. She must go around the workhouse to the alley, and there, except for this door, is the long, cold, brick wall that encloses the helpless of society. She is not one of them she reminds herself; she has her proper place in society.

The wall is well known. Here the unwanted infants of London pass through to the jurisdiction of the parochial authorities. Oh, how she hopes that this is as good as it sounds. Yet, who is actually there on the other side of that door? In truth, they pass through to the unknown. She denies the perilous position in which she has placed her child. There is little chance of survival, and no chance of a proper upbringing.

Mary has no recollection of conceiving the child. That has been blotted out. Her only memory is that of holding the child to her breast, a still and silent moment stuck in time. She was sixteen and unwed. Alone and frightened, she ran away to have her child in secret, fully expecting to keep it. After only a few months, however, her money ran out and she was seized upon by an idea: she would leave the child at the workhouse and go home.

She never mentioned to her family what had happened—she never spoke again. Her family brought in a physician. Obviously, something was troubling her; she had run away and returned unable to speak. What could be wrong with her they wondered? The physician had a suspicion, when, during the examination, her breast expressed milk. He said nothing for propriety's sake. Soon after, she was brought here.

I held both her hands in mine and stroked them with my thumbs. I spoke to her softly of hope and upon my suggesting she look forward to new life and let the past be the past, she allowed a single tear to roll down her young cheek. After this, Mary's spirit lifted a bit and the grieving lessened. We sat together in silence until it was time for her to be brought back to her room.

After George took Mary out, I sat alone unable to read or concentrate. Reed's absence haunted me. I sat at the empty table until I could endure it no longer. Though risky, I decided to look about for him myself. I slipped out as soon as George went for his nap. Reed must be in the tunnels I thought, perhaps hurt, perhaps wedged into some opening just a bit too small. I pictured him half dead in the half light of the dank tunnels. Only on the stairs leading down from the ward was his scent recent. It disappeared in the laundry room. Following a scent of him from days passed, I knew he was not there, yet, I entered the tunnels, refusing to give up hope.

Just then, the slam of metal startled me as a coal chute thrust itself into the small, casement window high in the wall of the coal room. Coal poured in skidding across the already mountainous pile and out the archway, a few bits rolling out and resting at my feet. My thoughts flew to visions of little children, missing for days, only to be found asphyxiated under a pile such as this.

Collecting myself, I renewed my search. I found no scent of him or any trace of him. And, as it was imperative I return before George emerges from his hiding place, I hastened my step only to be stopped by Patient S. He was hissing at me. The nerve of the man, the gall! I had half a mind to rebuke him through the door when he called out, "I know who it is who speaks to you."

Astonished, I had to stop.

"I know who sends out his thoughts at night and who controls the beasts. We share his need for blood, you and I. When he thirsts, we thirst. When he feeds, we feed."

Could this be true? Could this idle fop be connected with the Master?

"The Master once held me as his favourite. The Master contacted me through my thoughts. Sometimes he spoke to me in a murmur under the noise of the throng. Sometimes his voice was in the wind that blew through the eves in the late evening, when I could not sleep. Sometimes he called me from the cracks and pops of the fire."

I turned and cursed him. This unbalanced mischief-maker has heard something he oughtn't and was trying to goad me for no other reason than his own lack of meaningful activity. But then I was brought up short. Struck by his next comment, I turned and approaching his door without hesitation, opened the trap and stared hard into his hollow eyes.

"He wants Mina now," is all that he had said. And since there is no way he should know of her, I had to speak with him if only to satisfy the burning curiosity that thrust itself into even the remotest capillary of my body.

"What do you know of Mina?" I asked, wanting him to confess all his knowledge of her.

"The Master is through with me, he talks to you now. Why should it be you? It is I who did his dirty work. I collected their blood for him.

"He had instructed me to go among the masses and perform an experiment, a test to find the best way to get blood without being detected. The blood was easy to find, but how does one get it out without spilling it? A good question, isn't it, for such as you? You're the clever one, aren't you? New methods were devised—dozens and dozens. Slashing the throat, that always worked well; the blood comes out in neat spurts. Sometimes I cut off their arms and legs and head, spilling the blood into jars, and then I floated their torsos down the river. That worked well enough, but soon the blood became putrid. I needed to try new methods. One a week and no one cared or noticed until, of course, those times I took their organs—only five were attributed to me. I had found that the organs contained blood and could be carried away for later extraction. The young and the old, no one noticed, but the women, they fought for their women, even the lowliest whores of the street.

"That's how they caught me, you know; I stayed too long collecting the blood. The Master was angry. Yet, he made the law put me here. They'd have strung me up. There went the gift he promised me.

"Then came you and Lucy, the Master did not need me anymore. The Master abandoned me. I hadn't been discreet enough.

"The Master is patient though, isn't he, Renfield. A few years pass and all is forgotten. The Master has come himself to feed.

"They say I'm dead you know. Poor me, died of the influenza, what a shame, what a pity. But I'm alive. I'm alive, I tell you! Alive!"

Suddenly realising the passage of time, I ran upstairs to the common room sitting down at the empty table as casually as possible. George gave me a long look, but he had more urgent matters to attend to (Reed is missing) and that was the end of it.

How did Patient S. know these things? Surely he is mad. Can he read my thoughts? Am I to become as he? The Master's influence had reached out to Patient S. and made him... it is unspeakable! Patient S. stalked the streets of London seeking... No, it is too horrible. No gift is worth this price!

Then the Master called to me. He heard my conversation with Patient S. He listens to my thoughts!

"His blood was no longer pure, Renfield. Though he procured blood from others, it soon became foul and black. Only his blood sustained me. He gave it to me willingly and freely. Then he betrayed me. His longing for flesh poisoned his blood. Now that I have returned, I will need a new source of fresh blood. I desire blood that is pure and I will have it."

I became faint. I felt a tearing the fabric of the air just before 2:00. "Lucy" I hear someone call as if far off. I see in my mind... This must be a fantasy. Dr Seward, at Lucy's denial of his proposal... must be thinking terrible thoughts. His anger must be appeased in this way. My mind swims with thoughts and pictures.

The Master is grieving. Lucy is dead! Berserker, the wolf, left his post to follow Tom, leaving Lucy unprotected. Dr Seward, aided by his cohorts, murdered Lucy. Can this be true? Is that why they were there in the cemetery? It is. The doctor believes Lucy was a … she…

The Master is angry and he will have his revenge. "Lucy," calls the Master. "Lucy," calls Dr Seward.

And then, seeing through his eyes, and feeling his desire and his thirst, I see Mina in Dr Seward's study.

Mina is next? Will she become as Patient S? This sweet child, this woman of pure, unspoiled blood, she will be the Master's new recruit. *Facilis descensus Averni*!

Later.— When it dawned on me that Reed had found the steam passage to the roof, it was too late. As I climbed inside the ever narrowing ducts toward the roof, his scent became more telling; fear, and its sharp odour, mingled increasingly with that of his blood. It was too late. Nonetheless, a thorough search had to be made, if only to reassure myself that I had done everything I could. *Dum spiro, spero*.

The ducts terminate together under the cupola that tops the main building. Underneath is a space where the steam merges and escapes through vents behind each of the cupola's seven pillars. A utility door opens outward in the centre of the pillars. And when I emerged, I saw London in the distance and smelled Reed somewhere near.

The ridge of the main roof stretches east and west until it meets the wings which fold back away from the street. I walked along the cloud like a cat on my toes, the steep slope of the roof angling down on either side. Nimbly stepping between the ridges of the tiles, I first travelled right, to see the far side of the west wing roof. The closer I got, the more I sensed that someone was there. I could not hurry lest I lose my step.

At the juncture of the peaks of the main building and the west wing roofs, I looked down to find no place for a man to stand. London, her many roofs in the distance, rose from a fog so dense that it appeared to be on fire, the red rays of the setting sun jutting up from behind its churning billows. At the far end of the wing stands a large, round water tower. Behind that lone structure there was something alive. I could sense it.

Standing, waiting in indecision, I reached out for the thoughts of that being, hoping upon hope that it was Reed. It was not. The glimpse of that mind shook me and losing my footing, I began to fall. I crouched down on all fours scarcely able to hang on. Blood! Images of Lucy, Tom, Dr Seward, and myself and the scent that we carry, the scent of our blood, loomed around me. It was the Master. After so long, the dream, the burning desire was to come to pass. I sensed that he was coming toward me and a glimpse of something dark peeked around the tower.

It was Ham. After rounding the tower, he mounted the cloud of the roof and headed quickly and noiselessly toward me. Though unsure, I stood my ground on hands and knees. He stopped just a few paces from me and through him the Master spoke to me.

"Do not fear me," he said.

Lifting my shoulders from their crouched position, I knelt before him looking down on Ham, his green eyes now glowing red from the presence of the Master. His words were soothing and he promised me life everlasting. He said, "You must remain faithful to me. I will keep contact with you from afar."

My orders were clear: I must keep Dr Seward and the others occupied while the Master returns to the East with his new bride, Mina.

"Yes, Lord and Master," I said, confident once more of the Master's faith in me.

Yet, the Master was not satisfied. To prove to me his power and his resolve, he asked me to look back toward the cupola. To my astonishment, Reed stood against the white pillars holding on to either side for support.

"Renfield," said the Master, "see that your vision comes to fruition. All your visions, your strength, your confidence, come through me. Look now!" And he pointed his chin toward Reed who was stepping away from the cupola. I stood up, intent on reaching Reed, but I was prevented. "Should you disobey me, here is the fate that lies before you."

My confidence vanished and my fear of high places returned. In a moment my knees became weak, my breath stopped, and my lungs seized. My eyes lost their focus and the world moved forward and back as they tried to adjust. I teetered, losing my balance, and half blind, toppled over and slid slowly toward the edge of the roof. Scratching at the tiles, my hands, wet with sweat, could not hold on. Finally, at the edge, I jammed my elbow into the gutter and held on, my body hanging over the edge as the sun slowly slipped over the edge of the earth behind me.

"Know my power! Do not take my gifts for granted."

At this, I begged to be reclaimed as his slave, that I may have the return of my strength. He hesitated. As I felt myself no longer able to hold on, I promised unfailing fidelity.

Ham's eyes, two shadowy red flames, mocked me as he confidently and easily walked down the slope of the roof toward me. "Your strength," he repeated, "comes from me!" And with that I was restored. The roof came back into focus as did Ham who loomed there above me.

I wondered why I feared to fall for only three stories up is no great distance. Pulling myself up onto the roof, I found my footing was more secure than I had previously imagined and easily ran up to the peak to look for Reed. Yet, I was too late. Reed stepped forward and, with the downward slope of the roof giving him momentum, he ran forward to his end, just as my vision had predicted.

Later.— I cannot sleep to-night; I am having bad dreams, bad dreams. In the dream the revolving door of Mary's thoughts squeaks and turns endlessly, yet, it is not Mary who is sending me these thoughts. Mary is awake and thinking of her home. Besides, the attitude is all wrong. When Mary thinks of the door, she grieves for her lost child and holds back the anger toward society that put her in that position. In my dream there was a feeling of hunger, like that of waiting at the table until everyone is served so one might eat. I just realised that I have been salivating. In the dream I'm inside the wall and the door revolves inward, the tin box is full and squealing. Stepping out of the shadows from my hiding place, I remove the child from the box. Then I awoke with a start. What could this mean?

Is it the Master that waits in the dark for these children? He said that he preferred pure blood. Pure blood, yes, he said he wanted Mina's pure blood.

This evening's ordeal on the roof, was that a dream as well? No, I'm sure it was not, yet I wish that it was. Will the Master take Mina away with him? Will she end up as Lucy? How can I be sure just who, or what the Master is? I must find out quickly, before it is too late.

Later.— The Master—he commands. I have been entrusted to watch over Carfax. The soil of his homeland must be guarded until his return. The boxes! First, he must away one last time. He must return home. Mina, his beloved, will accompany him. Soon, she will be his bride.

He is satisfied. The trial is complete. He will leave the *Bosendoffer* of the *Wald* behind. Submerged in the multitudes of the London slums he will hide and thrive and feed.

Matron's voice calls from the main door. She greets … Oh the doctor is home and with him is Dr Van Helsing and… Now is my chance!

I slipped down the stairs to talk to Patient S. once more. I must ascertain just how he knew of Mina. Does he hold the key to who the Master really is?

When I arrived in the incurable ward, the corridor was full of people who spoke in hushed tones and seemed to be waiting—but for what? Without letting on my true role, I acted as if I belonged and walked directly to the photographic room. I closed the door behind me, leaving it slightly ajar so I might watch the goings on.

The well-dressed ladies and gentlemen who stood at a respectable distance must have been his family. George, of course, kept his distance as well, directing the warders and the workmen from across the corridor. A man with a doctor's bag replaced his top hat, signalling he was leaving. After him, two men in leather aprons emerged with a body on a stretcher. They were heading my way. So, thinking on my feet, I stepped to the far wall and feigned interest in the photographic studies.

No one paid any attention to me as they carried in the body and sat it in a chair. Metal braces were unfolded, and what I thought was a doctor's bag, contained an actor's makeup kit.

The bag displayed the advert: Mr Treat's *Momento Morie*.

Patient S, thus readied, the "mourners" were ushered in alone or in small groups and set *in tableau* with him seated before them. The flash of the powder, as each photograph was taken, filled the air with smoke and a burnt chemical smell. I was thus imprisoned there for what seemed an hour until, finally, all was completed. They left me alone with Patient S. laid out on a table covered with one thin sheet.

I stayed behind, perhaps to keep vigil, perhaps to hold onto the insane idea that I might obtain the information I needed. Satisfied they had gone, I glanced down on the body trying to detect the outline of the man under the cloth. What did he know? Why did I not believe him when he told me of the Master?

I waited in silence, and, after a discreet pause, pulled back the cover from his face for one last look. Startled by a noise behind me, for an instant I believed the body had moved. Turning, I found Angie shyly looking in from the door, her body partially concealed by the doorway. I nodded recognition and, she, stealing up behind me, observed the body from the protection of my shoulder.

"Not such a swell after all, is 'e?" She said commenting on the thinness of his face which was akin to those who die in poverty. (She had not seen the back of his head that, ravaged by disease, bore no resemblance to living flesh. Free from hair and skin, shown his bare, pockmarked skull.)

Reaching around me, she pulled the sheet back to the waist, revealing her true purpose for entering the incurable ward—she intended to rob the corpse. Patient S. was dressed in a fine evening suit as if on his way to the opera. This addition, no doubt, to please his family and to cover up the fact that he always had been locked in his room unclothed. Holding onto me with one hand, Angie slipped the fingers of the other into his coat pockets. She was happy for my company, where I, of course, felt extremely awkward. Next, his waistcoat was revealed, a deep wine colour that only the rich could possibly pass off as fashion.

Angie stopped the search though clearly the gold watch chain strung across the front of the waistcoat was just the sort of thing she was after. I sensed she was staring at his face, as if she had seen him somewhere before. Her body, pressed against my side, stopped moving entirely. I could tell that she had stopped breathing.

What was happening I wondered? She first showed no fear of the corpse at all and then suddenly, and for no apparent reason, she was petrified with fright. Then her

262

thoughts hit me. And, though they only lasted an instant, her thoughts showed me a complete scene from her past.

It is night. She is on her way to see Emma. Entering a dark alleyway with the light of the gas lamp behind her, she walked right into a smartly dressed gentleman exiting from the dark. Drunk and tired though she was, she immediately made a play to earn her doss. He declined her offer, saying he was satisfied and pulling his coat aside, he reached into his waistcoat. Angie, expecting a coin, was disappointed when he merely checked his pocket watch. In the dim light from behind, she could see the shine of his fancy burgundy waistcoat and the glitter of his gold watch fob.

Then, ripping me from her thoughts and back into the photographic room, Angie screamed, "Murder, bloody murder!"

Burly and George came running in. They had been just outside the door. They peeled her long-nailed fingers from my arms and dragged her away. Delighting in the short work required (for they were already in the basement) they thrust her in Patient S's former cell.

They soon returned for me. Why had I lingered there? Robbie is in the quiet room since yesterday, so they brought me upstairs to my room, which, because it now has barred windows, seems suitable enough. So here I write; my privileges removed yet again. The pain of Angie's nails, agonizing as it is, is no match for her shrieks which hurt my ears still. And Angie—I can still hear her screaming.

Letter, R.M. Renfield to Queen Victoria

"29 September.

"To The Queen's Most Gracious Majesty.

"Madam,

"A terrible scourge is upon us. London is being attacked by a force the like of which has never been seen before. This has been a long time in coming, but nature will have her way. To quote Darwin: "Man tends to increase at a greater rate than his means of subsistence."

"We are like a pestilence whose only intent is to multiply, whose only purpose is to multiply, returning poison for all we take in. We have become as parasites infesting the host, yet, if the host dies, so shall we. I pray you, who are the leader of the vast empire that is our England, to use your influence to stop this madness.

"The balance of nature must be restored and if we do not do it consciously, ourselves, nature will do it for us. Man will be like unto the lower orders, the vermin that are the fodder of larger carnivores. He has come who is the predator of man. "The dead walk amongst us, a plague that must be stamped out!

"Beware the dark dawn.

> "Your Majesty's
> "Loyal and Humble Servant,
> "R.M. Renfield."

30 September, 12:30 am.— Renfield, you have saddened me. Where is my faithful servant, my confidant? Did I not share with you all my gifts, my strength, my will, my vision? Why have you betrayed me, in this my hour of triumph? Would you keep Mina for yourself? No, I know you would not. You are a gentle and giving man.

You have angered me, you ungrateful menial, and for this you must be punished. All those who dare oppose me are punished. It is a gross error to oppose me. Yet, I am generous and have a long memory. For your service in the past, I will grant you two more gifts before I leave you. First, I will relieve you of the burden of the many souls you carry within you. Second, I will grant you the power to see the future one more time...

Suddenly my hand is free! The Master has written the above passage by taking control over my hand. Oh merciful heavens, how horrible to read those words from my own pen! The Master has the power to use my hand to produce immediate dictation.

He is no longer in my room with me, yet the Master is still here in the asylum, I know it. His presence poured in through the trap and slowly took the shape of a man—but shape only, it had no substance; He was as a vapour that gathered itself into a vertical pillar. And, in this guise, He loomed and laughed. He laughed at me in my folly. How could I have mistaken this evil for God?

The Master spoke, saying, "Renfield, see. See the truth, it is time. See through my eyes. The people of Whitby are safe."

And thus Whitby is shown to me. It is a crisp autumn day and life has returned to normal, the tourists having retreated south. Fishermen repair their nets, children scamper to and fro, and housewives bustle up the market street with parcels in hand. The herring gulls' ceaseless call, mocks the idle prattle of the idle who sit along the quay.

Then the Master spoke again, and said, "It is not these souls you contain. It is the souls of your first congregation you feel. They have reached out to you from afar. Your heart heard them, but your mind did not. Your mind has played a trick on you. It stopped you from understanding the truth that is too much for you to bear. You know that the burden of guilt has followed you all the way from Africa. What will become of the Ndebele village? What will become of the children who you taught to read and write? What of King Lobengula? What of your wife? You see her large brown eyes before you, calling to you. Yet you are back in England. She screams so piteously. Lobengula has ordered all the *kraals* in their path set afire, but it is too late, the Europeans have already arrived.

"You see, Renfield, this is the boon I promised for your past service. I have relieved you, for now you know there was no fire in Whitby." And then he laughed. I heard him laughing in my head. Make it stop! Far from being relieved, I am tortured with guilt all the more. The "Master," whoever he is, has given me the truth: In my mind, I can see where our village *kraal* once stood under the *kopjes*. There is nothing left but charred earth. Nothing.

Chapter 7

LOVE

RENFIELD'S JOURNAL

(*Continued*)

30 September. Sundown— Madness will surely take me for I cannot endure the anticipation. I see, as if in a dream, the Master coming for me. The vision I have is so clear and I know how it will end. In my mind I see the mist gather into a flowing river of vapour over the grounds of Carfax. It is seething and winding its way towards the asylum. Is this because I know the Master is angry with me or is it somehow more sinister to-night? This vision will not be shut out. I must write it down now for I fear I may not have another chance in the future.

This was no daydream or delusion, it was a vision. I have seen, nay, experienced the unimaginable. The air became heavy. The electric globe outside my door began to tremble and then swing as if the wind blew inside the corridor. A shaft of light swung back and forth through the trap as though searching for me. Then, suddenly, the light was blocked.

I felt His presence outside my door. Sparks flew as the electric globe burst. A shower of glittering particles of glass rained down, ending in the delicate tinkle of a Christmas tree as they hit the floor. Darkness. A strange burnt smell, as if the air itself were ignited, lingered in the corridor.

The mist from Carfax poured in through the trap in my door, and gradually, whirling and writhing, it took shape. It was the Master. Accusing red eyes fixed on me and I was pinned to the wall. Somehow, I did not know by what force, I was lifted so my feet did not touch the floor. My toes reached down but to no avail.

"You have betrayed me," said a voice, but I could not see from where, for my eyes became blinded with fear.

I could not disagree for I knew what He was referring to. He knows I will warn Mina. He has heard me contemplating the consequences in my mind. Who can stop thinking? Who can stop deliberating in one's mind when in such a predicament?

Then I was lifted still higher, lifted to the very top of my tall, narrow room. My head bumped against the ceiling, the rough surface scraping the flesh from my scalp. I tried to cry out, but no sound would come; it was as though a hand were constricting my throat. I struggled, kicking my legs and twisting my neck free. I dropped to the floor. No sooner did I realise that I was not seriously injured, that I was lifted again. The next drop was more damaging and I found the wind knocked out of me. As I struggled for breath, I looked up from where I lay on the floor at the swirling cloud before me and begged forgiveness. Circling around me, it drew up my legs and lifted me once more, but this time feet first. I could not struggle for I had not the fight left in me. Thus suspended, I heard him speak again.

"I have come from afar to claim my rightful place as the Corrector. Nature has sent me to cull the young, old, and weak from the multiplying hordes of humanity. All those who oppose me are punished. All those who stand in my way are swept aside. I will correct human error."

Promising cheerful compliance to his will, I begged to be released. I begged for another chance to serve him. Yet, he can read my thoughts, I cannot lie to him.

He spoke again saying, "Did you think I was God? To you, Renfield, I *am* a God."

Then, with tremendous force, I was thrown from this great height, my head dashed against the floor.

Silence. The presence was gone in an instant. My body lay prostrate and listless, my strength gone. I could not feel the right side of my body. (And though this revelation happened hours ago, I still feel a tingling on that side, reminding me of that horrible vision.)

My consciousness faded in and out. I heard footsteps outside my door. They quickly departed and I was alone again. I lay on my side unable to move. My hair sopped blood from a sticky pool on the floor. The taste of blood, my own, sprang from inside me. Then softly, almost silently, the door opened.

I could see but little in the darkness. The faint rustle of cloth approached—the skirts of a woman. Arms reached around me from behind, gathering up my broken body, and a soft, tentative voice said, "Mr Renfield, please do not go away." Was this Mina? Had I warned her and thus sacrificed my life? I could not turn to look. At first I thought it must be she, yet it was not Mina's voice I heard. Kneeling behind me, she laid my head against her breast cradling me in her arms. And there, she wept tears of pity for me. She sang softly to me a lullaby, and wiped the blood from my eyes.

Footsteps, hard and hurried, sprang down the stairs and toward my room. Presently, Dr Seward and Dr Van Helsing entered. As they examined my wounds, I tried to tell them, to warn them, but I could hardly speak. Oh horror of horrors, at last they would listen to me and I could not speak! I searched for strength and looking around with only my eyes, I noticed the woman had gone. Without my noticing, she had vanished.

Is this what will happen if I do, indeed, warn Mina or can I change the outcome by keeping silent?

Later.— George has placed a chair outside my door for I am under careful watch—my punishment for being caught, yet again, out of bounds. Oh, how alone I feel. He could never know, could never suspect, that his presence outside my room is the only comfort I have. While he is here, I need not let the voices frighten me.

Something is wrong, I know it. Also, George has been acting peculiar to-day. Perhaps the arrival of Dr Seward's friends has unnerved him. They are upstairs in the doctor's suite—a strange place to stay really. Would one readily admit one was staying in a madhouse? "Oh yes, of course, you were visiting the doctor who is an old friend of yours," you say, but they are really thinking, "a likely story."

The world seems different, somehow. Could it be the arrival of Dr Seward's guests that caused this change? Faint thoughts, a mass of concerns and fears, filter down through the ceiling tugging at me to align my thoughts with them. At first I blocked these thoughts out, for they are as tangled and mad as those of any of the inmates of this house.

Mina's husband, Dr Seward, and the others have gone to Carfax. I watch them as they go, patting each other on the shoulders and reassuring one another. Will they find the Master? Will they see his face before I do? They lift their flaming torches high and I can see them clearly, they are heading for the chapel. What would they with my Lord and Master?

Mina's husband is mad. A brain fever has left him impotent and delirious. He believes he is being pursued by a vampire. (And they call me mad!) He has gone to pursue his phantom and has left Mina here, alone. She is in Dr Seward's apartments directly upstairs. Mina, in her thoughts, revels in the idea of consummation. Will Jonathan ever be able to give her children she wonders as her mind wanders to thoughts of motherhood?

I heard the men talking over their plans when they decided to leave her here. They seek to protect her from the evil that lurks next door. There is no safety here! The Master is not restricted by these walls. Why did they bring her here?

You fools! You have taken from him his protégé, his concubine, Lucy. Now he will have yours. Hear my thoughts, I pray God you can hear my thoughts. Oh, dear Mina—strong, intelligent Mina—run while you still can!

What is this? Something is at the window. It cannot be a sparrow for they do not fly at night. It is a bat! Lord, it is large and fierce and somehow I know it wants me to open the window.

"I have come to collect the souls," I hear it say in my head, but I will not open the window. I beg it to stay away. It wants the souls of my congregation that I keep safe inside me. I screen out the sound of its wings by concentrating on my writing. I must carefully replace the dripping wax of the candle. There are only a few hours of wax left. Without the Master's gifts, I can no longer read in the dark.

Oh, it is gone! I have discouraged it with spirit and resolve.

But wait. The front door chimes distant and faint. George gets up reluctantly and lumbers downstairs. He is in charge again tonight; Dr Hennessey is attending a vivisection conference at Guy's Hospital. As George opens the door, the chime, which was irritating my ears, finally stops. I see through George's thoughts. They reveal a well dressed man waiting at the door. Tall, dark, and aristocratic, the visitor speaks with an Eastern European accent.

"I am Count DeVille," he says slowly and deliberately, "and I wondered if I may enter, if you would be so kind? Madam Mina is expecting me."

George invited him in and has left him with Matron.

(This article was torn from a newspaper and placed in Renfield's journal between the dates of September 30th and October 1st. The insertions are my best guess as to what was written in the missing corners of the article.

272

Perhaps his interest in animals prompted him to keep this. S.D.)

[Horro]r on the Heath

[Septem]ber 30

...a man about 30 years of [age,] found dead to-day on Ham[pstead] Heath, not yet identified by police.

Police were reluctant to affirm this as yet another animal attack and denied similarity to the recent rash of animal attacks on local children in the Hampstead Heath area. "Bite marks found on the necks of these children were most likely caused by a dog," the coroner said. "The long incisors or canines creating two round punctures about one and a half inches apart." The coroner further stated that in this case, because of the extensive damage to the neck, it is difficult to say for certain whether the marks were indeed teeth marks or stab wounds from a circular instrument, such as an ice pick or awl. The investigation continues as to whether this murder is related to the other incidents in the Hampstead Heath area.

Not since the Ripper murders has such devastation of the body been witnessed. The victim's throat was torn open with great force. Lacerations of the face and torso, displayed a knowledge of human anatomy far beyond that of the average citizen. The coroner's report states that the liver and kidneys, having been ripped from the body, were missing. The face, slashed by a sharp instrument, was mutilated beyond recognition, except for the eyes which sustained no injury. Witnesses reported that the staring eyes of the corpse reminded them of one possessed.

No identifying marks were found on the body. The victim's trousers, however, bore the laundry tag of a lunatic asylum just 20 miles east...embroid[ered] the initials T.T...

RENFIELD'S JOURNAL

1 October. Midnight— I fear tonight will be the night, the night he comes for me. I feel it in my bones. Dr Seward will not let me leave. I begged him, humiliated myself before him. I dared not tell him my fears—I have said too much already. The Master is angry.

Dr Seward actually thinks I am mad. Delusional! It is Dr Seward who is delusional. I see the hard bed, the bugs, the dirt—this is real! He does not see that no one in the ward has come out, yet he thinks his medicine is real—he even thinks he is a good doctor. The proof, my friend, is in the pudding. If no one is getting better, then his treatment is not helping us. If he calls for the same treatment, over and over again, without realising any benefit, he is not a good doctor. So if the doctor believes he is a good doctor when all proof says he is not, it follows, QED, that *he* is delusional.

What is more, he thinks his "science" is real! Psychology is nothing more than a name, a label, for that which is unexplained. Yet, it is a word without a definition, it cannot be defined. And the treatments! Locked in rooms, chained to walls, dunked in cold water, are these treatments or punishments? If one gets "better", it is only the patient avoiding these treatments that appears as "better." *Graviora quædam sunt remedia periculis!*

Have you cured anyone? Dr Hennessey believes the cure for madness lies in the past. Silly, really, to search the past for the germ of the situation. What is needed is action. Angie agreed with me on this point.

And, the mechanism by which the mind (another ambiguous label) can be treated is unknown. Has this been studied, statistics gathered, mathematical formulas ferreted out? No! How does it work, dear doctor? Or do you not know yourself? Ah, you try one thing and deduce the feasibility of the treatment from the outcome. The Outcome?! Yet, you *suggest* to the patient that this or that treatment should work and what the result will be. This is no science, my good man, this is voodoo! The results come only if the patient believes in them. This is the black magic that the strong, those whose will is strong enough, protect themselves from by exercising their self-control. A science requires no faith, for science, by definition, is the roster of the proved. If faith be required to heal, let it be faith in God.

Later.— Mina has just visited me. I reached out for her thoughts but her mind was full of revulsion. She was repulsed by my actions. She had seen me eating flies and found it disgusting. How could I explain I needed the strength such nourishment supplies? If I had not eaten the flies, I would not have the courage to speak to her—to tell her what I must, but cannot. "Please, please, please listen to my thoughts," I tell her. My tongue is tied but my mind is not. She is receptive to the Master, but cannot hear me.

I got the courage, I am not sure from where, to reach out and grasp her hand. "Run, Mina, run," my thoughts begged her, but she politely snatched her hand away, not lingering longer than would be expected in polite company. Surely, as we touched the message must have passed through to her, though it was only a moment. I pray to God, the message was passed.

Apologia pro sua vita

(This title is Latin meaning, "Apology for my life." S.D.)

It is the most difficult thing I have ever had to do, but I now admit that I have been fooled by the Devil. The devil of Want. The devil of Pride. Pride and Want have led me to delude myself; I did not see the Devil's temptations for what they were, because I did not want to see them.

Of the sins of the flesh, I participated fully. Pride led me to wallow in sin and debase myself before God.

When I arrived in Matabaland I was full of energy, verve, and dedication. My dearest desire was to bring the bosom of Christ to any and all who were ready, to bring the love of God to the farthest-most reaches of the earth. I started out with my best foot forward, and, immediately built a church. Yet the church was a structure only, for within three years of its establishment, I knew… I knew that conversion of these heathen was hopeless. Dr Livingston had long since ceased his correspondence and I was on my own. There were times when my hope rallied, but at no point was I ever convinced that my mission could succeed.

In me, from my earliest memory, there was a wanting, a waiting, for purpose, for something to come into my life. This something was passion—a passion to understand why we, people, were here, and what the purpose of humankind, with our superior brain, was. Our sophisticated language, our science, our ability to build and to write, wonderful as they are, comprise an extra layer above our basic survival skills. They are not needed. What could be the reason for such as we? I found a kindred spirit in those who sought to understand God like my dear, dead friend Monk, who died before I returned to England. It was just such questions as these that made them stand out as religious. My study of religion was clearly a means to an end. I wanted to know—why.

In the bush, however, there is no such need, no such need to know. Life is natural and celebrated every day. Joy is commonplace—not an exception, but the accepted. And, the disruption of this joy is not taken lightly. Life is not conducted with subtle political goals. No! It is lived, and expected to be lived to the fullest every day. I lived with the hope of finding the answer to-morrow, they lived with the knowledge that to-day is a good day.

In my thirty years in the *bandu*, I made not one convert. It is not *I* who converted *them*; it is *they* who converted *me*. Soon I became as them, relishing in the natural world and its seductive power, living for to-day. It was not the hope of eternal life that carried me through, but the delight in the day to day joys of nature. The trees, the grass, the antelope, the elephants—all seemed right.

All was right with the world. I began to live as an Ndebele. I suspected that my superior, Livingston, had done the same. I insist, however, that the choice I made was entirely my own.

Once I became as them, I participated fully in their culture. I took a wife, exchanging two cows for her, which I paid for from the Missionary Society's allowance. We had three children, though two died in childhood. My surviving son took to travelling soon after reaching the age of adulthood. He brought me much pride.

My greatest pride was that King Lobengula had sent for me as a translator. He trusted me and asked me for advice. He was a strong king, able to keep the Europeans dwelling to the west, east, and south, at bay for decades. Yet, when the pioneer column assembled below the Limpopo, I was called by the Missionary Society to return to England, immediately. I do not know if the society knew just how strongly I supported the natives. I do not know if they had heard of my "conversion." I do know that I left the King when he needed me most and for that I can never forgive myself.

As I was leaving, I heard two voices arguing in my head. The first said, "Stay, help the Ndebele! You can be their advocate because you can speak English, and you are a member of the native group. You can translate the words of the miners and protect the Ndebele from being deceived." The other voice said, "It is your duty to obey the Missionary Society. You must return to your home, your native land, it is calling you. Come home. What use are you? You are not persuasive or diplomatic. What can you do against such as these men? Come home to where you belong." The voices debated as if I were merely a spectator. They gave me no peace, no rest.

I do not know if the Missionary Society was embroiled in the mineral rights controversy, but I do know that I was afraid to admit to them my failure, the failure of my mission. I was afraid to declare that I wanted to bring my common-law wife back to England with me. How could I plead my case with such a record?

Elizabeth (that is the name I chose for her) was understanding. She believed the wait would only be a short while. I would send for her as soon as I was established as vicar. They would not contest the authority of the vicar, or so I wanted to believe.

Imagine my folly, my chagrin. My arrival at Whitby ended my hope of an easy assimilation of my mixed marriage. Whitby is not the simple village I expected. It is not a rural community where a curate is respected or acknowledged. I dared not broach the subject. I thought if perhaps I could establish myself, I might assert my right to bring my family, but I was regarded as a charity case, a nothing. I felt unable to ask for relief of my simplest needs, let alone the largess of understanding required to pay the passage of an "unwed" woman. I am so ashamed. I am so lonely. God forgive me, I never told them about Elizabeth. I hid from the shame of this lie only to live in the truth of my loneliness. Elizabeth!

I now know who it is who calls to me, calls to me to sin against God in God's name. And, I now know what I must do.

1 October.— Dr Van Helsing entered, and, as he did, he pictured a woman sitting on a stool in the middle of a small room. I recognised the room; it is the same one I occupy now, but I was not there. In my place, his mind substituted his wife, 20 years now in the attic. "You are dead to me," he tells her, but she will not yield. Stubbornly she stays seated on my stool though his thoughts order her away. She glares at him, accusing him. He shuts his eyes, but she it still there occupying his mind. Her eyes, disembodied, float before him.

His head is a jumble of philosophy, folklore, and "modern" medicine—the worst being the last. His brain theories are stuff and nonsense. *Quandoque bonus dormitat Homerus.*

These walls so cold and bare, the window barred now with heavy iron bars, bolted deep into the window frame, the door, trap open, George standing guard, makes me feel more a prisoner than I have ever felt. I resumed catching flies and spiders, yet, my interest in them has waned. I must occupy my mind lest the Master catch my unguarded thoughts.

I must get away from here. I must protect the souls I carry within me. My people are alive within me. Will I take them with me? Is it too late for Mina?

If only I can make it to the morning, the Master never comes in the day and George naps in the afternoons, I know I could get away and be safe, like Tom.

If only...

After staring at these words, bathing myself in regretful tears, they began to form a picture. The "I" stands proud, the "f" reaches out with its stubby arms toward the "o" that is the head of a cat, "n" the poised foreleg and shoulder, "l" the arched back, and "y" its tail...

Later.— I have just had yet another visit. Dr Seward brought several of his visitors with him. Lord Godalming, the man who won Lucy's hand (the Master won her heart) entered with a Mr Quincey, an American, from Texas. They wanted to know what I knew of the Master, and yet they did not ask. I listened to their thoughts and found there a compassion and understanding I did not expect. The Texan thought with a twang. The Lord thought in slow distinct phrases. I took the opportunity to appeal to them for immediate release, for I saw their eyes were not blinded by this "science" of psychology.

In their presence, I begged Dr Seward to set me free. If only I could tell him—I thought surely the other men with him believed I was sane and would help my cause. None of them spoke except Quincey, who, feeling the pain of my plight, stated briefly that an Indian native friend of his once said, "The white man may have the gifts of the arts and sciences, but we red men do not throw people away." The words he spoke had the same drawl as the words in his head, yet his statement was compassionate and compelling. His appeal, however, fell on deaf ears.

Later. —I beg for redemption, not so much for me, for my work is done here, but for those who will carry on. Robbie, may he know what friendship is. Angie, may she find peace. Daisy, may she grow and prosper. Mary, may she find someone on whom she may share her nurturing nature. Who knows if Tom and Reed are still alive? Wherever they are, may they find what they are looking for. As for Dr Hennessey, I have no respect for his ways, but his intentions are well placed and he is dedicated and hardworking. May he gain the knowledge that he needs to help these poor people. Dr Seward, I know he and I have had our differences, still I feel a special bond between us. My dearest hope is that he finds a new object to adore and that he may have the affection he so deserves. So too, Matron.

George is a difficult case. More often than not, I was made to hold my temper while this misguided miscreant mistreated, may I say, abused my fellow patients. Yet, it is easy to be harsh. I now see how I made his work more difficult. My wanderings caused him strain and my pets, distress. Perhaps if George were released from his terrible memories, his spirit would lighten and that would be a benefit to all.

The Bishop, the target of my wrath, deserves my thanks as well as my apologies. Was not the Bishop, mediator between me and the archdeacon? He shielded me from my immediate superiors, knowing my inexperience and hotheadedness would only further their contempt of me. It is clear now that the Bishop only wanted to help me. He sought to secure my living by giving me a post in his own parish. I repaid him with my ineptitude. And though he facilitated my incarceration, he saw to it that I was provided for as a gentleman.

The minutes refuse to pass. My abdomen feels full though I have eaten nothing. My palms are moist and the pencil slips in my hand. God, lessen my fear. I count the minutes until dawn; I know I will be safe then. I wipe my hands on the thighs of my trousers yet instantly my palms become wet again. Of all situations fear is the worst. I cannot control it or its cause. I am helpless. Oh, God, give me the courage to endure this nameless, formless dread.

Is life a personality, a soul, a spark of electricity? What is it I so desperately do not want to lose?

The pain has returned, only now it is constant. Sleep, let me sleep, and thus shut out this phantom horror that overwhelms me. With false graciousness, I asked George to take away my tray with the excuse that I was not hungry. Yet, I am hungry. I hunger—but for what?

What happens to the soul after death? It once seemed a childish question. Now, that Death sits quietly with me, waiting, such questions have lost their banality.

Oh Lord, abide with me.

The Lord is forgiving. This worry is for naught. I will prove to him that I am faithful. I have already spread out my sugar to begin my experiments again. Yes, a new study with careful measurements so I may make exact calculations. When the sun rises I will catch the last flies of the season. Soon the sun will rise on a new day. Tomorrow I will begin again.

Death is nothing. I fear nothing.

Note to Dr Hennessey from Matron
(*October 2*)

Dear Doctor,

Though it is not my place to point out the shortcomings of the male members of the staff, I feel it is my duty to direct your attention to the ever worsening situation in Ward D. I appeal to your dedication to this hospital in hopes that you will hear me out.

As you are surely aware, many strange things have been occurring in Ward D as of late. The situation has become intolerable. It is difficult enough to keep things running smoothly even when Dr Seward is present. Now, with the announcement of the doctor's imminent departure, I fear the ward will become total chaos for Simmons cannot possibly maintain the ward without proper supervision, as was amply proved last night.

Last night, Simmons was stationed at Mr Renfield's door per Dr Seward's orders. Elwood was occupied with Miss Smithe all evening. She had fallen into paroxysms as soon as she was placed in the newly available room in the incurable ward. She claims she can still feel the presence of Patient S. though I promise you that the room was thoroughly cleaned after his body was removed.

Simmons cannot have been at his station all night, because I saw Mr Renfield standing in the stairwell at about 1 o'clock AM while I descended the stairs from the Women's ward. Though I stood, out of sight, on the landing two floors above him, I could see him clearly. He stood on the landing between the first and the ground floor facing down the steps. I thought he would make for his escape, but instead, he stood there for some time in deep reflection as if he were making some important decision.

Then a thought came over him and he turned back with some determination. He did not return to his room, but rather continued upstairs to Dr Seward's chambers. I know this because I slipped downstairs and followed him. There he found the room of Dr Seward's guest, Mrs Mina Harker. He spoke to her through the door, but when he tried to enter, I blew the whistle.

Elwood came running from the basement. Simmons came from Ward D and we confronted Mr Renfield on the landing. He again insisted that he was in grave danger and must leave immediately. The three of us returned the patient to his room. I could have done this myself, for I found the patient's superhuman strength seems to have been the pretext of lazy warders. We had no trouble whatsoever in returning Mr Renfield to his room. Mr Renfield was secured and I set Simmons off to perform his rounds.

This was not the end of the evening's goings-on. At about 4 o'clock AM, I was on duty outside my ward when I was startled by a patient from the private ward. She insisted I follow her. I was preoccupied with other matters (the Women's Charity Ward had set to howling again) yet I neglected my own duties to return with her to Ward D. What I found was a disgrace. It seems that all the doors of the ward had been unlocked and the patients were roaming the corridors at will. It was no surprise to me that yet another patient had gone missing. Robbie Smalls was nowhere to be found. I went to fetch

Simmons, but found him asleep outside Mr Renfield's door.

Mr Renfield lay on the floor of his room in a terrible state surrounded by a pool of blood. The flesh in his scalp was torn and abraded with what looked like bits of plaster. His torso was twisted and limp, his right side rigid. The furniture remained undisturbed, yet I noted a distinct bloodstain on the ceiling.

I fetched Dr Seward immediately who was assisted by Dr Van Helsing. It was then I realised Daisy was no longer in tow and set out to search for her.

As to an explanation of why all of Ward D's doors should have been left unlocked, that is still a mystery. Simmons insists that he locked each door of the ward as usual, at 7 o'clock PM. However, this morning I found all the doors open, yet un-tampered with. Robbie Smalls is still missing, but Daisy had planted herself in the dayroom. My concern is with Miss Jones as she was quite shaken by Mr Renfield's death. In fact it was she who fetched me this morning before sunup and said simply, "Mr Renfield." Again, I detected another of Simmons' tales, for he claims that this patient never speaks.

I must insist that Simmons be replaced with a more competent warder. Dr Seward appears unaware of this man's shortcomings. As you know, Dr Seward has made sudden arrangements to travel to Eastern Europe with his acquaintances, the Harkers. We are short staffed as it is, so I must suggest, humbly, that this position be filled with due expediency.

G.R., Matron

Letter to Rev Renfield from Mrs R. Johnston

(*Unopened*)

"13 October, Friday.

"Dear Rev Renfield,

"Sad news. We have lost our battle to save the St Ann Chapel-of-ease. It has been ordered locked by Bishop Fairfax. We hope and pray for guidance and accept that though we believe that our cause was a noble one, we must put all in God's hands.

"Our hearts are with you and we pray that this letter finds you much recovered. The bishop informs us that you are ill and will not likely be returning to us. We will all miss you and your kind nature. It is impossible to thank you for all you have done for us here in Whitby. We wish you all the happiness in the world.

"One cheery note to close. Ham has reappeared. I know how fond you were of him. He returned all scrapes and scratches and was ever so dirty. It is a wonder that we were able to get him clean again. He is not as rambunctious as he was and not so prone to those playful bites. He much enjoys sitting with Auntie and me where he receives many pats and scratches under the chin. He must have had quite an adventure. What a story he could tell if he could talk!

"Yours with faith, hope and love,
"Rebecca."

Letter, Queen Victoria to Rev R.M. Renfield

(This letter was most likely written by the queen's confidant called "the Munshi" who handled the queen's correspondence during this period. The Queen's time was too valuable to deal with this sort of thing.   S.D.)

"31 October.

"Dear Rev. Renfield,
    "The Queen writes to say: We are not amused."

288

30443667R00178

Made in the USA
Columbia, SC
28 October 2018